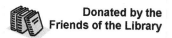

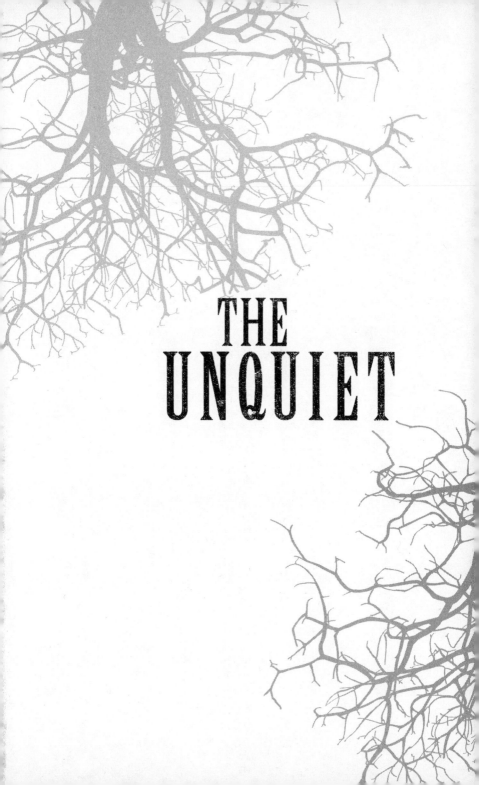

THE
UNQUIET

mikaela everett

THE UNQUIET

GREENWILLOW BOOKS
An Imprint of HarperCollinsPublishers

The Unquiet

Copyright © 2015 by Mikaela Everett

All rights reserved. No part of this book may be used or reproduced in any manner whatsoever without written permission except in the case of brief quotations embodied in critical articles and reviews. Printed in the United States of America. For information address HarperCollins Children's Books, a division of HarperCollins Publishers, 195 Broadway, New York, NY 10007.

www.epicreads.com

The text of this book is set in Celestia Antiqua Std.

Book design by Sylvie Le Floc'h

Library of Congress Cataloging-in-Publication data is available.

ISBN 978-0-06-238127-9 (hardback)

15 16 17 18 19 PC/RRDH 10 9 8 7 6 5 4 3 2 1

First Edition

 Greenwillow Books

for deseg,
because I am not me without you

"The road to death is a long march beset with all evils, and the heart fails little by little at each new terror, the bones rebel at each step, the mind sets up its own bitter resistance and to what end? The barriers sink one by one, and no covering of the eyes shuts out the landscape of disaster, nor the sight of crimes committed there."

—Katherine Anne Porter, *Pale Horse, Pale Rider*

Part
ONE

I have been a cottage girl for eight years now. Any cottage girl will tell you that eight years are long enough to set her bones in stone. "I fought it in the beginning," she might say. "I fought hard, but I am older now, and I am more this than anything else in the world."

We arrive at the cottages in the woods as prisoners. We are six and seven years old and do not know any better than to be afraid of them. So they lock us up inside bunkers underground and train us there until we have learned to like the gray of our uniforms, the brown leather of our shoes. Until we are obedient, compliant. Even the boys, rowdy as they were in the beginning.

Down there in that dark place with no windows we fantasized about the one thing we would do once we were allowed up. It became a movement, passionate and angry, our morbid revolution. Some boy would carry the knife, we said. A butter knife we'd hidden after dinner once and no one had noticed. He would not be afraid to use it.

"Where will the knife go?" someone asked.

"The heart right here, maybe the neck."

It was hard to know who spoke what words in the dark. It was our bedtime, but none of us were sleeping.

"And then we'll tie her up?"

"Yes, we'll tie her up and go left. We came from the left."

We could hear our hearts beating faster. Thump, thumping a song. There was murder in it, blood and guts spilled, the price of our freedom.

Then someone else whispered: "I thought it was right?"

We knew that when we'd arrived, the woods were filled with trees and that we would have to find the river again if we ever wanted to escape. In the end we agreed to listen for it. In the end we decided that if we did make it out of the bunkers, it did not matter what direction we went.

Eventually there had to be a road somewhere.

Nobody asked the biggest question; we were not ready to tackle that part yet. Nobody could say the words, but I knew we all were thinking it: Once we escaped the bunkers, how would we get home? How do you climb back into the sky when you have already fallen from it? Because that was where we had come from.

They had stolen us from the other Earth.

It was Alex's knife, now that I think about it. All I remember his saying back then was: "We'll go home. We'll find our parents." And everyone hooted and cheered and thumped him on the back. That was how he gained his popularity, I suppose, and it was not that we actually expected him to save us. Perhaps we knew even then that he couldn't, but there is something about a person who says that he wants to protect you. Regardless of who that person is, and what promises he can keep, you start to want him around.

On our first night outside the bunkers, the cottages were soundless. We looked at one another. I think we were waiting for someone to say the words, to initiate the actions. What had happened to all those plans to run? To find the river? To press that cold blunt knife into the delicate wall of our housemistress's artery? Not one word. Somehow, without any of us really noticing, they'd become nothing more than memories—those children with their blood-hungry eyes. We were ten, eleven, twelve by then, and we'd already started becoming the people we would be for the rest of our lives. No one even remembered where we'd hidden the knife. When we were finally released from the bunkers, it was because we understood the world enough. We took our blue and white pills. We knew that we must never go beyond the wired fence of the garden, that we must always be quiet, always be good. Our lives depended on it. But it was also because we had learned to use the guns in the training rooms and learned to use them well.

The problem with the system of raising children like us, I've decided, is that everything hinges on some dramatic effect. We are not told what we are; we realize it for ourselves. I want to say that finally understanding what we were and what we were for brought us some semblance of peace or made us ready. I want to say that we became brave little children then, inside those bunkers. I want to tell all the lies in the world.

About a hundred of us were in the bunkers in the beginning, so many that it was like maggots wriggling around a festering wound. Sometimes we were five to a single bunk with hardly any room to breathe. We would fall asleep at night and wake up gasping for stale air, pinned by somebody's heavy arm or leg. We fought over who got to sleep in the bed that night and under it, and sometimes a particular corner of the floor would be marked for the biggest, meanest kid who'd learned to get what he wanted with his fists. Nearly all of what I remember involves fighting, scratching at one another's eyes until the lights flickered out.

And then the first of us started to disappear.

Because that is how it was. You could be talking to someone or lying in a bunk next to someone who suddenly wasn't there anymore. This, we learned, was what it meant to be from the other Earth. This was how our people died. They call it the dominance theory. If two copies of the same thing exist and only one is necessary, then the other one will eventually disappear. It applies to people, to planets, even to the rocks. So we were fewer and fewer, even though we were once many.

"There's a high chance that we're going to lose one another soon," Edith said one night in the dark. It was Edith, Gray, Alex, and me. The four of us—the difficult four, as we were dubbed—were best friends by then. I was the youngest at eight; Alex was nine; Edith and her twin brother, Gray, were about to turn ten. "We're too many," agreed Gray, wiping the crumbs from his bruised face. We all were covered black and blue with bruises, the only visible evidence of the things we were learning to do with our fists and with weapons.

They'd snuck into my bunk bed, and we were eating all of our shortbread, all of our chocolate, everything edible we'd so painstakingly preserved until now. We got like this sometimes, finishing everything off because we were suddenly more uncertain of tomorrows than we'd been during yesterdays, because Edith had had a thought or a bad feeling, or because Alex had seen a boy disappear right next to him and once a boy was gone, we could never remember his name. Malcolm? Freddie? Emerson? We got this way because of the guilt, of being here, being alive. Each night we fell asleep together, and when we were still there in the morning, it meant that we'd lived through another day.

Now it has been six years since that night on my bunk bed, and there are fewer than a third of us left. Plus one Madame and one Sir. The boys have moved out of our dorms and in with their Sir. The four of us are no longer friends. Edith is tall and beautiful now at almost sixteen. She sits with the girls who whisper secrets into one another's ears and laugh a lot. We barely speak anymore. Sometimes she offers me a quick smile, and sometimes I offer her one back, but perhaps even that is only a memory. I don't know. I've almost completely let go of everything about myself from back then. I don't think children realize that any moment of their childhood is worth something while they're living it. It's only later when you're older and reach back to find dark spaces.

The empty beds remain, as does the wooden table at which we usually sit clustered together, ignoring the other giant end as if it does not exist. Our voices travel around a room that was never meant to be this bare. On occasion there is a lost sock found and no one it belongs to, but we are good at pretending that those things don't happen. The ones who are here today but gone tomorrow, we tell ourselves, were never really here. We have come a long way in eight years, those of us that made it this far. We carry that perpetual twinge inside us. It is not emptiness, exactly, just something close.

This morning Madame gathers all of us in the dining room for an announcement. First we stand at the table and sing our sleeper anthem. Then she tells us to sit down. "I am pleased to say that your final examination is in one week," she says, in her no-nonsense sort of way. "I believe you are as ready as you will ever be. Congratulations." And then she leaves the room.

Not one month or one year, one week.

We look at one another in silence for a long time. I don't know why; we have known since we arrived that there would be an examination. Still. "I thought we would have more time," one of the girls whispers, her voice a croak. "More warning."

We tell ourselves that eight years of training cannot be in vain.

If Madame says we are ready, then we must be.

We are not what we were at the beginning; those children are now history.

My own history is shaped like a little girl, with her big gray eyes and her angry smile. Madame had so much trouble whipping her into shape I wonder now that she ever made it. I was careless with her. I was ruthless, and now that little girl inside me, the one from the ocean, from the sky, is dead. I cast her out, and I buried her in the woods. Sometimes I spy the color of the dirt and how her tears and her bones look underneath it, an old red dress covered in worms, and I wonder, as I step over her hump of earth, how I could ever have been her.

CHAPTER 2

It is early evening, and we do our washing by the river with buckets and bars of soap. We use our generators sparingly, for our training and for electricity during the evenings but not for much else. We don't have washers, and we fetch whatever water we need from the river. We live off the grid and on natural resources as much as possible because anything else would lead to unwanted questions from the authorities of Earth I.

The river swishes back and forth beside us in the wind. Madame, our housemistress, does not understand why we enjoy the outdoors so much. She does not know how spending so many years underground makes our lungs burn constantly for the fresh air. Yet here we are outside, sniffling, pretending that we are not terrified of the river and that the wind that pushes past the trees is not also biting into our skins. I suppose this is as close to defiance, to a desire for freedom, as we will ever get.

I was six years old when we arrived. I did not have anything, not even a suitcase to my name. Since the portal that connects the two versions of France sits right in the middle of the ocean, we were soaked to our bones when we were pulled out from that one ocean into the other. Madame cut the wet clothes right off my shivering body, as she did with the other little girls and boys. They had not given any of us shoes; they were afraid that it would make us sink right to the bottom of either ocean or perhaps in between somewhere, watery ghosts floating between two worlds if such a thing were possible. They'd stolen us from one world and brought us to another; we could tell, even then, it was imperative we lived.

I am only fourteen now; that isn't nearly long enough to have grown old, though I feel it. But my mind is sound, the best it can be. I have not lost anything. I did not drown my stories in the ocean, did not, I confess, give up enough pieces of myself to do so.

Edith tugs on my shoulder, jolting me from my thoughts. "Your shirt sailed away. See?" She points out something white bobbing down the river. And then the other girls laugh when I start to chase after it, one hand trying to keep my sweater on my body, the other holding on to the woolen hat that keeps blowing off my head. I mutter a curse and run faster. It is not my favorite shirt, but it is the only white one I have without stains on it. Madame is already unimpressed with me enough and the mess I make with paints. "You have to be considerate," she often says, as if my attempts at re-creating the hills and valleys around where we live are somehow an affront to her.

I stop running.

A memory floats shyly on this part of the river like ice at the first hint of winter. I will not go near that spot, and so I watch while my shirt lingers there. A story used to run around the dorms when we were younger that once someone looked into the water at this exact spot and, instead of seeing his own reflection, saw someone else's—a person who was already dead. He'd apparently looked a lot like Solomon, a little boy who had arrived with us as children but did not live long. They say that he is living in the water now, either haunting us or keeping us safe.

I wait and wait until the shirt has passed that spot, and then I pick up a stick and lie at the edge of the river, as far from the water as I can. That is where I am, trying to coax the shirt back over to my side, when some of the boys turn up, boots stomping loudly on dead leaves as they move. One of them whistles. "Looking great down there, Harrison."

"Leave me alone, Alex," I say without turning around. I can smell all the things they have hunted. The blood of rabbits and deer on their bodies, their sweat and dirt.

We are proud to say that we cottage children have never been anything less than self-sufficient, right from when we were young. The cottages are well outside the limits of any major cities, hidden deep inside the woods, and when we are old enough, we begin to train with knives, with bows and arrows, with rifles. First we test these things out on the natural world, hunting for food, but eventually we turn our weapons on one another. Humans are far less predictable. We are now good at more than staying alive. By the time I was eleven, I knew how to murder a grown man with nothing but my bare hands. It has become our second nature, this art of killing. But we are safe enough in these woods, whether because of our skills or because of the trackers we wear inside our wrists that allow Madame to always know where we are.

The river pulls my stick away, and just as I'm about to pick another, my hat flies off my head. Then Alex jumps into the water for me. It's a stupid thing to do, especially on a day like this, when the wind is blowing and the river is starting to churn. If he is afraid of the water, like we all are, he does not let it show on his face. Brave, brave, Alex. "For a kiss, of course," he says when he reaches the bank, grinning, blond hair floppy on his head. His voice is deeper now, his body built like the strong trunk of a tree, but he has the same hair and impish eyes he did when we were children. Gray stands on the bank, watching us, and Edith is still talking with the girls.

"Of course," I say, and take the shirt from Alex.

I lean forward, lips puckered, eyes half closed, but when he gets close enough, I push him back into the water and leave him there. I wouldn't say that I run away exactly, shirt clutched in my hand, but I don't wait around to find out what the other boys want to do to me as revenge. I meet Gray's eyes as I walk past, and he forgets himself long enough to offer me a shocked smile.

The water takes Alex upriver a little, and I hear him splashing against it. He yells, "You're going to pay for this, Harrison." His friends laugh.

The girls are already leaving, and I grab my remaining clothes, dripping wet, and drop them inside my bucket. I wring the water out of the shirt. It is hopelessly brown with dirt, but I am only interested in the fact that Alex does not come after me. These are the small things to look for among the four of us, the few threads that are left. Alex will tease almost all the girls mercilessly but rarely me or Edith. And since Gray is always working, chopping wood somewhere, hunting, training, he never causes anyone any trouble. You might walk past Gray twenty times in a day, but the occasional nod of his head is the only indication that he sees you. I worry sometimes, in moments of weakness, that because he is never here, one day we will lose him without ever noticing. Then we will become a triangle, not a square, then a straight line, then a dot, and the world will be smaller somehow. It shouldn't matter, of course. I don't even really remember how I felt the day Madame made sure that the four of us would not be friends anymore.

"Wait for me," a voice rasps. I turn around to find one of the girls hurrying to catch up—Julia, with her eyes watering, her nose red as a tomato. I slow down until we're side by side.

My skin is covered in goose bumps, my hands are like prunes, but Julia looks worse as she stumbles to keep up with me. The paleness of her skin, the fevered yellow of her eyes make her seem like some otherworldly creature. Well, I suppose she is. We all are, but each time she coughs, the other girls look at one another, wondering whether this is how she will disappear. After everything, will she be lost to a cold? I can tell they write her off because of it, and I am the only one who ever washes my shirt next to her, the only one who has to listen to her talk.

Julia is a frail sort of girl, with spindly legs and hair so pale and long it falls to her back. She is probably beautiful, because when the other girls whisper about her at night, I can hear their underlying jealousy. "At fifteen she has no breasts," Jenny hissed just last night, as if it were the worst crime in the world. Which is strange because if she looked down, Jenny herself might be surprised to find herself somewhat breastless, too. A year after we moved out of the bunkers, Julia came here from another cottage in another country. Her target family had moved to these parts, and so she had to as well. For years she did everything in her power to fit in, but we were already set, and there was no place for her. Her accent and overeagerness did not help.

"I've got some shortbread," she says now, out of breath. She is clutching at her chest with one hand, her bucket swinging in the other.

I know she wants to exchange the shortbread for an hour braiding her hair. I start to tell her that I am planning on reading a book tonight, but Jenny speaks over me, saying, "We haven't made shortbread for weeks. Where did you find it?"

Jenny doesn't wait for an answer before turning back to the others. Julia blushes and stares down at her feet. The thing about Jenny is this: she does a pretty spectacular impression of anything she hears, and if she doesn't like you, she speaks to you in exactly the same voice you speak to her, like a parrot. In Julia's case it's a nasal/throaty combination that's hard on the ears.

"You've got to stop doing that," I say quietly. Julia gives me a confused look. "Our accent. You don't want Madame to hear it. You're not supposed to go against your training."

She shrugs, but her face turns redder. Perhaps she thought that she was finally starting to sound like us in a good way. She runs her fingers through her hair and sighs. "I'll cut it all off if you don't help me. I don't know how anyone can walk around with hair like this."

I say nothing.

"It's the kind you like," she whispers hopefully, "the one with the raisins in it."

"Poor Julia," says Jenny, smirking. "Did you save your stale shortbread for her all these months? Do you want her to be your best friend?"

Julia mutters something in another language, which I'm pretty sure is an insult. Jenny, who is actually this tiny human being that contradicts her personality, nudges Julia hard with her bucket. "What did you say to me? What did you *just* say to me?"

"Jenny, leave her alone," I say tiredly.

The surprising thing is that she listens. She doesn't exactly stop glaring at Julia, but she does move her bucket away. I suppose Edith and I are what Alex is with the boys: the unofficial leaders of the girls in our dorm rooms. I think it's because we survived, our whole group intact, while theirs did not. They lost their friends every day, yet here we are, I and the others.

When we were children, there were rumors about which of us had good luck and which did not. It was agreed that you wanted to be around those who did not seem to be disappearing. It's not true, of course; we cannot choose whether we stay or not, yet that silly sentiment still lingers. Now, though my influence is still there, only Edith wants to be that with the girls—their compass, their good-luck charm. I've learned to function better when the spotlight is not on me, while Edith thrives on it. Julia gives me a grateful smile, but I ignore her. I go back to putting one foot in front of the other.

As for the shortbread, I know it's not stale. I know the place behind Madame's cabinets where she hides all her sweets.

The truth is that I can stand Julia because she is like me.

They say there is something about us, the children they find in orphanages on Earth II. There aren't very many of us at this cottage, two or three. Nobody wants their old stories from before the cottages to stand out from the rest, so if we can help it, we never mention it. They say we orphans are emptier than all the rest, colder behind our eyes. We were broken long before we got here. We fitted in just right. We already bore the knowledge that all cottage children must have: that nobody loves us but ourselves.

CHAPTER 3

The boys have started an argument with us. They follow behind us at a small distance. Nelson tells Greta, loudly, that the mosquito bites on her chest don't actually need a bra. (Somehow everyone always seems to be talking about breasts these days.) He asks why she bothers, wasting her time like that when she could go shirtless, and then we have to hold her back, to keep her from charging.

"What?" Nelson calls, laughing. "You're not strong enough to come over here?"

Greta fights harder to free herself, but there is nothing

she can do against all of us girls. She talks loudly about the size and shape of Nelson's head. "Like a watermelon," she says, which is true.

"Leave it alone," we tell her. "He's just trying to get you in trouble."

Several more insults and curses pass between us. We are like this now. The girls against the boys, an only half-joking game. We have a saying: making friends with a boy is like dousing yourself in gasoline and then waiting in an empty field during a lightning storm. The older we get, the more we separate ourselves.

Something sits there between us all, you see. Something seductive and dangerous, certain boys giving certain girls looks that sometimes Madame catches.

We all lived in the same cottages, even the same rooms, until a few years ago, when the boys got their Sir. Now we are absolutely not permitted to frolic with members of the opposite sex. That is what Madame says in her shrill voice. But it happens anyway. It happens when she is not looking: a boy and a girl sneaking off, the sounds they make, the flushed looks they give each other in the morning. Some of the older girls, seventeen or eighteen, say, "I want to know what it feels like before they send us out there. I don't want any surprises, and I don't want to feel like I missed out on anything." For some of them, kissing seems to consume all of their leisure time.

And then there are the rest of us: prudish and proper in our uniforms, white shirts always buttoned, gray skirts always at least an inch below our knees, socks pulled up as high as they go. If we are missing anything, chances are we will never know what it is.

We arrive at the cottages and immediately break up to do various tasks. Some sit at the piano, some read books, some are in charge of dinner tonight, while others have the leisure of sleeping off their busy day. "The fridge and cupboards have been restocked," Madame announces, and we know it must have been at great risk to her. It always is whenever she goes into the city for the things we need.

We sound like little schoolchildren, our voices harmonious when we murmur our "Thank you, Madame."

She nods.

For all we know she was chased by a wild bear just now, but you would never know it from the way she strides off into her office, her best dress devoid of a single wrinkle, her brown leather shoes still shined, her bun still severely secured atop her head. "Stand tall," she likes to say. "The ones who live the longest are always the proper ones."

Our Madame is not what you might think; anyone who imagines her small must adjust her size to at least three times bigger, and if in your mind an ogre appeared, then you must think of a smaller, softer sort of woman who could not hurt a fly even if she wanted to. Madame is neither small nor big, neither powerful nor weak, but she owns us. She owns us in a way that we did not understand as children, still do not understand now. We respect her, are afraid of her, are enamored with her, are disgusted with her, all at once. She has a shrewd face and a sharp nose and eyes that are piercing. She is good to you at the exact same moment that she is cold. As long as she is standing in front of me, she is solid, but the moment she is gone, she becomes undefined in my mind. I suppose what we've decided, collectively, including the boys, is that as far as Madame goes, we do not really know what she is.

The smell of sizzling onions perfumes the air. The radio is on, our only connection to the outside world, and some of the girls are swaying to the music. We seem simple enough, yet we are not what we seem at all. A sort of violence sings in our bones, an unquietable hum just beneath the surface, like the fire of a volcano. Madame calls us carriers, for now. We only carry the ability to do what is required of us. When we pass all our exams, we will become sleepers.

We have been training for these exams since the moment we arrived; it is all we have lived for. When we have passed, when we are sleepers, we will leave this place. Until then we must remain hidden inside these woods. The problem, you see, with two versions of a person now existing in one world is this: someone might recognize us and mistake us for someone we are not, and then everything—coming here, hiding in their woods all these years—would have been for nothing. So we stay hidden until it is time to leave. That is the most important rule.

Tonight the conversation is easy. Jenny and Greta have just finished reading a book by Hemingway, and they are trying to recount the story to some other girl who has yet to finish it.

"Well, there is a man," Jenny says.

"And there is the sea," Greta says.

"And I swear to God, that's pretty much all that happens," Jenny says.

I tune them out. The sunset sneaks up on us, turns everything gold for a moment before stealing away again. I am watching from the window, marveling at how it never gets old. We did not miss the windows when we were in the bunkers; that sort of thing is not important until suddenly it is. We do not take anything for granted now.

You ask, What is one cottage girl to another? We stand one another well enough to live together. But we have learned that the only way to protect ourselves is to trust no one else. We have been taught to be selfish. We are very good at it.

The radio continues to play, someone hums, someone else sets up a board game, and I watch Edith wash the dishes. I am still sitting on the windowsill by the kitchen sink, only half awake, the echoes of old memories beating at my tired chest. I wonder sometimes what someone standing in the dark outside our window might think if he looked, really looked, at us. Are we punctuated by our secrets? The question marks of the future, and all the exclamation points from the past?

You wouldn't know from our faces that the final examination is in a week. Afterward there might not be any of us left.

CHAPTER 4

For as long as anyone can remember, there have been two planets. It was as easy to take for granted as the idea that we need air to breathe. Earth I and II. The original planet and its alternate. Everything has a reflection. It is only a matter of whether you can see it or not. The funny thing is that back home, on our planet, we were the first Earth. We were original, and they were alternates. Now this is Earth I, which means that I am second. I am the alternate. Everything is a matter of perspectives.

The two worlds look exactly the same. The sky is just as

blue; the cities are just as windy; the snow is just as white. Mirror images, yet two ways any single story can play out. When you were four years old, you were entered into the interplanetary registry. I was five the first time I spoke to my alternate via satellite. "*Bonjour*," I said, to another girl named Lirael who lived in Paris, who looked like me, smiled like me. We were the same in almost every way and yet different in others. She giggled a lot. She never played with her hands, and no one had to remind her to look up or speak louder. The monthly satellite conversations were supposed to be a way for everyone to learn to be content with her lot in life. You start to think that if your life is so terrible here, maybe your fortune can be made elsewhere, and then you learn that your alternate took that route and her life is either better or worse for it. In the end, if you compare and contrast the two, their differences are either very few or very many. Most still live in the same look-alike cities, are still essentially the same person, but less commonly, some are so vastly different that they might be unrecognizable to each other. It didn't always make everyone content with their lives, but at least we knew what the other roads looked like. It turned out that the knowledge itself was the most powerful thing.

I think I had just turned six when relations finally broke

down. Six when it was no longer permitted for us to be in communication with our alternates. Interplanetary communications in general were cut off, and all there was of that other world was the dot in the sky. Suddenly I didn't know anything about Lirael and her life, and she knew nothing about me. What had been normal became something to fear, to worry about. Many said they'd always suspected it. That it is impossible for two parallel worlds to coexist indefinitely. That at every moment our two planets, atmospheres, even our stars are fighting each other and have been for years. There might be two versions of everything, but only one can stay. Only one reflection is real.

We call this period now, when the two planets officially no longer communicate, the Silence. It is harder for some—those older men and women who have known their alternates for sixty years, who feel like they have lost their best friends, their other halves. But even they understand that the Silence is meant to be a period of introspection. Even our presidents stopped speaking two years ago.

Earth I also meant it to be a period of good faith. A standstill. So that the two planets could each search for a better plan, one that might mean our two worlds wouldn't have to go up against each other. *The Silence.* That they even came up with a standstill proves one thing to us: that the people of this world, of this Earth, are the better, moral versions of us. Their mistake is not understanding this and assuming that if you lock two people up in a prison with only one glass of water and a knife, the knife will lie where it is on the floor, untouched whether the water is still there or not.

At the end of the Silence, one Earth will fall; there can be no two ways about it.

By the time they realize that our sleeper program is in effect, that we are coming to take over their world, it will be too late.

I spend an hour in the training room before bed. The examination is in a week, and I am afraid to fail. There is nowhere for failed carriers to go, and so they are killed. I am not the only one here. The training room is full despite the time. It's hard to fall asleep when all you're thinking about is that you could die in a week. For some of us, what we do with this final week in the cottages will determine the value of our lives. *One week*. I swallow hard as I turn on the screen and watch footage of my alternate's life: her sitting for dinner with her family; her alone in her room. I watch the summarized footage of everything she has done today, doing my best to emulate her. To sit like she does and use the same hand gestures. I do this every night. By the time I am finished the cottages are quiet. I stumble into my bed.

I close my eyes and let myself fall into that space between sleeping and waking. Sometimes I see an old man in my dreams who speaks to me, who has been there since I was young. If he is not there, then I do not dream. The old man is waiting for me again tonight. He should not be there because the children of Earth II no longer dream. They say it was a sign no one noticed. Sometimes, when we were younger and still friends, Edith would shake me awake each time I got too loud, thrashing in my sleep, in case one of the other girls heard. Now I have learned to be frozen and to scream silently inside myself no matter what I dream about. Sometimes I feel as though it is only inside these dreams that I am myself, with all my fears and weaknesses exposed. It is the only way to know me.

One week, I think, and even in sleep I can feel my throat starting to close.

But I know who I am, I tell the old man.

Lirael.

My name, for as long as I have known it, is Lirael Harrison. I am fourteen years old, and I am from the other planet. I have spent the last eight years of my life in these woods, training to become someone else, learning not to love the things that I love, not to want the things that I want, not to walk the roads that I would have. In the end I will be the version of Lirael that only the people of this world recognize. In the end, without a second thought, we will kill our alternates so that we can take over their lives here. There is no other choice. Some of the cities are already chock-full of sleepers. People who look and talk and act the same as they always did, who are not the same people at all, who are only pretending until all of this is over. People who trained where I have trained, who understand the importance of this mission and that many lives far greater than ours depend on our ability to stay secret, to never make mistakes, to always live two steps ahead. It is easier for the young ones like me, who did not grow up with their alternates, who can do the things that our parents cannot.

Madame likes to say, "Who says wars need to be fought with guns and bombs?"

CHAPTER 5

There are fourteen girls in my group and nineteen boys, and we have been very careful over the years not to love one another. It is a mistake to grow attached to someone you might never see again. A mistake to make friends you cannot keep. To form bonds that will have to break. We could not understand this when we were younger. We held hands in the dark and told stories about our families and how scared we were to suddenly be here, not there. They'd taken us when we'd least expected it, rounded us up like animals without telling us why we were chosen or where we were going until we were here in this world. It's possible that some children were volunteered by their parents, and it's possible that they were not. Who knows? Who has those insignificant memories anymore? It is the sort of thing that would be a burden to remember, a weight forever on your shoulders. All we could ever say for sure was that one moment we were in our houses, the next moment in dark vans, the next coming through the portal.

We used to have little confessionals. "They took me while I was shopping with my mother," one boy would say. "They killed my mother, and *then* they took me," someone else would say. Alex, of course. It was a game to see who had the worst story. I still don't know if any of Alex's stories were true, but they were always the worst, sometimes so bad I would even cover my ears, and he loved that, frightening me.

Madame hated us those first few months when we were stubborn and angry. When we would not eat or sleep when she ordered us to. "Why us?" we kept asking. "We don't want to be here. We want to go back through the portal. We want to go home."

I don't remember her reply. I don't know if she even had one.

I am the youngest of all the carrier girls. Most are at least a year older than me. But Madame says we already have the minds and the maturity of adults, and so that is how she treats us. She says our eyes are the window to our souls. When she looks, she sees only blackness there. That's how it's meant to be. That's what it means to be the stronger version of a person, the version that survives. Genetically, physiologically, we are the same as our alternates. Same brains, same DNA, except somehow for the darkness.

I remember one of the boys crying one night and the sound of it echoing through the room. It kept us all awake. Finally some of us climbed out of our bunks and surrounded his. His older sister, he said, had been sick and dying of cancer. He knew that he would never see her again. He could not stop crying. Someone hugged him, I think. Someone whose face I cannot remember because it is no longer here, because it has evolved into a face like mine, detached over time. I think back to that night often, how we comforted him, and I do not know whether we were better people then, but I know we were more like *them*. The people who live here in this world. The people who are not sure that they want our lives to end when we have already decided on theirs.

I linger a little when it's time to get up today. New children have replaced us in the bunkers, and I am supposed to be downstairs with them. It is the job I hate most of all, chasing after them, making sure they don't injure themselves. It is not time for them to know yet. They have not realized who and what they are.

When the time comes, they are the ones who will break their own spirits.

There are still so many of them. They are as angry as we were, and I wonder whose heart they intend to cut out. Which way they plan to run once they're free: to the left or to the right?

There is nothing I won't trade with the other girls not to be on the schedule. Unfortunately all the others in my group feel the same. Still, I spend most of my chore time begging whenever Madame has her back turned. I am very good at popping up when I am least expected—on the other side of a fridge or out from a cupboard just before it's open. It's easier to beg someone you've just made laugh. It's the one time I intentionally make a fool of myself; I am desperate enough.

Finally I run into Margot, a tall, big-boned girl with her fluffy hair in ringlets. She's coming out of my room even though hers is the one across. "What are you doing?" I ask her, narrowing my eyes.

"Well, what's that in your hand?" she asks, one hand on her hip.

"Nothing," we say at exactly the same time, dropping our best attempts at bribery inside our pockets. What other options do we have? How do we get out of this?

"I've hurt my leg," Margot says, gesturing down. "I think maybe you should go downstairs without me."

I let out a horrible cough. I say, "If you abandon me, I'm going to die of pneumonia right here on this floor. Do you want to see?"

She sighs, and her hair bounces on her head. "I swear those kids are worse than we ever were. Let's just go in there and present a united front. That always works for Jenny, and she's like a midget. The kids love her."

"It's probably not smart to say that to her face, though," Julia calls from her bed, with the air of someone who has all the knowledge in the world. Margot and I poke our heads back into the room and see her sitting with a book. "She might try to kill you in your sleep or poison you at dinner."

"Are you speaking from experience?" Margot asks solemnly, even though I can tell she wants to laugh.

Julia lies back on her bed and mutters to herself. We're leaving, but I think I hear her say, "Even if I was, no one would do anything about it."

Margot and I both look away. We cannot dispute it. Julia

knows she is less valuable to us and to Madame than Jenny.

The chance that Julia will be alive after our examinations is slim.

I follow Margot down the stairs. On the other side of the door there is yelling. I yank it open, and Edith looks grateful. She swears underneath her breath and stumbles past us, half dazed, as if she has been starved of fresh air. Inside the room there are several fights going on, and the kids are yelling at one another. Margot and I stay standing at the door. "So," I hear myself say unenthusiastically, "I guess I'll take that corner and you can take the other side."

"We were much better than them as kids, right?" Margot says.

"God, I hope so."

She holds the door open, and I'm stupid enough to walk through it first. Naturally it shuts again behind me.

"I just need some time," she says from the other side. "I just need one minute," but I think she's really hoping that I'll settle the kids before she has to deal with them. Some of the other carriers are tougher than us, and meaner. They are the ones the children are afraid of. They are the ones who command fear and perfect silence, but I have not mastered the art of such cruelty. It is too fresh in my mind: the memory of living in the bunkers, myself; the memory of how the older kids would punish us with their fists when we did not obey them. Alex is a firm believer in this method. "It's common sense," he said once. "You show them what you're capable of a few times, without Madame ever knowing, of course, and then they learn to fear you."

I'm a disappointment to Margot when she finally enters fifteen minutes later. She wrangles two angry seven-year-old boys apart and then howls in pain as they converge on her hair. Her voice is high and scratchy. "No," she says. "Sit down. Don't do that. What is wrong with you people?"

A spitball lands on my neck. When I turn around, four dozen straight faces stare back at me, but the moment I look away again they're giggling, hands over their mouths. I run my hands through my hair, and more wads of paper stick to my fingers.

"Okay, who did that?" I ask, narrowing my eyes.

Nobody answers.

I shake my head. I am trying to seem angry, but the truth is that I envy them this. I think both Margot and I do. This camaraderie will not last forever, will not even last much longer than today.

"Everyone, please sit at your information desks and put

on your headphones," I say, gesturing to the cubicles with small white screens protruding from them.

"I don't feel like it," one of the boys, a notorious trouble-maker, says.

I ignore him. He changes his mind when I reach for a box of biscuits on the shelf and pass it around. "Only if you are sitting at your cubicle," I say, and I breathe a sigh of relief when he reluctantly obeys. Bribery is my only friend downstairs. When they are finally seated, I flick the switch that turns the screens on and watch their eyes glaze over as they are given information, each of them something different, some history that will help them take over their alternates' lives when they are older. This is how it begins: hours of surveillance, of learning about the way your alternate walks, talks, sleeps, laughs until it enters you and you cannot breathe anything else, until you become that person, and then the real training sessions begin. By the time these children are eleven years old, they too will know how to kill.

There are sleepers whose sole task is to collect the information needed for training. To plant cameras and compile it all into data that play on these small screens. We don't know much about them, and I suppose we never will since they are little more than background noise to our lives.

While the children watch the screens, Margot and I sit by

the door, flicking through books and magazines. I have two more to read before I am ready for my literacy test, before I know exactly the same amount of information that *she* does. I cross my legs and work with a highlighter. For a while the room is unnaturally quiet. There are no sounds from upstairs, no smells, no voices. Down here the younger carriers are not even sure whether it is day or night; they only know what we tell them: that when they have proved that they are willing to learn, to train, they will be allowed upstairs. *But they are not all ready yet*, I think, looking around the room at the rebellious ones, the angry ones.

Some are almost ready, though.

A girl named Lillian-Grace smiles at me whenever I look her way. She is much too old for the teddy bear she clutches in her hand, the thumb she sticks in her mouth, yet I think she could have been me. She has the same look of terror, of uncertainty in her eyes, although it grows dimmer every day. It is as though we understand each other. I would not be surprised to learn that she also does not know who her parents are, that for her this bunker is infinitely better than the orphanage they took her from back on the other Earth. I wink at her, and she flashes her missing teeth at me before turning back to her screen.

Margot and I have five days left; less than that. Five days before our time here is over, and we are torn between the things we want to do and the things we should be doing. Margot flinches when I lean over to see her book. The one she shouldn't be reading falls out from between the pages. But when I smile, she smiles embarrassedly back at me. "Do you think we'll be any good at this?" she asks quietly, and I notice for the first time that her eyes are blue with flecks of green in them. How is it possible that in eight years I have never noticed such an obvious thing? Why am I noticing now?

I shrug. "If we're not, the testing will kill us."

She plays with her hair. I can tell that she is not satisfied with this answer. "Do you think we'll miss this place after we've left?" And then before I can answer, she blurts, "I know a boy and a girl who love each other. Who say they can't help it." Her cheeks are bright red, and she does not look at me when she says this.

My mouth falls open. "Did you tell Madame?"

She plays with the corner of her book. "I was going to. I don't want any trouble."

We fall silent. We both know she should have told. I realize suddenly that she is fighting the urge to cry, and I don't know what to say, how to comfort her.

Love each other? Why would anyone be so stupid? Even the ones who sneak into each other's beds, who kiss and secretly hold hands, live under no delusions of some happily ever after. We are not here to love. I stare at Margot until she gets herself back under control, and then she shakes her head. "Dumbasses," she mutters viciously. "Let them get what is coming to them."

I nod my agreement. This boy and this girl Margot knows, I am sure there have been countless others like them before us, and there will be more after. Perhaps even now in this room, with these children, two of them will lock eyes and decide on each other in irrevocable ways and choose their emotions over their world, their lives. It happens. They are sheep who fall out of the flock, who do not have what it takes to survive this world like we are meant to.

They won't pass the testing. It is the most excruciating examination any of us will go through, designed to weed out our mistakes and to eliminate those who are not up to par. They do not have even the slightest hope of passing it.

Margot and I refocus our eyes on our books, both of us shaking our heads in disgust, both of us silent.

Love is what *they* have. The people of this Earth. Not us. Look how weak it has made them.

I am afraid that my ability to dream will make me weak, too.

I cannot figure out why this particular man is stuck in my head. I remember his face from the orphanage. I was four or five years old, and he was a janitor. I tripped over his mop one day, and when he helped me up, I heard him say under his breath, "You poor, poor children."

I froze. It was the way he'd said it. Before that moment it had not occurred to me. That I was something to be pitied, but after that I never forgot it.

A few nights later the alarms in the orphanage went off. The man ran into our room with a rifle in his hand. He ran right up to the girl in the bed next to mine. "My name is Emilio Dupuy," he told her. "Your name is Elsa Dupuy, and I am your grandfather. Your parents do not want you, but I do. I am here to take you home with me."

He did not have to say much more than that. She went into his arms willingly. Not because she believed him—she probably didn't—but she was like any orphan there. We all wanted to belong to someone, and we didn't even really care who that person might be. Nothing could be worse, we thought, than the orphanage.

As voices drew nearer in the corridor, the man picked the

little girl up. They rushed for the door, but at the last moment he turned to look at me. "You can come with us if you want," he said.

I don't remember agreeing, but suddenly the three of us were running. We made it out of the building and across the yard. We reached the gate. We were almost free when several security guards appeared, their guns drawn. The man was carrying the other girl in one shaky arm and holding his rifle in the other. It wasn't even pointed straight. "Stay with me," he told me, his voice low so nobody else could hear. "Just stick with me, and I'll get us all out of here."

I remember the cold. I was wearing my nightgown and no shoes.

When he let his rifle fall to the ground and reached for my neck instead, that was the last thing I expected. "Let us go or she dies," he said. His hand was not tight around my neck, not enough for me to believe now that he really would have snapped it. But my minders believed him. I did not fully understand the look of fear on their faces then, but now I do. They did not like to waste their potential carrier, especially when there was already a good chance I would disappear. Every orphan counted.

We inched backward, out of the gate. The man started

to say something to me, but he only managed a syllable. The single shot went right through his head. That it hit Elsa, too, was an accident. They both collapsed on top of me, and when I was rescued, I was covered in their blood.

I never thought about escaping again.

I learned later that he had gotten the job as a janitor in order to save Elsa. Every once in a while our minders would talk about it, thinking we were not listening.

It is one of those things I have been trying to let go of ever since.

On the day before the testing, the day before we are supposed to leave this place, I am using one of the punching bags in the training room when we hear a scream. It is early morning, the sun just risen, and usually we are either doing chores or about to start our training. Those of us already in the training room rush outside and find some of the girls huddled together by the cottage. "What happened?" I ask, but they are so shaken I can barely get them to speak.

Finally someone tells us.

Alex and Margot were found hanging from a tree near the river.

One of the boys, Alex's best friend, found them a few

minutes ago, already surrounded by blackbirds. My head shakes automatically in disbelief. I think of Alex as I knew him, trying to kiss me at the river, Margot, trying to get out of basement duty. *Why would Alex and Margot be hanging from a tree?* I want to ask, but I cannot form the words. I move past the shaken girls instead and walk until I can see what they have seen.

I stand there next to Madame in shock.

On the tree they are nothing but broken necks and pale bodies speckled with blood where the birds have pecked. Their eyes are wide, their hair falling over their faces, and I cannot reconcile any of it. I cannot tell myself that it is them I am seeing. My mind spins backward and makes my body retch. Madame wears a grim look and orders all of us back to the cottages, back to our training, as if nothing has happened, as if they were never even here. We follow her orders silently, but we're all shaking. It's not supposed to affect us like this.

The note says that they wanted at least to leave on their own terms, together. Not in a testing room, not because they did not meet the necessary standards. Their hands are tied together by the gray ribbon from Margot's hair, the same type we all wear in ours.

I know a boy and a girl who love each other. Who say they can't help it.

What heavy lies we must tell to keep the truth from floating away from us.

CHAPTER 6

What happens next is that I cannot breathe. I lie on the hard floor, held there by a weight pressed against my neck. Nothing I do changes it: no movement, no fight. I imagine that I am turning a terrible color, that all the important events of my life will begin to flash before my eyes as they leak away. The tree from today. I climbed it with Alex and the others one afternoon and broke my arm when a branch snapped. It was possibly the most definitive moment of my childhood.

I remember Madame shaking her head over me, a half smile, half grimace on her face. I was an example that day, lying there, howling. "Why should I help you?" she said for everyone to hear, her voice cold and angry. "Why should I make you feel any better for disobeying me? Do you think the rules are for my amusement, you foolish girl?" But eventually she picked me up and carried me to the room we use as an infirmary. There she cleaned and wrapped my arm, and in my delirious state, I told myself she loved me. That she loved us all in spite of herself. She had to; we'd been with her since we were six or seven years old, all of us. Madame was the only mother most of us remembered. But she made me tear up the drawing I'd made her earlier that afternoon; with her watching, the pieces of charcoal-patterned paper scattered over my infirmary bed.

Then she removed her glasses and stood at the edge of my pillows. "Look at me," she said, and I couldn't. I focused on the mark beneath her chin instead. I could tell I had done something wrong. As it was, I was already trying not to cry, trying not to look at the drawing I'd etched so painstakingly, now nothing.

"Lirael," Madame said, eyes boring into my skin, "never again. Do you understand me? The things you think you know, the things you think you should do, always ask yourself: Am I following protocol? At the end of the day it is the only thing that will save your life."

I could not tell whether she meant the drawing or the tree I'd climbed. And then she leaned in close so I could smell the cigarettes on her breath, could see the hairs and wrinkles on her upper lip. "And if you ever disobey me again," she whispered against my ear, "I will kill you myself."

That threat must have been issued to every single one of us at some point because over time other backs became as straight as mine, other faces less enamored with the idea of mothers and love. I stopped climbing trees. I stopped talking to Alex with anything other than contempt, stopped talking to the boys in general. We girls became allies. Allies, but never friends. Like a person you can share a toothbrush with if necessary but whose eye color you might never know.

I cannot erase the image of Alex. Alex, in our tree. Alex, dead.

I have always followed protocol. Until tonight, when I cannot breathe. When the boy leaning over me is killing me. Protocol means always finding a way to win, but I'm not looking. I'm not even trying to save myself.

"Come on," Ezra says, but he doesn't budge an inch.

His fists press harder against my windpipe. He smiles.

He is drunk with the power of it. Power to make me want to beg. Power to determine my fate.

No one else in the training room asks him to stop. Everyone is engaged in some kind of violent sparring of their own, with their hands and their training knives and sticks. There is another room full of treadmills, another for target practice, another where you have to assemble your gun with your eyes blindfolded while knives dart out at you. Every room is full tonight.

Perhaps we feel like we need to be punished.

None of us are really speaking to one another right now. Some mutter about how selfish it was of them, Alex and Margot. To kill themselves on the day before testing, as if they had wanted to take us down with them. Others see it as part of the test: to fall apart now would be to fail, and so they fight harder.

Margot and Alex were sparring partners. From what I could see they did not even get along. That is what I am thinking, lying there, when someone says, "Get off her," and Ezra is suddenly ripped off me by Gray.

The two of them fight until they bleed.

Training sessions started light when we were younger, but there is no mercy in these rooms now. If you are worrying about how best not to break someone else's leg, you might just find yourself paralyzed before you can do anything about it. We are feral, almost heartless, when we fight. I wrap my arms around my chest. My breath comes in huge, painful gulps, and still, not nearly enough enters my lungs. Finally I scramble out of the way and lean against the wall.

Ezra has always been my sparring partner. Short and stocky but with arms of steel, a brick wall when he wants to be. Gray is taller, and one and a half years older than us, with his tie loose around his neck, the sleeves of his white shirt rolled up his arms as they've been since I first knew him. I can tell that he is looking for a fight tonight. He is the one who discovered Alex and Margot, the one who saw the worst of it. For that, it is probably smart to stay out of his way, and Ezra knows that. He scuttles away with a bleeding nose. Gray has plenty of vulnerabilities, from my vantage point, but tonight even the other boys cannot look at him.

When I am strong enough to stand, I glare at him. "Why did you do that?"

For a moment I regret it because he flinches. I am afraid he will say he didn't want to see me hurt, but he doesn't. He blinks at me as if he has no idea who I am, where we are, and then finally he shrugs, swipes at his brow with a severely cut-up hand. "Why not? I need someone who will not make this easy for me."

He looks me over, up and down, appraising my state. Perhaps it is easy for him to see that though I stand tall, my ribs hurt and my left knee aches. But perhaps he cannot see anything at all.

"Come on then." His eyes challenge, his lips pull up in a slight sneer. "Whoever wins does all the dishes in both the boys' and girls' cottages for a week."

"It doesn't count when there is no week," I say, but even to my ears this sounds like an excuse. To his credit, Gray does not call me out on it. I try not to hobble over to the knife stand. I choose this because those kinds of fights are over quickly. Sometimes a winner is declared over a little spilled blood. It's a gamble, a game of luck, and tonight, with my aching body and wandering mind, that is the only game I am willing to play.

Gray is good with knives. I have not sparred with him in at least two years, but we have all seen him train. I pretend not to notice the overconfidence spreading over his bruised face, pretend not to care. And when he lunges at me the first time, I even let his knife graze my side. But with the next swipe, I twist his arm as my knee connects with his chin and then his belly. It's almost too easy to make him fall, to watch him snap in two. I stand over him, my bare foot pressed to his neck. I hate the look in his eyes, the one that says, "Alex?" and wears his grief. I hate him for showing it to me, to all of us. As if any of us still mean anything to one another. He is pathetic, lying there, and that only makes it easier for me to find the words. "The thing is," I say, my voice low and empty, "you're making it easy for us. We all feel sorry for you. Look around you, Gray. Nobody wants to fight someone they feel sorry for."

He pushes me away and stands. He opens his mouth to say something, something to everyone watching him silently now. "I . . . ," he begins, but he changes his mind. We watch him leave instead, the door clicking softly behind him.

Once, when we were younger, one of the girls swore she saw him sneaking away from the cottages every morning and, when she followed him, found him tending to a bird with a broken wing. Those old tales, old stories of the people we used to be.

But even that doesn't make me regret hurting him.

Madame enters the training room moments later, her arms loaded. She ignores the tension hanging over us. "Their things," she says, dropping books, clothes, old radios and toys and filled diaries on the floor. She does not have to tell us who they are. "If you want anything, take it now. The rest goes downstairs."

Lying at the top of the pile, that damn gray ribbon they used to tie their hands together.

I think there's even a little bit of blood on it.

At first none of us move. And then one by one, we slowly approach the pile. I don't want anything, but we all have to show that we are fine. That we are ready for our exam. That Alex and Margot mean nothing.

I touch the ribbon in my braid and wonder what story about it, about the girl who passed it on to me, I will never know.

CHAPTER 7

We each own a suitcase, and all of our lives can fit into them. I own one pair of shoes, brown, worn leather that is repatched each time it tears. Two drawing books, a set of paints, my pills, a nightgown, and an old children's book. Every girl's suitcase is different. A girl named Leah, who sleeps in the bunk below me, has a suitcase filled almost entirely with her animal-shaped origami, a different one from every week of her cottage life. She is actually a better potter, but clay is too heavy, hard to pack. These things no longer belong to us; we cannot take them with us, but we pack as if we can. As if we were only going on a trip that we will soon return from. Our pills: they are the only things that we will have with us in the end. We are healthier than our alternates because of them, less prone to falling ill. If we pass our exams and become sleepers, vulnerability is not a risk we will be able to afford.

Now that night has fallen, a sense of sentimentality in the air threatens to tear us open, spill us out onto the carpet. For just this night, we smile shyly at one another again as we pack. *Tomorrow.* Tomorrow everything changes, but not today, not yet. And so we regress. Hover on the verge of being children again. Watch a film crowded on the living room floor together, braiding one another's hair.

It becomes too claustrophobic for me, and I wrap a scarf around my neck, follow the scent of cigarettes to the old tool-shed near the vegetable garden. On the other side of it, Gray leans against the wall and stares up at the sky, and I suddenly don't know what to do. I do not know how the boys are commemorating tonight in their cottages, not to mention the fact that I humiliated this one just hours ago. He doesn't turn to look at me, but he knows I am here. I take a step forward and then a step back.

"It's much cooler out here," I say, but he ignores me still.

I am not Alex, after all. I turn around to leave and walk into Edith. "Oh," she says.

I do not know whether she followed me or she was here before, but she offers me a guilty smile just the same. "I've stolen Madame's best bottle of wine," she says, holding it up to the light. "Not to get drunk, of course, but just to know. The way she hides it, you would think it was worth her weight in gold." She laughs shortly. "Actually, it probably is."

She sits down, and after a moment I join her. My uniform will be dirty from the rusted nails poking out from the shed, but I pretend it does not matter. Edith fiddles with the bottle, one eye on me and the other on Gray, where he stands ignoring us. This is the single thing that reminds me that he is her brother. Like us, Edith has been good about ignoring the boys; perhaps in a way tonight she hopes to make amends for that. Or, I think suddenly, maybe this is something they do all the time, sneaking out to stare up at the moon together. Maybe they've been close all this time, and we've just never seen it. Like Margot and Alex. Secrets make everything else so unsure.

I cross my legs and pull my skirt down over them. "Won't you know after tomorrow anyway?" I say, gesturing to the bottle. "I mean, surely your alternate drinks."

"Yes," Edith says, popping the cork out, "but it will be a different type of knowing. And besides, you won't be around to drink with then, will you?"

I stare at her until she adds, "Not that it matters." She sighs. "It's not supposed to matter."

"No," I agree, looking down at my arm. At the scar from breaking it. My memory of our friendship, of our time in the trees won't leave me tonight. It's Alex's fault. I see a tree and automatically associate it with laughter, with all of us, and then suddenly before I know it, the memory turns gory. I see the boy and girl hanging from that tree. And my arm hurts, as if it were snapping in two again. As if I have weighted our whole history on a single fleshy branch. And when Madame cut it off as she removed their bodies, she cut off a piece of me, too.

I ignore my arm. I look at Edith instead.

In this one moment of weakness I can admit that it is still strange to me. How we'll never be friends again. The four of us. I used to feel as though we were meant to know one another forever.

Tonight I shake my head to clear it, to end the looking, and smile at Edith. Her ponytail is loose, the top two buttons of her shirt are undone, and her socks rolled down low, as close to her shoes as possible, as if she meant to hide them altogether. It is fashionable, I suppose, the reason why the boys flock around her and why we are so different for it.

I retie the scarf tighter around my neck. The fact that I am fourteen and Edith is nearly sixteen doesn't matter to her. I like that. I barely remember it myself, even though I am the youngest carrier taking the examination this year.

Edith swirls the bottle around a bit. She takes a swig before handing it to me.

"This is probably a bad idea," I say, but I take a sip, too. Some evenings, when we've been very good, Madame will open a bottle of wine for us to share around the table. But it's the cheap kind, the kind that she herself rarely drinks. Somehow you grow used to the taste, the tanginess of sour grapes. In comparison this expensive wine is too sweet, too rich, as it swirls around in my mouth. I take another sip and whisper to Edith, "I'm pretty sure Gray wants to kill me."

She frowns at him and then whispers back, "No, not you."

I say nothing.

Crickets are chirping, and the leaves of the forest rustle. A pair of owl eyes glower down at me from a tree, a group of fire-flies sidle past, and the wind starts to sing an eerie song. Now that darkness has fallen, all the things of the night are awake, aware. We should go inside, but I am afraid that I belong here more, to this wind, to this song, than I do to the sound of voices, of people. I always have, even before we left home.

"I'm going to bed," Gray says quietly after a while. Am I imagining the way he looks at me? He straightens from the shed and inhales what must be his third or fourth cigarette by now.

Edith startles. "Oh, okay," she says too cheerily, but I can read the disappointment in her voice. "You want some wine?" He doesn't answer, so she hands me the bottle, and then she stands. "I'll be right back, okay?" she says. She walks over to her brother, and though they whisper, I understand that Edith is trying to coax him out of whatever depression he has fallen into. She touches his cheek, but he flinches, as if her touch burned. She wraps her arms around him, but he stands there stiffly, blinking past her at me. Her shoulders are sagging, too, by the time she lets go.

I leave Edith where she is standing desolately and follow him, and I don't even know why I do it. "You're going to be okay tomorrow, right?" I hear myself asking.

He stops, waits for me to catch up. "Do you care?" he asks, the toe of his shoe scuffing the ground. That question seems like a test. A small test masking a larger one.

I tell him the truth. "Not really. I don't think I've even really thought of you before tonight. Not since we were kids. But . . . now I can't stop thinking about all sorts of weird things."

"Like what?" he asks, curiosity stirring his expression for the first time tonight. His eyes burn mine in an old familiar way. They've always been so serious. A cricket hops right onto my left shoe and sits there.

"Do you care?" I say, in the same tone of voice.

For a moment, silence. Then he shakes his head at me as if he is disappointed, hands me his cigarette, and walks on. Alex is dead. Gray is angry. Edith wants to drink herself to sleep. So much for our lucky group. We haven't even started our missions, our lives yet, and we are already this small. This tired of ourselves.

When I come back, Edith is sitting at our spot, still drinking. "Are you afraid you won't pass the exams tomorrow, Lira?" she asks me.

Of course I am afraid. I am *terrified*. And I wish we wouldn't talk about it now. It will be bad enough trying to fall asleep tonight. My heart is racing, and there is a heaviness that has clawed its way into my stomach. But I refuse to let it show, not even to Edith.

"I saw Jenny throw up three days ago," I confess instead. "I don't know whether that was fear."

Edith nods. "Jenny has been having little panic attacks all week. She thinks nobody notices."

"Everybody is afraid," I say. I am surprised to find myself defending Jenny.

"See, but that's not a good enough reason. The exam is the scariest thing that has ever happened to us. It's fine to be scared, but then we're supposed to get over it. We're supposed to think that after training with one another for eight years, there's a reasonable chance we'll make it. Panicking isn't going to solve anything."

"Is that why you've chewed your fingernails raw?" I ask her.

She tucks her hands into the pockets of her coat. "Is that why you were going to let Ezra choke you to death before Gray rescued you?" she asks me.

I don't answer.

Alex is gone. This is what we really want to say. Want to talk about. But we can't.

I know she is thinking the same thing I am. Alex's being gone somehow makes the possibility of our death tomorrow that much realer.

Edith sighs and shakes her head as if she's trying to clear it. Her voice is lighter when she speaks. "We're rich, you know?" she says. "In this other life we're going to. On our Earth we were living on the streets when they found us. Our parents were gone, and Gray was good at figuring out who we could steal from without getting caught. We lived beside garbage cans, slept in alleys, that sort of thing. We had to roast rats once for breakfast, and now we're here. And apparently we're going to be rich with two parents in some giant house in the city."

"Is that good?" I ask.

"I don't know," she says. "I guess we'll find out."

My own family consists of two grandparents and a sister and orchards in the countryside near Paris. We have no parents, my alternate and I. I suppose we have this one thing in common: that we were not meant to be loved in that way by those people.

I say nothing. Edith moves on.

"On the radio they're saying *alternate* is a vulgar term now. That we're duplicates, not alternates. Like what a thing is called is more dangerous than what that thing can do to you."

I suck on Gray's cigarette and wait for the real thing I

know she wants to say. The thing I was waiting for Gray to say. The reason I am out here to begin with, because I could read it on him when we were fighting earlier in the training room. We might not be close anymore, but I can read it on Edith now. After a while I do not think it is coming, and I have almost decided to go back to the training room and practice for tomorrow, to forget them, all of them, completely. Then Edith puts the bottle down and runs her fingers through her hair. She does not look at me.

"He doesn't think they did it," she says after a moment, staring down at the ground. I don't ask what she means, I am too frightened to, but she elaborates anyway. "He doesn't think they killed themselves, not like that. He says they had ideas of how to be, outside of here. That they might even have made it."

I rub my hands together because they're suddenly too cold. Because the wind is singing a crueler song than even I can bear. And then she makes it worse. Presses her lips right against my ear, where there is no risk of being overheard. "He thinks Madame did it to them because she found out," she says.

CHAPTER 8

We are always waiting our turn. Waking up in the morning and then lining up to use the single bathroom. Some of us go outside to brush our teeth because the line is so long. Some of us sneak out a piece of toast when no one is looking, just so we do not have to wait for breakfast also. This morning I fill up the kettle and set it on the stove.

I practiced my knife skills until I was exhausted last night, and now I pick up my book and keep reading from where I left off to tune out the noise. One girl is running around the living room half naked, iron in her hand. Another polishes her shoes while the radio plays. Everyone's suitcases are starting to pile up by the door. These suitcases will be rifled through by Madame when we are gone, and sorted, their contents passed on to the next cottage children. The next generation of us.

Toothbrush still in my mouth, I walk outside barefoot, toward the chicken coop for eggs. There are just two. It's getting too cold for laying, and soon enough Madame will cook these chickens and get more chicks after winter has passed. And whoever replaces us in the cottages, the children downstairs who are ready, will pluck feathers until their hands hurt. I put the eggs in each one of my pockets, but I've barely gone two meters before the book is snatched from my hand. This is my fault. If I'd been paying attention to anything but reading, I might have noticed that I had company.

"You know," Davis says loudly, voice filled with equal parts cheer and amusement, "most of us threw our hands up in the air last night and left it all up to fate. Nothing we can do about the examination now, but not Harrison. Harrison has to study right up until the last moment. And what's this book going to do for you anyway when you've got a target to shoot and no loaded gun?"

I try to snatch the book back, but he's too quick. I don't

think about it; I spit as much toothpaste as I can manage on his clean leather shoes. He's still exclaiming about this when I take the book back. I say, "Harrison passed her final math exam with the highest grade this year. What number were you again, Davis? And what was it Madame said about the size of your brain? Was it the size of a pea or not even that big?" Because I am just as good at this game as he is.

But even as I am speaking, I cannot help thinking that he's acting like Alex. That cocky tease-the-girls/make-everyone-laugh Alex routine. As if someone has to take his place now that he is gone, and maybe he does. Maybe that's the only way this day will work for the boys, for the girls. Maybe it is all of our jobs to play along.

The examination tests everything from the capabilities of our minds to our bodies with only one question: Can we live perfectly as our alternates? And there is only one right answer.

By the end of today I might be dead.

I think about that, *dying today*, and feel the latest, deepest twinge of fright. So far I have done my best not to count time, but it has run out on me anyway.

Davis might be lying in the ground right next to me in a few hours.

We don't want to know this. No. We don't even want the chance to think it.

"See, this is why the young 'uns shouldn't be graduating so soon," Davis says, throwing his hands in the air dramatically. "Now they think they can talk back to their superiors."

A small smile flickers on my lips. "I heard Madame say that half the kids in the bunkers will be ready before you ever are."

He looks quickly behind him before lowering his voice, his eyes nearly panicking. It won't do to have the other boys hearing these things about him. "She was joking," he says out the corner of his mouth.

"I've never heard Madame tell a joke in my life," I say out the corner of my own mouth. "Have you?"

He presses a hand to his chest and groans. "Oh, you wound me, Lira." But his pain must be gone pretty quickly because he's back to his normal self shortly after. This time he leans forward. I lean back, but that doesn't stop him. "So, listen," he says underneath his breath, and even though I can already tell that I shouldn't, I do. "We all know that you're pretty innocent around these parts. But pretty much every guy here has made a bet that he's going to be your first kiss, and I was thinking that maybe you could do me a small favor."

"Nope."

"Are you sure?" he asks. "Do you think Julia would go for it?"

"Why do you have to be so immature?" I say, shaking my head.

He offers me a dimpled smile and straightens. "It's in my alternate's personality. It's *your* alternate's family I'm concerned about. They might try to return you." Before I can form a retort, he and his friends are ambling off to find someone else to pester. "Don't forget to take your pills, Lira," he calls after me, and wriggles one brow. I wave back, and in a way I am sad. That was our best attempt at a good-bye.

I turn back toward the cottage.

Carriers never forget their pills, not from the moment Madame explained that they are the most important rule we must keep. A carrier without her pills is like a gun without any bullets in it. If we are not stronger and smarter than our alternates, how can we expect to defeat them? In our eight years as cottage children, most of us have fallen sick only once or twice. It's because of the pills, we are so healthy. But that is not their only use.

I remember sitting on the floor in the bunkers when I was six, along with the other children. We'd been there only a few days. "It goes against the nature of things that we are here in their world," Madame said, pacing in front of us. She'd brought some of the older carriers downstairs with her to help control us. We were only half listening when she held up two pills—a blue and a white one—and said, "Without these, you will die soon enough in this world."

That got our attention, and the noise died down a little.

"Every planet has its own set of rules," Madame said. She told us that we could not expect to leave our planet and enter an alternate one without some kind of reckoning. She explained the gruesome outcome of not taking our pills, sparing no details. "Without the pills, you will begin to feel disoriented. Then your bodies will shut down, but only after you have begun to bleed from the inside out."

After she was done, my entire body shook from fear.

Needless to say that now taking our pills is the first thing we do when we wake up every morning.

When I reach the cottage, Jenny is in the kitchen. "I have to go get ready," I tell her, retrieving the eggs from my pockets. She can afford to fry them while I get ready, but although we both hold out our hands, the two eggs hit the ground with a soft splat.

Jenny and I lock eyes, but only for a moment. Jenny bends to wipe up the mess, but I step away.

Neither of us knows whose hands the eggs fell out of.

Afraid, afraid. The words echo around us.

Her, not me, I tell myself.

I am not afraid.

I am not going to die today.

The boys are first for their examinations this morning, and by sunrise they are dressed in their best suits and ties. It is so uncharacteristic of them to do *anything* before us, much less be ready, but they are. Edith is the only one who goes outside to say good-bye, the only one to hug a boy, the only one to wish him good luck. The rest of us stand at the window and watch them disappear one by one into the woods, suitcases in their hands, backs rod straight, as if they are marching to death.

There is a brown cottage there, deeper into the woods, that we have never been allowed to go to. We used to like walking past it on our way to the river, but not lately. Now we pretend it's not there at all.

The morning flies away from us like this, with us watching. Finally it is our turn. Madame looks her best today: tall and severe, but in a suit, not just a dress, with shoes that click when she walks. She's smoking like a chimney each time she comes to collect one of the girls.

I look around the room. Everything in the cottage has been put back into place, every bed made, every spoon washed and dried so that it is as if we were never here. We haven't even left yet, but we are already blending into the wallpaper like ghosts. I close my eyes and think of the ocean, the great vastness of it. That blue place where the two worlds connect, and I still don't understand how they, our government and scientists, found it. I don't know how it is possible to know that somewhere, somehow, if you jump into the water at exactly the right spot, a secret spot, you will not drown. The water will pull you down, down, crushing your lungs until you realize that you are actually being sucked upward, toward a new sky. And what was here is there, and what was there is here.

I remember being so small, so afraid.

It happened the same then, too, with the waiting, and then they dropped us small children into the water one by one, asking, "Can you swim?" It didn't matter the answer; they dropped us anyway, and then Madame was waiting in a boat on the other side, younger but with a cigarette in her mouth like today. "Welcome home, carriers," she said, and pulled us out. "Breathe."

CHAPTER 9

This is what the other Lirael Harrison is not doing right now: she is not sitting on the floor of a dark room with her hands tied behind her back. But imagine that she is. Imagine that she is being asked a hundred questions about herself, about her life, questions like: What is your favorite food, and what is your favorite time of the day? What do you think of your family? What do you want to be when you grow up? What are you most ashamed of about yourself? Which parts of your body do you hate? What makes you most insecure? What makes you angry? Show me what you look like when you are angry. When you are happy. When you are frightened. When you are confused. The knowledge test. A check to make sure that the facts are there, embedded inside her mind. This is the nearest thing to being stripped naked without ever taking her clothes off, and a single wrong answer could have immeasurable consequences. She does not know what those consequences might be, but every now and then the stale smell of blood drifts up from the ground around her. From today or from a year ago or even the year before that, as if this were a place meant only for death.

There are two men and two women, interviewers apart from Madame, whom I have never seen before. In fact, Madame does not stay, although she returns silently every little while with cups of tea and biscuits that we did not know yesterday we were baking for our examiners. The two men and two women sit in front of a long table across the room, near the curtains, their shadows contrasting the lightness of the wall. They take turns with their questions and listen attentively. There must be other rooms in the cottage with other examiners because my exam alone lasts nearly two hours, and in all that time I am wondering whether this is it, whether the hype over the examination was just that. Two hours that make my head spin, not just because of the questions but also because I am working the rope from my hands. Because even though I haven't been told to, I don't like the idea of being tied up, of being held in one place like a lamb, waiting for the wolf. Despite myself, I start to relax at the two-hour mark. I tell myself that this *is* it. That the hype over the examination *was* just that. Then the light flickers fully on, and I realize how wrong I am.

There is a woman sitting across from me. A young woman, beautiful, who cannot be much older than her mid-twenties. All this time we have been sitting right across from each other, so close, and yet unable to touch because the woman's hands were tied also and her mouth is taped. All this time, never knowing she was there. I stare at her. I have not been given any orders, yet the people sitting behind the desk stare at me, as if they are waiting for me to do something. That is when I see it: the gun lying in the space between us. It is only a matter of which one of us can get our hands free quickly enough, and then, I suppose, it is a question of morality versus self-preservation. I cannot stop staring at the girl. I ask myself questions I immediately wish I could take back. Who is she? What has she done wrong? Why did she wind up here like this?

It is as if the examiners have read my mind. "Her name

is Harriet Cummings," an older woman says, her voice raspy as she lifts a cup of tea to her lips. "She was a girl just like you once, living in the cottages some years ago."

If the woman is at least twenty-five, then she left the cottages just before I arrived. If I'd been here even just a year earlier, I might have known her.

But that is all the information they offer up, and it is even worse. To know a name but not know a reason. To watch a girl try desperately to free herself in front of you, tears streaming down her cheeks. She has been given some kind of toxin that makes her hands shake, that makes it hard for her to move properly; that is why she is so slow. But her eyes have the same fire as mine, that same intense desire to live; it is almost as if I am staring at some future version of myself, just a few years from now. My hands are almost out. Just a single tug and I am free. When one of the examiners stands from her chair and ambles over and frees the other girl, everything changes.

Now there are two free girls and one gun.

We both are frozen. Surprised or afraid, and I don't know which is worse.

I think again of the ocean.

The smell of cigarettes and whiskey, the pain of broken arms and dead friends come back to me unbidden. This is how any future Madames will be born. Just like this, in this room, with this gun, with this choice.

We react at the exact same moment. She lunges for the gun, but I lunge for her because my body is stronger, faster. There is a horrible crunch when my fist connects with her face. Once and then again and again. When I am sure she is weaker than I am, I inch forward on all fours toward the gun and wrap my hands around it.

This is only test number two.

CHAPTER 10

The picture slides into a small crack in the mirror and hangs there. Not a picture of me but of *her*, and in a way she is more beautiful than me. I remember thinking that even when I was five, watching her on satellite, though we looked exactly the same. But she had rosier cheeks and eyes that glistened whenever she smiled. I had my hair in pigtails, per orphanage regulations, and when I smiled, it was this difficult practiced thing that really depended on my muscles' level of cooperation that day. I was wearing a yellow dress that did not belong to me, that the orphanage minders would put on whichever girl was going to talk to her alternate next, pretending that they were caring for us better than they were. A canary yellow dress with beading down the front, a large black bow at the neck. I remember loving the feeling of wearing that dress yet thinking that it could never really be mine because two dozen other girls loved it, too. I remember the bruises underneath my dress and the way my ribs still hurt from the fisted hand that had punched me there earlier and wondering whether instead of smiling, if I frowned, if I burst into tears, would my alternate care enough to try to save me. If I said the words out loud despite the minder sitting next to me, told her about what really went on at the orphanage, would it matter to her?

Please . . .

I turn the water off and straighten. I am remembering those things because somehow I have to let go of them now, along with the tears that do not have my permission to fall, along with the bile that bitters the back of my throat. My hands are shaking over a pair of scissors; my hair is wet over my shoulders. The last drops of blood, soap, and water swirl down the sink, purged from underneath my fingernails, my hands, my arms. I am wearing a piece of wire wound around my wrist that signifies everything that has happened. My success. My strength. My courage. I stay where I am, blinking at it, until someone knocks on the door.

"Fifteen minutes," a male examiner says.

I nod my head, then realize he cannot see me. "I'm almost finished," I say, to my reflection in the mirror. I am almost finished cleaning up. Almost finished getting ready. Almost somebody else.

Then I begin to cut my hair to match *hers*. Shoulder-length brown hair, blunt bangs in front.

Please, she begged, staring at me. There was blood running down the side of her face.

The more I cut, the more my hands tremble, the more my eyes well up. I let the tears fall. I am crying, but I can still see myself clearly through my tears. I can still cut my hair exactly the way the picture demands. These are not the kinds of tears where you lose yourself for a moment and then have to search, have to refocus. I know who I am and what I have done, and I am crying right through that. And when I am finished, I will still be me, the girl from the cottage, and I will still have done all the terrible things I have just done.

CHAPTER 11

"Come closer, Lirael," Madame barks, and makes me sit in a chair. I am inside another room in the brown cottage, and she is talking with somebody she keeps calling Agnes. Agnes, who dries and perfects my hair and then applies a thin rim of kohl to my eyes, a glossy lipstick to my lips. Agnes, who pierces my ears because they have to be, and holds the tattoo gun to my rib cage and writes the excruciating words that will stay with me forever.

I do not want the permanence of her words, the weight of what they mean to her.

It's funny that I can get this far in the training, this far past the examinations, and then suddenly my mind snaps, and I am mad. That is what Madame keeps saying while she pins me down: "You're mad, you're mad, you foolish girl. Do you want to fail? After all these years do you want to lose everything over a few words on the side of your ribs? You think life comes at no cost, eh? You think this is supposed to be easy?" She glares at me as if I am the stupidest girl in the world, but she doesn't let me go, even when she can. Even when she should. Even when, because of this one small thing, I can be considered a failure. Perhaps for Madame this is as much as the eight years between us can ever mean. But afterward I do not hug her. I do not thank her. I just shrug into the dress I am offered, the boots and scarf, and stumble toward the door, knowing that after today I will never see either of them—Madame or Agnes—again.

A bus waits to take us away from the woods, and standing by it already are most of the boys and the girls from the cottages. I look around, trying to figure out who is missing. Emma with the fiery red hair is gone, but she was no surprise; she had a bad memory and could never hit a target. Jason with the deep voice. I can't see Rebecca Matheson, who played the piano almost every evening, anywhere. And no Greta. *Where is Greta?*

And then I realize Edith is shaking next to me.

Gray isn't here.

I am so shocked I cannot move. How can her brother not have made it? I scan the group again and again, and Edith's teeth are chattering together so loudly I can hear them.

"Maybe   he . . . ," I begin, trying to offer her some explanation.

Edith watches me hopefully. But I cannot think of anything else to say.

She looks away.

We line up in front of the bus. I try not to think about her as I hold my hand to my chest and sing. Our sleeper anthem. We sing like we have every assembly morning for the last eight years. We sing for the last time. We pledge our allegiance to the other Earth. Halfway into the anthem, when Edith is biting her lip so hard she has drawn blood, her brother finally turns up. Shirt buttoned wrong, hair a mess, and dried blood on one hand, slinking into the line, as if he had never been gone. "I see you both made it," he says out of the corner of his mouth. He doubles over when Edith slams her elbow into his side.

"You idiot," she says, but she breathes a sigh of relief.

There is an eerie silence afterward as we board the bus,

different from any that has ever been, and everyone either looks down or stares out a window. All of us are now in on the secret. We have spent the last eight years here reprogramming our bodies, our memories, but this last day is proof that somehow along the way, we reprogrammed our morals also. What is right and wrong. What we can and cannot do for our country. For ourselves. The examination was never truly about what we remembered; it was our final lesson: that we are capable of anything.

It is strange that we are supposedly ready for this, for our new lives. I do not feel as though I am truly any different today from yesterday. But we will begin our new missions. We will live as our alternates and wait for the day when the war really truly begins.

Handlers will keep track of us once we are away from these woods. A routine check-in once a month when we must give account of everything that has happened, when health checks are performed and our pills are refilled. My handler, they tell me, will be a person named Odette.

At the very last moment before I board the bus, I turn to Madame, who suddenly looks so old and pathetic. My voice is soft but not kind. "You didn't pass the examination, did you?" I say, because I understand now that it is not us she hates.

"That's why you're here. If you'd passed, you would be in the city. You would have claimed your alternate's life."

Her eyes widen for a moment, and I cannot tell whether she is surprised at my frankness or my daring. Normally her girls and boys are supposed to be meek, obedient. Then the look is gone. A silk scarf billows up around her neck. "There is no such thing as failing the exam for some *special* people," she says, breathing smoke onto my face. "If they cannot pass in the usual way, they pass in other ways." She gestures back to the cottage, to Agnes, and I suddenly imagine myself as a hairdresser, a tattoo artist, even the person who collects surveillance on alternates until we're ready. It is not such a bad life. It is only a punishment because you had the chance to be someone else, someone better, someone more important. Because you, out of everyone, will be the person never to get on the yellow bus that comes.

Madame runs her fingers alongside my left cheek and smiles. Her teeth are yellowed, rotted, and despite myself, I smile back. I even hold still when she leans forward suddenly and hugs me. My chest warms in an old childish way, as if even now I am only a marionette in her game, still waiting for her to piece together my drawing and to tell me it was beautiful. Waiting, like a bird at the mouth of a rifle.

Why do we always want the things that will hurt us the most? Madame's hand is rough where my tattoo aches, and her voice is full of malice when she whispers, "*Vous êtes faibles, mon enfant.*" Weak, weak, little girl. "Don't worry, it will be our little secret." I pull away, as if I have been slapped. I stumble on board and sit at the back, press my face to the glass, and watch the cottages disappear, swallowed up by the trees.

I will never call them home again.

CHAPTER 12

The road is long and straight; it seems to go on forever. The hours that pass feel like days, but it's the minutes that are worst. You breathe and breathe forever, waiting for it to end, and then find that only two minutes have passed. That time is moving like winter on a day when everything is frozen.

We hold on to our seats with white hands and pursed lips and hearts that beat horribly out of sync. With every slow-passing minute the sky dies a little more, the day peeled back by night, until, finally a murmur of excitement buzzes from those who can see the city lights. They already feel the energy of our new world, and it is different, better, yet exactly the same as they had imagined. Everything we learned in the cottages to survive—how to hunt, to cook, to be self-sufficient— must now be hidden in the real world. We are not supposed to be able to take care of ourselves. Kids our age are not even supposed to want to. There are high fives and hurrahs. I hear someone in front say that our real test isn't our ability to kill; it's our ability to make friends, to pretend to care about our clothes, our homework, learning how to drive cars, and thinking about colleges.

"Here's to our pretend futures," Davis says, raising an imaginary glass in his hand.

"To our pretend futures," everyone echoes.

The bus roars with laughter.

This is it. *This is everything*, and I make myself smile with them, press my face to the window. I want to be as happy as all the other sleepers. I don't want to sit here missing the familiarity of the past.

When we first found out we would be sleepers, I used to imagine a horror story. It was always the same one, which left only one version of me alive, but it was the wrong one. There would be a battle of good and evil, and the good one of us would prevail. She, and never me. I was always dead, but that was not the worst part. In my story no one would ever know. She would go on living, and I would be the one forgotten, lost, because there was never enough of me to begin with. I had not left enough of an impression in the world. I would think these things and then shake my head quickly mid-thought. "My name is Lirael Harrison," I would say, snapping my fingers. "I am fourteen years old." My name is Lirael Harrison.

I think that sometimes we walk toward the stories we have already written for ourselves, or perhaps they are forewarnings of the things that are coming. Perhaps, deep down inside, we already know how our whole lives will play out, everything has been decided, and I am already dead somewhere.

I jolt awake when Gray says, "Lira," softly on the bus. I open my eyes, see him turned around in the seat in front of me, concern making his eyebrows furrow. My look must be the same as the one he gave me in the training room because for the longest flicker of a moment I do not understand who he is, and then I do. I get the impression that this is not the first time he has called me either. He looks tired, but he leans in closer, as if he has forgotten all about yesterday, as if I am in a bad enough state for this moment alone to matter. Edith is staring at me, too, and that is when I notice how cold I am. That I am shaking. The hand wearing the wire shudders the most, as if it might be trying to remove itself because it already knows that it will kill another girl today. It might as well be screaming: "You are afraid." I've been twirling the wire on my wrist so hard and for so long that there is a bruise forming.

"What should we do?" Edith asks. They're talking about me as if I am not here.

"She's fine," her brother says, but he doesn't turn back to the front, just watches me. "Think about something else, Lira."

Except that there's nothing else to think about.

I sit on both my hands. I stare straight ahead and pretend that that is all there is: the road and the journey without any destination. About five kids are left on the bus when it finally stops for me, and this is what I want to be able to say: that I found her in a tree, in a green dress and black rain boots. She did not see me coming. She did not notice the way I slid the wire from my wrist and unwound it until it was long and strong enough to wrap around her neck. I want to say that there was murder in my eyes. I want to say that I did not feel fourteen for the first time in my life. But I did. I did, and I do.

My training never presented the possibility that my alternate would see my face before I saw hers. That is what threw me. She was not supposed to be in the barn; she preferred the trees. She stood there, frozen, but a friendliness crept across her face when she recognized me. It stopped me for too long, and by the time I recovered I had already forgotten how to be a good sleeper.

I say all this as though it were past, yet I say it inside a moment when I have lunged for her, but she is steadier than I am, and stronger. Blood is running down my arms and down the side of my face where the rock hit me. I am lying on the ground, and her hands are around my neck.

I cannot breathe.

I am going to die.

I want to beg her, tell somebody, please don't forget the history of me, that I was here. That I tried. That I failed.

It will happen quickly, and this is how it will go: I die and she lives, but the moment I am dead, our people come to silence her before she can reveal what she has found out. If I am still alive somehow, they will kill me, too, and then we both will have ended.

But then suddenly the blackness around my eyes begins to fade, and Edith is pulling me up. "It's okay," she keeps saying. "You're going to be okay."

Gray does all the work. He removes the evidence. I don't even hear her scream. I gasp for air until my eyes clear up and my throat stops hurting. They wipe the blood from my forehead, from the corners of my mouth, and I am ashamed of the way I feel, like a little child needing to be cared for. I am crying and shaking, and I don't know where one stops and the other starts. How did they get off the bus? When? Why are they here?

"Don't say anything," they tell me when I open my mouth and shut it for the third time. "Don't say anything. Just go and be a sleeper. This part doesn't matter."

They don't wait for my response. They blend into the dark as they hurry away.

My enemies, my friends.

Over time I turn this night into a dream, a myth, a false memory. It never happened, and I have begun the rest of my life with more secrets. They heap themselves on one another until there are nearly more than enough to bury me, but I will wear this face. I swear. From now on I will wear it well.

Part
TWO

One Year Later . . .

CHAPTER 13

My grandfather sends me into town once a week with a box of apples and apricots on my bicycle. No matter how early or late I leave, Cecily insists on coming with me, her lip bitten in concentration as she rides over the bumpy road on the tricycle she should have given up two years ago. "It's good for me to know," she says in her serious voice, "everything you do in the city so that I can take over when I'm older. Right, Lira?"

I nod in agreement. She looks pleased with herself. "Someone has to take care of the trees," she adds.

My grandfather, Da, has been putting all sorts of ideas in her head about the family legacy, about how the well-being of the orchards will fall to us one day. Some afternoons he gets the sudden urge to walk us both through the trees and vines again, make us take everything in while he watches, as if within twenty-four hours we might have forgotten what apples look like, what unripe grapes feel and taste like. As if he can teach us to love his life, his job, his orchards as much as he does. I neglect to mention to Cecily that since I am barely fifteen, it's very unlikely that she's going to take over anytime soon. "You look ridiculous," I yell instead, turning back to laugh at her. "You're going to have to learn to ride a proper bicycle soon, because that thing is going to give out on you. Just look at the rickety wheels."

She makes a face and pedals faster, although that gets her nowhere. Sweat trickles down from the sides of her pink helmet from the effort. "I don't get in your business," she growls, "so why are you getting in mine?"

"You're six," I say. "I'm *supposed* to be in your business." I wave back at the fishermen by the river who are readying their boats. The river is only a few minutes from the orchards, easily visible to those passing by on the road and often filled with fishermen who have done this job all their lives. Some afternoons they bring back something for us. "For your grandmother," they'll say.

"Well, I'm old enough to mean what I say," announces Cecily. She sticks out her tongue, licks her sweaty upper lip, and I laugh again. Her hair is matted to her forehead, and I slow down. For my efforts, when she reaches me, she rides her tricycle directly into me. We both go flying into the grass on the side of the road, apples and apricots sprayed everywhere. "No, no, no," I groan. I jump up and immediately begin picking them up in case a car comes. If Da were here, he would cry. "An apple is worthless," he would say, "if it has a single bruise on it. I am the best orchardist for miles, Lirael. People respect me. People expect the best from me." His thumbs would press against his eyes to hide the tears; he would clear his throat as if it were itchy. And I would remember how small he is, how stooped his back gets when he walks, how old and wrinkly and breakable he is.

I squint over at Cecily. "You saw that on television, didn't you?"

"Of course not. If I did *half* the things I saw on the television, Lira," she says cheerily, "you would be dead. Race you." And then she is gone, dust from the road billowing up in her wake. I wipe the fruit carefully on my dress before putting it back inside the boxes. Cecily pedals as fast as she can. She couldn't beat me if I was walking, much less riding my bike, but she doesn't let that stop her. She turns back to grin at me, eyes wide, voice squeaky. "I'm winning, I'm winning. Oh, my God, I'm actually winning."

"No, you're not. I'm coming to kick your butt," I yell.

But I let her win. Not just because she is my sister but also because there is no sorer loser in this world than Cecily. I let her win because it is the thing to do and because suddenly I am tired of having to smile, having to make conversation. It happens. Sudden moments like these when I am heavier than usual. Despite myself, I turn my eyes up to the sky much more frequently these days. I am waiting for something. I just don't know what. But then I think that maybe I am remembering what I did, not waiting, and my head hurts.

I let her win because I have never forgotten that I am not really her sister.

A lot can happen in a year. A body can grow taller, bonier; eyes become bigger, grayer; hair darker, longer. I am her but harsher around the edges in a way I am convinced she would never have been. *This*, I tell myself, *is not weakness*. It is the subtle reintroduction of myself, the old me, in a way no one but I will know. My old self wasn't enamored with food, didn't care about her appearance so much, didn't care about pleasing everyone else. That is what I tell myself when I look in the mirror. Secretly I am afraid that I might be about to fall apart.

Each dawn the same robin sits on the same wire fence, singing the same song. Night hands over morning in the exact same state it was given. There have been no rearrangements of the clouds, of the stars, no big surprises. Everything in the world is a whisper, and now more than ever, I understand what it means to be a sleeper. Counting time, counting days, always on edge, yet doing nothing. I was trained for much more, but my orders haven't come yet. The worst that has happened is that my grandmother is sick, my grandfather is unhappy with his apricot trees this year, and he is blaming the nippiness of the weather at night, the lack of workers because all the boys over fifteen have run off to the city to sign up to become soldiers, to become men.

It is not just them. Most parts of the countryside are emptier now than they were ever meant to be. The Silence has made people antsy. The possibility that it might not be resolved with simple conversations or negotiations. If the world falls apart, people want to be ready, people want to be doing something. They're not stupid enough to be completely defenseless, so every once in a while, protests surge around the world, and men and women hurry to sign up for the army, to pledge their allegiance to a possible war, but it won't be enough. They have no idea what they will be up against.

Some people think the Silence will last forever; others, just a few more years. The effort is less halfhearted in the countryside, where the boys are bored, and running away to big cities seems better. In school, before I finished last term, there were empty desks, and the teachers pretended not to notice. People seem to think that in bad times, being surrounded by more people is some kind of defense. Perhaps it is. Perhaps if a rocket falls from the sky and there are ten people standing together, at least one will survive. On any given day on my way home from school, some family was always sitting at the bus stop with suitcases and a look of unease on their faces. They worried about going to the cities to live in cramped apartments and breathe in the polluted air, but they did it anyway. That stopped nearly as quickly as it started, though, and it's gone back to waiting now. Waiting for war; waiting for the Silence to end.

I am still not used to the idea that my life as a cottage girl is over forever. Every once in a while I sense that I am being watched. Those times are the only reminders of a sleeper world. My fighting muscles are completely useless to my everyday life, and my mind still turns, trying to assimilate new facts of the world that I dare not miss. Like the new things that make my grandmother tired these days, that make Da worried, that make Cecily sad. Sometimes I catch my sister staring at me, and suddenly I cannot meet her eyes. I know I am still living in the cottages inside my head even though I am here. I am guilty of that. Today I have to remind myself twice that the apples and apricots are for the baker's wife and that the money will buy Gigi's medicine for the week. When we reach the shop, we tie up our bicycles, and I have to remind myself that I am not *supposed* to be shy. Da says that I am a good haggler, almost as good as him. I tell myself these things and become *her*.

I get by.

I smile and get by. I'm all alone. Even if I were permitted to, I could never love them as much as they love me—I must be incapable of it, I think, must have lost the ability somehow, somewhere along the road—but we all get by. There is blood on my hands, but it doesn't count if nobody else can see it.

And somehow I have reached Safe status.

CHAPTER 14

I was nervous to meet them, and then, once I did, I was afraid to know them, to really, truly know them beyond the things that a screen had taught me all those years. Not afraid exactly, but wary, like a girl who suspects her hand might be reaching out for a heap of hot coals. It was bound to burn me. I was bound to mess up. I already had, outside, just moments before with Edith and Gray. I had messed up in the worst way a sleeper could, and I was almost surprised to still find myself alive.

I still am, sometimes.

***

On My First Night:

My grandfather is an old man with white hair and a full beard. The suspenders make his pants too short, but he likes to see his socks. Likes to make sure that they're the same color and that they match his shoes. There is a long line of stories scribbled on his face that I could trace with my fingers, and the first time I meet him I want to say, I *know you*, and I want to say, I *have never seen you in my life*. Instead I sit down to dinner and pretend because his lined face looks angry. Once the food is served, he doesn't like to wait. He waited twenty minutes for me, yelling my name throughout the house and finally outside. "Where have you been?" he asks with gritted teeth, but I don't answer. He says a prayer, and I dump some mashed potatoes onto my plate without any gravy. Everyone is quiet. I, too, sit in silence, fork at my mouth. When the old man leans forward, suddenly I jump. "All right, Lira," he says, tenting his hands in front of his face, "I'm just going to say what everyone is thinking."

I know I am about to be chastened for being late. But before he can begin, a large hairy creature jumps off the top of my head and scurries across the dinner table. Everyone screams. We scramble away from the table, as fast as we can, splashing food everywhere. No one ever really likes spiders, but nobody reacts like me. Nobody does my strange dance around the room, afraid that something else might fall from my clothes, half screaming, half crying.

I can't even remember whether my alternate is supposed to be scared—of things, bugs, of *giant* spiders. I don't even know whether it is about the spider or a residual effect of what happened outside with Edith and Gray. It's like I am standing outside my own body, watching myself overreact, and I cannot do anything about it. Is that what a panic attack feels like? Where is my courage, my strength?

I am Lirael.

I am the cottage girl again and horrified. I didn't even last five minutes.

The old man is looking for his glasses, but he is too slow. Eventually the little girl stomps on it with her boot. The hairy black thing that becomes a blob of goop because she doesn't stop at fifteen stomps or even twenty. Twenty might not be enough for a thing that big and that hairy.

When it's over, we reclaim our seats at the table. My face is hot and sweaty, my hair sticking to my temples. I clear my throat and pick up my fork. I try to tell myself that this is nothing. That it doesn't matter, but I can feel everyone's eyes on me as we eat. I force the food down my throat.

It is the old man who laughs first, and then the old woman. The little girl stares at me for a moment before she laughs, too.

They have not seen my failure. They have not recognized this moment for what it really was, with the girl who is not their granddaughter or sister. They think it was perfectly normal.

The old man clutches his belly, and his laughing voice is a loud boom, a contrast with when he talks. "I was going to ask why there were twigs in your hair," he says. "Seems like you've answered my question. You keep climbing those trees and you're going to break your neck one of these days." But his chastisement is lost because he's laughing so hard he can barely form words.

Say something, say something, I think.

"And I suppose you wouldn't notice until dinnertime."

"Twenty minutes past at the very latest," he promises.

They spend the rest of the evening falling into fits of laughter. The whole time I am afraid they know, afraid that they can smell it on me, the fear, the blood, the death of their Lirael. *She is right outside in the ground,* the voice inside my head says. *I was not climbing any trees.*

I don't want to laugh. But I do. And it sounds loud and sincere coming from my lips.

My heart thumps inside my chest, my hands sweat, and I realize that I am afraid of them. Her family. *My* family. I arrived scared and ugly, only half a person, and now I have to learn how to hide it. I have to get used to it. The strangeness. The fear. The unpredictability of living in the real world.

I wake up every day from Mondays to Fridays, from Saturdays to Sundays, and suddenly one month, two, three, ten months have passed. I am not used to it. The ripple of time. The sound of laughter. No Madame. No cottage children. No sleeper anthems. I am growing old faster behind my eyes. I am aging from the exhaustion of it all. Of pretending.

It was the old woman I met first, with the same shock of white hair as her husband. She was standing at the door, and she said, "Oh, hush," to her yelling husband, "here she comes now," and she smiled at me with her crooked teeth. "Dinner is ready, sweetheart," she said, gesturing to the table, where her husband was glowering.

I met the little girl last and liked her first.

We were praying right after I rushed in, and I opened my eyes and saw her, and she ran her finger across her throat and then quickly closed her eyes again. *You're dead meat.* I liked her because she expected nothing from me. Because it was enough that she was herself and all I had to do was close my eyes, too.

Months have passed since the beginning of my life. I am still thinking about the spider and how it seemed to say, "Welcome. We intend to make this difficult for you." But time is passing, and the dead girl is still dead. For a whole year she has been dead. . . .

There are other things I am not proud of. Moments I want to peel off my skin. "I thought you liked banana bread?" someone will say, or, "I thought you were never going to wear those shoes again?" Worse moments: "What is wrong with you?" or, "Why are you suddenly like this?" or, "Sometimes I feel like I don't know you anymore." Or, "Go to your room."

If there really is darkness in my eyes, then that explains why it is so hard, hard, hard to pretend to have a light shining there. The light can snuff itself out and become dark, but how does the dark become light? How do you start a fire with nothing? I have nothing.

Sometimes.

I wish I were never a cottage girl at all sometimes, in my weakest moments, when I am lying in the dark and there are no snoring voices in bunks all around mine, no schedules, when I wake up and find that this is the life I am in, this is the present that I was predestined to live.

Sometimes I write my words down; then I burn them or drown them or they never escape the confines of my skull.

And I tell myself that I don't mean any of this.

I am not afraid. I am not weak.

I am not. These things were never said.

CHAPTER 15

"You're going to leave me here again, aren't you?" Cecily asks as I pocket the money from the boxes. But she is already shrugging out of her coat and into an apron that the baker's wife hands her. We have an arrangement. The baker's wife looks after Cecily while I run errands and buy Gigi's medicine. She tells Cecily that today they are going to make croissants, which is an intricate process that only little hands can properly accomplish. "I'll just turn the radio up a little," she says with a wink, "and then we can start."

She is a short, round woman with dark, wispy curls and

reminds me of my grandmother when she was better.

I offer her a grateful smile as I turn to leave.

"It's almost as if there's nothing out there but emptiness right now," a crackly voice is saying on the speakers as I reach for the door. "All the folks listening who have lived as long as I have will agree that it has never felt quite like this before. Like we are alone in the world . . ."

The topic of conversation on the radio is always the same: the Silence, the possibility of war, the waiting. Most people roll their eyes now. At school I once watched a film about the beginning of the Silence. That initial panic has ebbed away. And they roll their eyes a little more every day, stare up at the sky, and *dare* them, whoever is out there, to come with their bombs and their missiles. B*eg* them to come. Anything but this waiting. Anything.

They have no idea what they are asking for.

"Be good. I'll be right back," I say, and step out of the shop, pull my coat tighter around my body. Even though there is a pharmacy nearby, I make my way right across town, taking the paths least trodden, avoiding people and their familiar faces. All sleepers exist in a state of paranoia. Always afraid that we are being watched. That the people here suspect us.

I am always looking. Backward and forward and sideways.

A woman is sweeping the front of her shop. I walk right into her pile of dirt.

"Sorry," I say quickly, but she swats at me with her broom anyway. It's all done rather good-naturedly because to her she has known me for years and I go to school with her daughter.

I saw a girl from the cottages once, one afternoon when I was running errands for my grandfather in the city. She did not notice me; she was walking with her friends, laughing, hands waving in the air animatedly. She was older. I wondered for a moment whether I had just conjured her up because I had run out of people to imagine seeing. But then I realized that we all grew up together so that we would be dispersed into a world close together. Even now we are a unit, a team. Since then I have seen more of us from the cottages, some who offer me a quick, friendly smile, some who look right through me. I have to confess; I am a lot more enthusiastic to see them, eyes always flickering about, always hoping. I overheard my handler say that over the last year people are moving through the cottages faster. That per the instructions of our government, there are no longer eight- to ten-year learning curves. As if some sort of invisible deadline were pedaling up to meet us.

* * *

A small flower shop sits on a dirty, lonely side of town, lost among the older forgotten buildings. The walls are skewed; they intend to cave in slowly and hope no one notices. When I knock on the shop door, a short, bespectacled man peers out at me before opening it. He is thin, made up of sharp, angular edges, has a pointy mustache, and reminds me a bit of a praying mantis. He says nothing to me, just holds the door open. Inside his shop there are so many plants that it is nearly impossible to move. He glares at me when I knock a flowerpot over, and even though I straighten it before I reach the counter, his scowl does not go away. His radio is blaring in the background. The air inside the flower shop is musty, as if the plants are competing with us instead of helping us, and the blinds are drawn, too. I pretend not to mind.

The man bends, reaches underneath his counter, and retrieves something wrapped in a frayed cloth. I know even before I unwrap it what I will find. The piece of paper with the writing on it. The syringe. The phone. I know he is watching, so I force my hands not to shake as I pick up the paper and read it. The rest I tuck away inside my messenger bag. A year ago I knew nothing about Safe status. I thought it was this simple: you took over your alternate's life after killing her, you lived exactly as she would have. Sometimes you would be given an older sleeper who was ill to look after until he was better, and that was it. But then I met my handler, Miss Odette. Now I know that you receive Safe status when you have been watched in your new life for long enough to determine that you are in an optimal location, optimal lifestyle to do more work for our people. More work does not always mean a syringe. Sometimes more work is a gun to deliver. A knife. A nail in the road to cause a car accident. Sometimes more work is carrying a bag of groceries to a seemingly abandoned building and leaving it there. Groceries like bread and milk, like medicine, for the ones still in the cottages, the ones like us. Sometimes work is good and work is bad, and I think that the consequence of failing either is to be sent back to the cottages to be a Madame, where little children and their bedtimes and burying bodies that hang from knotted trees become one's job.

The good thing is that Safes are no longer watched, at least not as rigorously as those who are not Safes. When I first left the cottages, they were everywhere. People following me. People listening in on every conversation I had on the streets. People pretending to read newspapers whenever I walked by, even though they knew I could see them. They weren't really trying to hide from me. They wanted me to know that they were there, that they were everywhere. But now it is quiet. I am mostly on my own. I have had a year to earn it.

I come to the flower shop once a week. I come in the mornings or afternoons to retrieve my missions, and then I fulfill them at night, when my family is asleep.

"Is there a problem?" the man says, breaking through my thoughts.

I blink back into the present, having read the string of numbers on the piece of paper. "Do I have a time frame for this?" I ask.

"By tonight, if possible," he says. "Midnight." He usually gives me a week.

I think of Cecily waiting for me, and my heart sinks. I can't do it now. And it'll be a few hours, at least, before I can sneak out of the house and ride back to the city. "I might be late."

The man says nothing, and I sigh. I am supposed to be able to find a way to fulfill the mission without compromising myself. I take the lighter he offers me and burn the piece of paper right in front of him and then leave. But I trip over the same pot again, and this time it shatters. Soil pours everywhere, including on me. The man curses and runs to clean up the mess. I only catch little bits of what he is saying,

" . . . clumsy people . . . stupid little girls . . . do not want any of your help . . ." He bends with a dustpan and brush. I shake my shoes free of clumps of soil.

I am not sure at what moment we both freeze and look at each other, at what moment the radio becomes more important than his precious pot, his precious flowers.

The announcer on the radio is speaking excitedly. Voice high, as if he just really wants to burst into tears.

"The Silence is over," he says, "and has been for some time."

The flower shop man lets go of his brush, and I straighten. We both stand there, frowning at each other as we listen.

Apparently a few months ago, the presidents from our planet reached out to the presidents here, and they have been having conferences—about relocations, about vaccinations, about science.

"There might be no war after all," the man on the radio says, voice still shaken. "Everyone might be safe."

After this announcement the radio goes silent. It is just me and the flower shop man again. But we say nothing to each other. I shake the remaining dirt from my clothes and shoes and leave the man to clean his shop. Outside, I hold the phone to my ear, dial the number that was written on the paper, and a voice answers. I used to think it was automated, but now I think that someone is on the other end and that his voice is muffled by some kind of computer. That voice gives me the name of the man the syringe belongs to, his location tonight, and how to reach him. When I hang up the phone, I destroy it. I catch a bus back to the bakery. It is faster than walking back. I ignore everyone on the bus, marveling at the joyous news, at the possibility that the Silence is finally over. The old talk about how they have missed their alternates. They tell their grandchildren how wonderful it is to know your other self, to know all the best and worst possibilities of yourself. Because one is always better than the other.

"Wait till you see, Annie," a white-haired woman in front of me says, her voice loud and crackly. She squeezes her granddaughter's hand, wipes a tear from her eye with the other. "You will love your other Grandma Josephine. And she will be so happy to finally meet you, but not nearly as excited as the other Annie."

This Annie's eyes are wide. Her little blond head bobs with either excitement or terror or both.

Everyone is telling stories like these. For them the end of the Silence means everything will go back to the way it once was.

I want to tell them all *no.*

Our people have come too far already; they don't know what we have done to them. What we will continue to do.

We are the worst versions of them; we never truly believed in this idea of two worlds to begin with. Forty years ago our first star disappeared, and no one thought anything of it. Then people started to disappear, vanished into thin air right before our eyes as if they had never been. And then buildings and trees, and massive holes appearing in the ground, causing earthquakes. Some days the sun would come out, touch us, and on others it would hide away. There are cold patches on our planet now. Places where the ocean has frozen over. Places where it never stops snowing. These are not stories that we had to be told. I lived in that world for six years.

We didn't agree to the Silence because we wanted to think about how to fix things. We agreed because we did not want them to know the truth: that our planet was collapsing on top of us. That the universe was literally choosing between every man and woman in the worlds, and ours was the one chosen to go, to die, to disappear.

We agreed because we did not want them to see what we were doing. What we were planning. Whom *we* were choosing.

I stare at the reflection the bus window passes back to me. I remember the girl I see from when she was younger, but no good is left. Not in her eyes, not in her hands, certainly not in the syringe in her bag. In this moment she is so empty I'm surprised to recognize her at all. The girl in the reflection says: I *don't think you can choose who deserves to live or die, not in this situation. I think you just choose your side, and you stay with it no matter what happens. And you have already chosen your side.*

I open my bag, stare down at the syringe. I do not know what the clear yellow liquid it contains is. I do not know what it will do. Those things are not my job to know. Those things are not my concern. I look up again and wear my face.

Not everyone has the option of weakness.

I have been gone only an hour, but it is already beginning to get dark when my bus stops. I return to the bakery and find Cecily curled up on a table. "Sorry," the baker's wife says. "She got bored with baking about five minutes in and decided to sit by the window and wait for you."

I stuff Gigi's medicine inside my coat pocket. I pick Cecily up, press my face against her soft hair. "I'm so sorry," I whisper. "Can we not—"

"Not tell anyone about this?" she whispers back, her voice groggy. "Da says you're not supposed to leave me alone."

I groan. "I said I would be right back."

She looks pointedly at the clock on the wall and then back at me again. "Right back" means fifteen minutes to Cecily, and not a minute more. I can imagine all the ways she will play this up and how Da will fall for it. "I'll buy you anything you want," I tell her.

"Good," she says, and then she leads me toward a candy shop that's just across the road. "Because I already know what I want. And it's going to cost you *plenty*."

This time, on our way home, I let her ride ahead of me in the growing dark, hoping she burns all the energy from her sugar high before Gigi sees her like this. One look from her, and Da will have my head. Cecily rides more slowly this time around so that I keep bumping my bike into hers. And she rides in zigzags along the road. There are always very few cars on this road, and especially today with the news. People will be glued to their radios and televisions, but I am still wary, still looking over my shoulder.

"Where do you go all the time?" Cecily says. "And how come you go without me? Da says you're not allowed to have a boyfriend until you're at least fifty, you know. Were you with your boyfriend?"

I shake my head and sigh, reach forward and ruffle her

hair. "You ask so many questions. What's up with that, huh?"

"I want to know what you do when I'm not with you."

"Why?"

"Because," she says softly, suddenly near tears, and I already know the answer. "Because I want to know what Mama would have done if she was here, and Gigi says you're most like her. And I want to know what that means because . . . well, just because." She bites her lip, and I know she's thinking very carefully about her next words. When she finally settles on them, she frowns at me. "Mathieu says that the reason why Mama died while she was having me was that I'm bad luck."

"That is," I splutter, my fingers tightening around my handlebars, "the stupidest thing I have ever heard in my life." Now it's my turn to study her. "Wait. Is this why you got into those fights at school? Because Da thinks you're mad."

"Meh," she says evasively. "Boys are stupid." She rides in her zigzag way again, and I think it's all forgotten, but when I catch up to her again, she asks, "Is Gigi going to die because of me, too?"

I frown. "I thought that dumb boy Mathieu was supposed to be your best friend."

"I know, right?" She smiles at me. I've stumbled upon the right thing to say for this moment and breathe a sigh of relief.

But then she adds, viciously, "Dumb boy," and barks a short laugh. Mathieu had better watch his back. My sister might be six years old, but in a way she is much older, much tougher than she seems. In that way she is the version of Lirael that Gigi was referring to. The type of girl who is strong even when she is weak. She, not me, is the most like her mother already, even now, even this young.

When a set of headlights flashes ahead of us, my first instinct is to pull us down onto the grass, let the car pass. But it's Da in his truck, come looking for us. He yells at me for keeping Cecily in the city so late, especially after the announcement that the Silence is over. "Who knows what is going to happen next?" I say nothing back. Finally he stops, catches me staring out at the sky, catches me not being who I should be. For months all I have done is complain loudly about the whole Silence thing, the way *she* would have. About the way everyone seems to have stopped living. "Let's pretend it's not even out there," I said, yet here I am looking up.

But I can't look down. My neck is frozen.

Cecily tells him she thinks I am coming down with something and nudges me conspiratorially. *Our boyfriend, our secret.* She doesn't say it, but I let her think better of me. Let her share our imaginary little thing.

CHAPTER 16

My first duty as *her*, as me, happened two days after I arrived.
I accompanied Gigi to the clinic not just because she was feeling ill but also because she suspected that whatever the doctor had to say, she would not want Da to hear. She didn't want
me to hear either, but I had been the one at home when the
doctor had called to confirm her appointment. Gigi thrives
on secrecy when it comes to her family. Always their happiness before hers. I'd known this before. I'd known it since I
was nine years old, sitting there in my bunker, but it was still
the sort of thing that made me nervous now.

The clinic was white, and the smell of it reminded me of some sort of perfumed bleach. It was very small, not as flashy as all the others in the city, but Gigi had been coming here for so long she said she couldn't remember her last doctor's name. The paint outside the building was peeling, the window rattling, and it was so hot that the secretary kept fanning herself with the files of patients she was flipping through. The radio was on, but the signal was so bad that there was more static than music. We chose a corner of the room to sit in, and I thought about Gigi's loyalty. I don't know how many times I sat in the training room, watching footage of Gigi doing or saying kind things, comforting everyone else. All through our training we'd been taught to expect the unexpected, to create margins of error for the people we were learning about. Not everyone would be exactly what they seemed all the time. But Gigi was. She was exactly what I had learned my grandmother would be.

Sitting in the waiting room, I listed all her qualities in my head as I had done during training, as I had done during my exam. I knew her whole history: That she'd grown up in a free-spirited sort of family, but she'd been good and innocent right up until the moment she met my grandfather, and as she liked to say, it was all "shot to hell" after that. She married Da and lost a son before she had my mother, and that was the most difficult part of their marriage. Once she had my mother, Gigi devoted herself to being a mother and wife. I sat there in that waiting room, counting all those things I knew, a lot of which the real Lirael would never have known because she'd had no file to read. She could never have been objective about the people she loved; she had to love them in spite of whatever they were and weren't.

Despite the fact that the clinic was half empty, we sat in the waiting room for hours. Every few minutes the secretary would sing off key in what she must have thought was her *quiet* voice, and every few minutes the old man sitting across from us would mutter, "May the good Lord take me now," or "May the ground open up and swallow me now." He was very dramatic about it, and Gigi and I were trying really hard not to lock eyes in case we started laughing.

When they finally came for us, Gigi stood. "Wait out here," she told me, and I complied. But once she came back out, I peppered her with questions. Her hands were shaking even though her eyes were dry, and I studied her face, perhaps even too long. She kept waving me off dismissively each time I asked what she'd been told.

Then we walked past an ice-cream parlor, and she said, "Let's go inside."

"But you hate ice cream," I said.

She *tsked* and ushered me inside. We sat on stools so tall that our feet no longer touched the ground. I ordered a banana split. The moment it arrived Gigi leaned forward, a deep crease between her brows. "That banana is brown," she said, not exactly quietly, her lips curling.

I shrugged. "Sometimes it happens."

I knew this was an insult to my grandparents. They held the world to the same standards they held themselves, as far as food was concerned. A browning banana. It was the equivalent of poison to Gigi. "You have to call that waiter back," she said. "This is unacceptable. Your grandfather would never allow this."

I made a show of holding the spoon to my lips. "Only if you tell me what the doctor said."

But she said nothing, just looked away. I ate the ice cream, brown banana and all. She ate her vanilla scoop, both of us hating it, neither of us telling each other the truth.

I spent the entire time surreptitiously watching my grandmother's hands, not just because they were still shaking but because they reminded me of my own hands just three days earlier on the yellow bus. My eyes were glued to those hands, so soft. The art of holding a paintbrush to create things, of using our delicate hands at all, had been passed down in the family. It was tradition to express ourselves creatively with those hands, the only way to stay sane, and it showed. We had fingers that could bend in the wrong direction, that could twist and turn to create whatever we wanted them to create, but that day those hands were stiff and frightened. They were the kinds of hands that knew all the things your mind and the rest of your body chose to ignore, hands that understood that something bad was coming.

Afterward we went shopping for groceries, our cover story, and Gigi bought me an expensive pair of gloves. For the coming winter, she said, but I shook my head. I tried to put it back down. "Gigi, it's too much."

She waved me off again. "Never. I can spoil my granddaughter all I want." But I knew what she meant. I imagined the words hard in her throat, struggling to find their way out. They were the kinds of words that changed things, the kinds of words that asked too much of you, and it was only once the bus had dropped us on the road and we'd started walking to the house that Gigi said them. "Don't tell your grandfather about this."

We weren't lying to everyone, exactly. We were just letting them be happy for a little while longer. "It's the kindest thing that one person can do for another person," Gigi said without meeting my eyes. I followed her into the house then, and inside my head I was trying to imagine what the real Lirael would do. On the one hand, if her grandmother was sick, she would want to tell her grandfather if only for the fact that it was better that someone else knew. It would be a betrayal, but at least Da could try to do something. On the other hand, if Gigi really was sick, then she would probably do everything in her power to get well, and in the meantime, wasn't it better that Da still wore that smile on his face? That Cecily never cried at night, even if just for a little while? Which was better? What was I supposed to do?

I wasn't sure.

I wasn't sure at all.

In a way this was my first real test in my new family, and I looked back on my training, my eight years in the cottages, and found it completely useless.

CHAPTER 17

I am upstairs in my room when someone knocks on the front door. I open my bedroom door, trying not to make a sound. Then I tiptoe closer to the staircase. I hear Da fiddle with the locks, and then Gigi exclaims happily. I haven't heard her like that in months.

It's their long-lost daughter, my aunt Imogen. Except she wasn't particularly lost; she just doesn't like to remember that she has family until she needs something. Or at least that is what Da says.

I lean over the banister to watch.

"Daddy, I haven't seen you in forever. How have you been?" Aunt Imogen exclaims. In a high-pitched voice and strange, unrecognizable accent. She's slurring her words, too, and her makeup is smudged. Her cheeks are puffy, and her smile keeps wobbling. Actually, she looks as if she has been crying.

Da says, "What do you want?"

He is especially not impressed when the front door opens again and more people come inside, most of them swaying like Aunt Imogen. Her friends, she explains, and they'll be here only a few hours. "They've never been on an orchard before. I told them you wouldn't mind, Daddy. Was I wrong?"

Da grunts a response I cannot make out. He is probably half hoping she means it because he stands at the edge of the room, waiting. He wants to show them his trees. Show them the ones he planted himself and the ones his father did. But the moment the words are out of her mouth, Aunt Imogen forgets them. She and her friends sit on the couch. They open bottles of wine and eat cheese. They cross their legs and point their toes in some sophisticated poses. They say that they are celebrating the end of the Silence, but all they really talk about is whether their alternates have found happiness with any of the boyfriends they've recently dumped. They are loud and raucous, clanking glasses, completely unaware of the time. "Just imagine," one of them says, "if John is the one I was supposed to spend my life with."

Da leaves them there eventually. He helps Gigi up to their room. He's muttering to her about ungratefulness and self-ishness, but I swear I see him blushing with embarrassment. Their bedroom door closes with a slam.

I stand in the shadows for a long time, staring down the stairs. Aunt Imogen was the person the real Lirael looked up to when she was a kid. She wanted to be just like her. One day her aunt was training to be a teacher; the next she'd decided she was going to be a doctor. Today she is wearing an air host-ess outfit, same as all her friends. Her lips are stained with bright red lipstick, and her hair is wild.

I jump when I realize I am not spying alone.

"You're supposed to be in bed," I whisper to Cecily.

"So are you," she says.

Aunt Imogen looks up suddenly. Her face brightens, and she waves. For a moment I don't react; I just stare at her. When her hand falls, I realize I've waited too long to be the girl she knew. The one who loved her. *Get yourself together, you idiot*, I tell myself, and straighten. I walk down the stairs with a false smile on my face. She introduces me to her friends. I feign wide-eyed excitement when she tells me and Cecily about her adventures on airplanes. The whole time I am thinking, *How would Lirael sit? How would Lirael stand? What would Lirael say now?*

Because I don't know.

It's one thing to be a granddaughter and sister; I know Gigi and Da and Cecily like the back of my hand. Everything I studied, every moment spent in front of those screens in the cottages were meant to fool them. But Aunt Imogen isn't supposed to be here. Nothing about her is constant, permanent. Nothing I learned two years ago about her and how to fool her even applies now. She has changed. Her hair—strawberry blond now, no longer brown—and even the way she walks are different. But it is her eyes that make me wary. Two bottomless pits that are not as sure and trusting as they once were. And she is expecting something from me, her niece.

I smile, but I don't want her here.

Everything has been going so well.

I wake up barely four hours after I put my head down. Four hours since I snuck back into the house, after completing my mission. Da knows early morning is when I am most vulnerable, when my eyes are wild and my body craves sleep. He ignores my guttural groan and hands me a hot flask. "Come on," he says, a man shape in the dark. "We're going to join the fishermen." He leaves the room, and that is his mistake. When he comes back a few minutes later, I am curled around the closed flask, reveling in its warmth, pillow over my head, and lost again in that dream of the old man who always finds me in sleep, who always speaks to me. I have not yet solved the riddle of why I dream about him, though I suppose, in a way, he was my answer to my life as a sleeper. I didn't have a family, so I created one of my own. I know he isn't real, but in my dreams that does not matter. In my dreams I belong with somebody.

We are standing together on a piece of the ocean, standing there as if on solid ground. *Look*, the old man says now, pointing to a memory that replays behind us like a black-and-white movie. *Look. This is your last good moment.* But before I can see it, the man and the movie begin to grow smaller, begin to shrink away from me. And though I try to chase after them, there is no place to go. I am suddenly in a room with four black walls that I slam into with each step I take.

"Lirael," Da says, yanking the blanket off me and forcing my eyes open. He smells like cigarettes and coffee and sleeplessness, the exact opposite of what I was dreaming about. His voice is deep and strong but chopped in places, as if it is beginning to wear out. He nudges me again, more roughly this time. "I am going to carry you to the river like this, but I expect you won't want Pierre and Philip staring at you all morning in your underthings. Then we'll drown for sure, with Pierre and his rowing skills."

This time I sit up. I hold the flask to my chest and scowl into the dark. He shuffles through my drawers, pulling out clothes like he has any idea what he is doing. He gets it wrong, of course. Pulls out a shirt that he mistakes for a dress, a torn woolen hat, two left boots, but I am still in no place to find him amusing. My voice is nearly as rough as his, as if I have been screaming all night. "You're only trying to punish me for the other night with Cecily," I say grumpily.

"Damn straight I am," he says without stopping. He yanks my curtains apart, lets the first whisper of sunrise on the horizon shine through. He reaches inside his pocket and retrieves a wrapped sandwich that has been smashed into a ball shape. "Breakfast," he says, but this time does not leave the room. This time he stands with his bent back to me, his breathing harried, as if this has taken all the effort he has and he suddenly finds himself worn out. Da is getting older every day. The orchards are becoming too much for him to bear, even with the workers who have stayed behind to help. I think he is tired. But if he is, he would rather die than admit that to me.

I climb out of bed, shrug out of my nightgown, and find the correct boots. I wish I could reach underneath my mattress and take my sleeper pills. If ever I needed my health to be perfect, it is today, out there on the river, but I cannot risk

Da's noticing. I will have to wait until I get back. I wear the torn hat, the shirt, a pair of leggings, and a coat. I do not comb my hair; I have nobody to look decent for. This is how we both—Da and I—prefer my life, and on this one thing we can agree. I tuck the greasy sandwich inside my coat pocket, grab the flask. I wrap the giant scarf Gigi gave me for Christmas around my neck twice until my mouth is covered.

"I said I was sorry," I say in a muffled voice.

Da doesn't answer, doesn't turn around, just marches toward the door and expects me to follow him. In the hallway he says, "I don't want apologies. I want you to show me that you give a damn. About your grandmother. About your sister."

"Of course I do," I say, with as much irritation as I can muster. We don't talk about the fact that sometimes when he can't stand to see how sick Gigi is, he gets sad and moody and stays out until he knows she has gone to bed before skulking into the kitchen, looking for dinner.

We tiptoe down the stairs. The worst fishing days, rare as they are, are when Cecily wakes up and decides that she wants to come along. Even worse is when we make her return and she is furious, but we can bear those days better than when we're halfway down the river and she's bawling her eyes out because the fish we've caught are *dying*.

"Funny," I say as we pass the kitchen. Da nods toward a couple of buckets in the corner, and I pick them up. "On the days you want to punish me, you think you're a fisherman. Why can't you be an orchardist on those days? Why can't we go pick apples like normal people? I *like* picking apples."

Aunt Imogen's suitcases are still sitting by the door. They've been there since she arrived two days ago, fresh off her divorce, but I haven't even seen her since that first night. That was what brought her here: the end of her marriage to a man Da specifically warned her against years ago. So he says, but don't all parents warn their children, and are children ever expected to listen?

She goes drinking and sleeps late. Da, Gigi, Cecily, and I barely speak to her. Only Gigi tries. Mainly because of the suitcases. Da says there's no use in investing time in someone who has no intention of staying. She comes, she goes, and she stays out of the way. Sometimes I hear her crying in her room at night.

Once I even knocked. It was what *she* would have done. But the crying stopped, and the door stayed locked.

She comes out now, as if I conjured her up, her hair sticking up in strange angles. "Oh. I thought I heard voices. What's happening?"

Da doesn't answer. I'm the one who says, "I'm being punished." I hold up the buckets.

Aunt Imogen smiles. "I remember Da taking me on those trips. I don't think I ever caught a single fish, though." She looks from me to Da and then back again, and there is something hopeful about her voice when she says, "Do you want me to come with you? I can help. I think."

Before I can say anything, Da snaps at her, "And will you bring your bottle of wine with you? Or perhaps you've found something stronger today. Your mother's missing pills perhaps?"

She looks like he slapped her. She turns around, walks quickly back into her room. Her door slams shut. For me there has never been a more awkward moment. But Da acts like she was never here at all. I know he's angry. Two years ago, Aunt Imogen married some man we've never met. Aside from one postcard, that's the last we heard from her. No phone calls, nothing. When she was younger, she and Da used to be very close.

It's hard to forget all the used-to-be's.

"You used to love to fish," he says, clearing his throat.

I turn away from the room Aunt Imogen disappeared into. "I was ten, Da. Now I'm lucky if I can get the smell out of my hair in a week, and you know how Pierre can be. You know how he won't leave me alone."

Da shrugs, shutting the door behind us. I think he is ignoring me, but then he speaks softly, his reluctant words not meant for my ears. "You're still ten," he mutters. "You'll always be ten."

"You're not my father," I say, which is the obligatory thing I always say to him when I am supposed to be mad. Supposed to be horrified at the prospect of having to spend the day with him. I don't think I have actually had a day in my life I've not wanted to spend with him. Da jokes sometimes that I am a better boy than I ever was a girl; there are certainly no girls who live near us who think that spending the day fishing with their grandfathers might be the best thing that has happened to them in weeks.

"Of course I'm not, and no wonder," Da says gruffly. "I would have done the whole damn thing better."

But he kisses my cheek with twitchy lips, and I climb into the truck.

The orchards are full of trees, but I have managed to convince everyone that I am now too old to climb them. I did not break any habits when I came; instead I collected them. The way she walked and talked and laughed. It was like a filled box that I had to step into, that I had to mold myself to fit, but I could never bring myself to love the trees. The truth is I am no longer brave enough to climb them. I stand on ladders, which I tell myself is a different thing entirely. A ladder will not betray me, not without warning me first at least, and all our ladders are sturdy things. But a tree deceives you into thinking that it is on your side. Once in my dreams the old man said the same thing he always says: *Look.* We were standing at the top of a tree, and for a second we could see the whole world from there. But then my branch snapped. I died in that dream, I think. Even in sleep, I cannot dream a sturdy tree properly. Whenever I draw trees, I draw them with thick unnatural-looking trunks, with branches of steel, three times bound in wood. I must draw the ugliest trees in the world.

The river is not the same thing as a tree. You cannot blame a river for your fear because a river never lies to you. Already, even before you approach it, it is dark. It has no bottom. If you want it to, it will even do you the very worst favor of your life. I remember watching this image in the bunkers: of a girl and her grandparents and her mother swimming in the river, splashing one another with water. The girl is young, eight maybe, and she laughs as if the whole world belongs to her and that river. She laughs as if she is unafraid of it. That girl, I think, the original Lira, would never squeeze her hands together before entering the river. Would take no deep breaths, nor have to remind herself to be brave.

"It's okay," I whisper to myself as I climb onto the boat. And I have to keep saying "It's okay, it's okay" as the boat rocks and my knees knock together.

They say that if you conquer the ocean, you can surely conquer something as small as a river or a lake. But I am not nearly so optimistic.

Back at the cottages, the transfer was not the only time when we drowned. Sometimes the older kids would hold our heads in buckets of water, per Madame's instructions, for however long it took for us to nearly die. "This is how tough it is going to get out there," Madame would say when we were coughing on the ground, clutching our chests. "This is what the world is going to be like and how it will feel once you leave this place. And what do you know? What do you say?"

"Our Earth first," we would chant. "Each other first. Soldiers first. Never them. Never them."

"Good girls," she would answer, nodding. And just when we found first breath, found hope: "Again."

"Quick, Philip," Pierre yells to his son when he spots us,

"go help them." As if we were incapable of rowing our own boat onto the water. As if because of old age and size, we were puny things with our fishing rods and buckets. Pierre, who I am convinced never bathes, raises a hand and waves at my grandfather, and they exchange pleasantries.

I pretend not to notice either of them. Pretend that the boat, which is really nothing more than a dinghy, is taking all of my attention. Da's teeth glisten in the early light, and he speaks without losing his falsely enthusiastic smile. "Smile, Lirael," he says. "They always catch more fish than us."

I shake my head. "It doesn't matter whether I smile or not. Look at this." I wear my most discouraging face, yet Philip wades into the water, climbs aboard our boat.

He shakes Da's hand, as if they were meeting for the first time, as if they were speaking a secret language, and then smiles shyly at me. "Hi, Lirael. You decided to come today."

I say darkly, "I wouldn't exactly call it my decision," and Da elbows me in the ribs. I think how much Gigi likes fish. "But I'm glad I did."

This basically cements my fate for the rest of the morning.

"There's looters down your way this year, sleeping in the orchards," Philip says. "Everyone's been complaining about missing things. You and Cecily should be careful about . . ." He sees the look on my face, and his words trail off. He laughs. "What am I saying? They're the ones who should be afraid." He wiggles a single eyebrow at me. "So, Lirael, which poor sod have you beaten black and blue most recently? Or have you been good since that school fight with Michael Stanton?"

"We don't talk about that," I say quickly, but it's too late. Da has already perked up.

"I would like to talk about that," he says.

"That's probably why we don't talk about it," Philip says, laughing. "Anyway, she seems pretty reformed now. Hasn't had a bad incident in months."

I laugh, too, dip my hand into the water and toss a handful at him, and Da gives me his look of approval. Anything for more fish.

"Fourteen," I say, staring down into the water. This is a guessing game we play.

Philip cocks his head to the side like he's thinking about it.

"Thirty-three," he says finally. "A little ambition never killed anybody."

I raise a brow at him. "Your greatest ambition is to catch thirty-three fish today? Really?"

He laughs. "At least I'll never go hungry."

To his credit, Philip does not look like his father. His clothes are cleaner, his hair less wild, and he certainly has more teeth in his mouth than Pierre. But they have the same objective, and their objective does not interest me. In fact, now that I am being homeschooled and it is nearing the end of summer, I do not know why Philip and I have to spend any more time together. He is supposed to be to Lirael what the kids from the cottages were to me. Somewhere in the world there are old childhood memories of a Philip and a Lirael, running through the orchards together, fishing together. But I look at him and never once see a boy whose head has been held underneath water, who has been beaten until he cannot speak—this not from Madame, but just because Madame was away and the older kids felt like it. The ones assigned to look after us in the bunkers, who didn't have patience. They knew that our trackers would send alerts if something truly terrible happened to us, but no one had to know that we'd been kicked in the shin, punched in the stomach; that was our life, and from that one small simple thing, this Philip can never truly know me. Never understand me. What could we possibly have to talk about?

And this is not his fault.

She cared about him. I cannot. If this continues much

longer, if I have to marry this boy one day, he will probably be the husband I pretend to smile at, pretend to want to kiss. That life is a good ten years away, I hope, but that does not keep me from wanting to yell, "Go away." He deserves better, but to tell him so would be to break protocol. I am not allowed to break protocol. I am not allowed to set him free.

Da and Philip switch boats, with Da going to sit next to Pierre. Even from our boat I can tell that he is not happy when Pierre wants to talk about the other Earth instead of fishing. Pierre says that when the Silence first started, he went out and bought as many guns as he could find. Filled his basement with them. "Gotta protect my family, you know? I said, 'Let those bastards come and see what we are made of.'"

I do not catch Da's response, but I see the way he flinches. My grandfather is the kind of man who wants to believe only in things he can see. The idea that the war has already arrived, that it is right on his doorstep, would be incomprehensible to him. Worst of all, any interactions he might restart with his alternate once communication is reestablished will only remind him that Gigi is sick. And if Gigi is perfectly healthy on the other Earth, then he would rather not know it.

We haven't talked about what the end of the Silence could

mean for our family, but I am sure that if there were an opt-out plan, Da would never speak to his alternate again.

Even Cecily isn't all that interested in meeting her alternate.

"That is exactly why your family was chosen," my handler, Miss Odette, told me when we met. "Your grandfather has no interest in starting any trouble. It is the perfect place for a sleeper to hide."

I wonder. If Da were a little more like Pierre, obsessing over the other Earth and stashing dozens of guns in some basement, would I even be here?

We row past a man in a small boat. He is wearing a suit. Looks too serious to be a fisherman. My immediate thought is that he is a sleeper, and he is here for me. Perhaps it is time, for Da, for Cecily and Gigi, and Philip. Am I supposed to kill them now? But we row right by him, and he says nothing, barely even looks at me.

I have to remind myself: I am a Safe.

They trust me.

I am so tired of forgetting.

They have not told me what will happen next. It could be anything. It could be today or tomorrow that the war begins.

I have to be ready.

The water rocks the boat ever so gently to remind us that it was here all along. That it is doing us a favor by leaving us where we are, that it is bigger and more powerful than we can imagine. It is nearly noon when Da and I go home, and he's in a good mood. Philip caught nearly all our fish and convinced his father to give us even more. Da makes up a song as we go, truck bumping down the road, and by the time we reach home I am singing along. Cecily greets us at the door with a look of fury in her brown eyes and pummels her fists into my thighs until Da promises her a fishing day of her own, soon. Gigi sits by the window, knitting a sweater she keeps saying she has to finish, a small smile on her soft face despite the pain.

I watch them. I watch us. And I do not once think, *One day you all are going to die.* And I do not think, *Soon.* No. And I definitely do not think, *Because you're not my real family at all.*

When I have a mission to complete at night, I drug them, especially Da. Nothing powerful, just enough to make them think they are sleeping soundly through the night on their own. On those nights I ride my bicycle back to the city. I deliver names, deliver weapons whose use does not concern me. How the man in the flower shop comes upon them, I do not know. I suspect he does not know either. He is only another piece in a very large puzzle. He plays his part.

Look, the old man from my dreams says, sitting beside my bed now. And in my sleep I see the memory of a tree, of four children standing at the very top of it. It's me, Alex, Gray, and Edith, laughing. The birds swoop down over our heads in a dramatic dance. Madame yells at us from the bottom of the tree in a fury, in a panic. "The trees are meant to hide us," she shouts. "You foolish children, come down at once," but our laughter drowns her out. We hold hands, the four of us, best friends. We promise never to let go.

This is your last good moment.

And I agree.

We have those eyes. Those eyes that would disappear the first time we fell.

CHAPTER 19

Is it today?

Are they going to die today?

Am I going to kill them today?

Fall asleep and wake to the same questions. Always the same questions.

And the same answer: I *am ready.*

Some nights when I sneak into the city for a mission, I am afraid that I will not make it back. Since the Silence ended, our missions have become more dangerous. The people of this world have let their guard down, and that is exactly what we wanted, but I am also summoned to the flower shop more often than before. "This is our opportunity," Miss Odette told me. "To erase as many threats to our cause as possible. You may be needed for more missions than you were before. Be ready."

Some jobs require a different type of look. A wig or a hat, a different set of clothes. Some jobs require an entire team of us. On those days the flower shop man will give me the address of an empty office building, and when I reach it, other people will be waiting for me. There will be a costume to wear, and I will have a part to play. Sometimes I am the only young one there; sometimes there are no adults at all. Today a mix of us are carrying out the plan. A city official must be killed, and it must be made to look as though he has had a heart attack. No questions, no answers.

Normally these jobs are quick. We never introduce ourselves; we get right to work. And when it is finished, we disappear as if we never met.

There are five of us. A college kid, in his early twenties, who still wears braces and a pair of round glasses. An older man with a greasy-looking ponytail, and a woman who looks to be in her forties. Those two come from a time just before they started training children like me. The rules are different for them, the ones who came before us, who came before our world realized just how ruthless sleepers had to be. There is a girl no older than thirteen, who is supposedly the woman's sleeper daughter. And me. We're such an odd bunch that under any other circumstances it would be funny. But I can sense the fissures in our team right from the moment we meet, and I know enough to worry. Our best-case scenario, we have been told, is to catch the man while he is out on his evening jog. The young girl is supposed to act as a distraction, while her mother injects the syringe that I brought. As the rest of us get ready, the man unpacks his sniper rifle, which he will set up in case things go badly for some reason, in case we need to be protected. He assures the rest of us that he is a very good shot, a comment that is rebutted by the woman underneath her breath. The college boy and I exchange a look.

This is only the beginning of how badly things will go.

I wear a long red wig over my hair, a baseball cap, and clothes that make me look homeless. I color my face with dirt, and the sneakers I have been given have holes in them. We have no qualms about taking off our clothes, about changing in front of one another. That's supposed to be strange, but it's just the way we are. Each of us wears a communication device inside our ears so that we can stay in touch. My job tonight is just to sit in the park and keep my eyes open for civilians. If there is even the slightest chance that our presence will be noticed, we are to fall back on one of several backup plans.

Everything is all set, and we're all in place.

Then our target changes his jogging route.

Not just that, but we find out that our information is wrong, and he has invited a jogging partner tonight. When we realize this, the man and woman begin to argue about what we should do next. Wrong information means that any other backup plans we had could be compromised as well. Should we take the chance? For about a minute I'm listening to them arguing over my earpiece. The college boy keeps coughing nervously, and I understand the way he feels. I'm sure these two are usually very professional and we've just caught them on a really bad day, but this is the difference between them and us, the adults and the children. We are much more malleable. We have been taught, right from when we were in the cottages, not to let our egos get in the way of our missions. The older sleepers have not learned their lessons quite as well.

There is something much more stoic about us children. Like soldiers, we leave our emotions out of it. Even the little girl watches her mother with an almost eerie calm.

Finally the new plan is decided, and it is much riskier. It

involves disabling an alarm system and entering his house, killing him in his bed right next to his sleeping wife. So we follow our target home. The woman and her daughter stand outside, keeping watch, and the man holds his syringe in one hand, his gun in the other, as we enter the house. It is a simple plan, and normally, when it is done by sleeper children, only one of us is needed. But the man insists that both the boy and I follow him inside, so there we are like idiots.

It goes badly because the man wakes up just before the syringe can enter his thigh. He wakes up and has the time to exclaim. That wakes up his wife, who in turn screams, and so that is that. Both their fates are set. The woman tries to run, and even though I catch up to her, we both stumble down the stairs. Then the gunman retrieves her and carries her, fighting, back to the bed. Tomorrow they will call it a murder-suicide, a dispute gone bad between a man and his wife.

After we are finished, it is the college boy who sweeps the scene to remove any evidence of us, while the man stumbles outside, nursing his broken nose. I tuck the unused syringe back inside the pocket of my coat and limp toward the back door, but before I can reach it, the sleeper woman outside hisses into her communication device. "Don't use the back exit," she says. "Someone is coming."

My heart slams inside my chest. Sirens blare closer and closer.

Someone called the police.

We have erased all signs of a struggle. The man and his wife are lying in their bed, and I make a point of not looking at them. The college boy and I make our way to the bathroom, where there is a tree leaning against the window. My foot throbs as I climb, and I have to grit my teeth to keep from crying out. I limp into the darkness as fast as I can.

We change in silence when we're back at our rendez-vous spot, some of us livid, some of us chagrined. The man is swearing underneath his breath. He's holding his nose, and he keeps saying, "I'm screwed. There will be repercussions for this."

After the man and woman and girl are gone, it's just me and the college boy. He runs his fingers through his hair. "The next time they want to give us a mission," he says to me, "they should probably avoid giving us an actual married couple. What the hell was that?"

"You think they're married?" I say, pulling my shirt over my head.

"If they're not married, they certainly want to sleep together."

I say nothing, and he shakes his head. "I don't normally do this stuff. They just sent me because the target's kid is about to be replaced and they needed someone watching. I'm the one gathering intelligence for the cottages, and we're lucky that kid was at a sleepover tonight. I mean, what the *hell* was that?"

I am only interested in the first thing he said. "You gather surveillance?" I ask. "You're the one who sends information about our families?"

"I know," he says, at the look on my face. "You're never supposed to meet us. But this is what we look like. Just like you. Less heavy on the fighting stuff, though."

I am surprised that he is so young. I want to ask how he got the job, but he reads my mind. "They pick you out right from the cottages. You've got to be able to notice things that nobody else does. And you've got to be able to do it while staying invisible. Stealing, for example."

"Stealing?"

He grins, and his teeth glimmer in the light. "I'm really good at taking things that don't belong to me. And putting them back."

He walks slowly with me as we're leaving the building, muttering to himself, as if he's still trying to process tonight. He's wearing a backpack, and I can see an economics book sticking out of it. Somehow this seems to fit him better than his job as a sleeper. "I'm putting in a complaint with my handler," he says. "The adults need to go, man. They're becoming obsolete. They're embarrassing themselves."

"That's funny," I say. "I'm pretty sure the adults are going to put in a complaint about us. It's always our fault, remember?"

"Oh, hell, no. Not tonight, it isn't. I mean, I know we're trying to do as many missions as we can while everyone's guard is down, but I swear I could have done this one better on my own, with my eyes closed. You're gonna put in a complaint, too, right? You're gonna tell them how stupid this whole thing was?" I nod, and he gives me an absentminded smile, and as he walks away, I stare after him. "This was fun," he says. "Nice not meeting you."

"Nice not meeting you," I echo softly.

There are police cars driving around as I retrieve my bike from someone's backyard. I use the back alleys until I am out of the city. I go home and open the fridge, find a frozen bag of peas. I hold it against my ankle until the swelling goes down. In the morning I will pretend that I fell.

CHAPTER 20

I run into Edith one afternoon. I am not expecting it, even though her life is only a train ride away in Paris. And it is not that rare that Paris dwellers visit our quaint town for things they cannot get in their big city. I am walking from the bakery with Cecily one afternoon, grimacing because every puddle she finds she insists we jump in. Aunt Imogen is exploring some store, and we're supposed to meet her in an hour. It's the first time she's shown any interest in us or the outside world since she got here.

"Remember when the orchards were wet last summer?"

Cecily says. "Remember we used to do this?" She doesn't wait for my response before she jumps.

I jump, too, right into the puddles. And whenever a passerby yells a string of expletives, I am the one who apologizes. Cecily shakes her head. "Old people just don't know how to have fun. Mathieu says that it starts to happen around your age actually." She pats my hand. "And that explains a lot."

"Hey," I protest, but she cuts me off by squeezing my hand.

"Jump," she shrieks, and this time after we do, Edith is standing there covered in mud, eyes round and horrified.

She is wearing a pale pink dress that looks like it might have been expensive, and shoes that are definitely expensive, and they all are ruined. My mouth flutters while Cecily frowns between us, and then, before I can say anything, Edith is squeezing the water out of her dress. "The only way you can make this up to me," she says with a small smile, "is to buy me a cup of coffee."

And Cecily, whose latest obsession revolves around coffee, mostly because she's not allowed to drink it and Aunt Imogen fed her some last week, immediately snaps to attention. "Yes," she says, grabbing my hand and dragging me along. "I saw a café over here."

We've already had an argument about this at least twice this week. "You're not addicted to coffee; you just think you are," I said. "But I need it to survive," she said, throwing her arms in the air dramatically. If she notices my reluctance, or even the way I stand between her and Edith, or the fact that Edith and I both veto the suggestion of sitting outside where everyone can see us, she doesn't show it. "I say we sit there," she says, choosing a spot right in the center of the room.

"You can go save our seats. We'll order," Edith says in front of the counter.

Cecily makes a face, looks Edith up and down before finally narrowing her eyes. "You're not supposed to order here. That's the waitress's job."

"Go save us a spot, and I'll bring you a croissant," I tell her. I don't mention that Edith will not be joining us.

Once she is gone, Edith and I stand next to each other, pretending to look at the range of bakery goods, shuffling from side to side. A woman looks over at me from her table and smiles, but then she turns back to cuddle her crying baby. I am wary. I do not know what it means to be standing next to someone from the cottages and to have no reason for it. Sleepers who were in the same cottages might run into one another from time to time. It's the stopping to have a conversation that is a problem. We're not supposed to have anything to say to each other. My hands tingle from fear. I have not seen Edith or Gray since the night that never happened. We both keep looking over our shoulders, guiltily, as if we're about to be caught. A permanent state of paranoia. I press my hands against my sides so my nervousness does not show. What I really want to do is wrap my arms around myself, though. What I really want to do is turn around, grab Cecily's hand, and leave.

Muddy water drips down my boots and onto the ground, but I pretend not to notice.

Edith is my opposite. Her legs are long and shapely underneath her dress; her fingers, adorned with all kinds of rings. She is wearing lipstick, which glistens in the dimly lit room, reminding me that we are supposed to be "real adults" now, or at least becoming adults, whatever *that* means. Growing up involves rewriting our faces, our hair, in ways that are still foreign to me. My own hair, I know, is matted to my head underneath my knitted hat. My fingernails are too short, some chewed as far down as I could chew. For once I wish I'd worn the dress Aunt Imogen gave me when she arrived, which is pretty and feminine.

Edith meets my eyes when she is finally ready to speak.

She smiles at me, a shy little thing, as if we were still children, and leans in close until we're touching and there is no space between us. Instantly I feel myself age down a year. It is our last night with Madame all over again, and Edith and I are sitting behind the shed with her best bottle of wine, reveling not in the drink itself but in the idea that we have it. Our f-you in a way that we could never have said out loud. "Gray sent me," she tells me, her voice barely more than a whisper, and I snap back to reality. "He said you looked terrible when he saw you, but I can't really see it now. I'm sure it's there when you're much drier. He's never wrong about people."

"Oh," I say.

I go hot with embarrassment. Gray has seen me? I haven't seen him. I can imagine what they think: *After what we did for her, this is all she is?* I regret ever stopping, ever coming here. I regret this coat, this hat, these boots. An unwelcome nakedness creeps over me despite my being fully clothed. I am not as round, not as tall as Lirael Harrison was projected to become. I am tinier. My breasts are small, my bones slight, my hips nearly nonexistent. I might have her face and her potential, but I am not living up to it. Today I feel stupid for it. Inadequate. This is the first time I have ever felt this way around Edith. I almost can't forgive her for it.

I frown. "He sent you to do what, exactly?"

"Save you," she says cheerily, clutching her purse in front of her dress.

"How?" I try to sound as neutral as I possibly can.

For her it's as if we're having a conversation about the weather. "I'm going to be your friend again," she says. "Never mind the fact that you hate us. We've decided to take you on as our latest charity case, the others and I have, and as Gray likes to say, may the gods have mercy on you." She smiles, but it fades quickly. "They don't tell us how lonely this job can be. Maybe the ones who know choose differently. That's Gray's favorite saying.

"Here." She reaches inside her purse, finds something, and before I can speak, she has dropped it inside my coat pocket. I only catch the smallest glimpse of something silver. "A gift for you, and you're not allowed to refuse."

I open my mouth to say the usual things: that I don't need help, that I don't need trouble, that I don't want her gift. I used to believe that if you stayed out of trouble's way, everything would be fine. Now I believe that if you stay out of trouble, trouble will come and find you, and that trouble is Edith. But what comes out of my mouth instead is: "When did I hate you? I never hated you." And my voice is baffled, defensive.

I look around quickly, to make sure our conversation hasn't drawn attention.

Edith stares at me for a moment before she shrugs. "Maybe you're right," she says quietly, and then she looks away, speaks to the ground, but not before I see the hurt in her eyes. "I suppose after a while it's okay to forget those things about ourselves—things that make us seem like less than who we think we are."

I repeat myself more vehemently, "I never hated anyone," but even as I speak, I suddenly remember saying those very words years ago: "I hate you, leave me alone." This is one of the visions the old man does not show me in my dreams, does not remind me of. I only ever remember up until the moment I fall from the tree. I only ever remember the way Madame makes me tear up my drawing. I don't remember what I said to my friends, or all four of us crying in the infirmary after Madame had left. Edith grabbing my good arm and begging me. Begging me to remember our promise just hours earlier in the tree: to be best friends forever. Me shrugging her away because I had realized what they had not and had started to turn a different way.

I was the one who ended our friendship. Now I even remember sparring with Edith once and beating her until Madame had to pull me off. "Good job, Lirael," Madame said.

"You fight with purpose." Edith limped around the cottage for a month.

I don't think that . . . I am a good person.

I am not a good person.

The proof of it is emerging more every day.

Edith is waiting for me to say something. I don't know what. Finally I ask, "Do you remember a kid named Solomon, who was with us at the beginning?" I can tell I have disappointed her.

"There were plenty of kids that were with us at the beginning," she says. "I can't say that I remember too many of them now."

But I remember Solomon, mostly because he never stopped crying. He cried when we trained, cried in front of the screens, cried during dinner. "Solomon, shut up" was our favorite phrase. None of us were particularly kind to him because he did not try. Because he still held on to whatever he'd lost, as if it were his lifeline.

This was no later than our first month there. That is a long time for a little boy to be crying. His face was permanently puffy; his lips were chapped. He would stop only when he ate but then throw up the food and start again. There were others like him, but Solomon was the worst. Once I tried to bring him into our group, tried to convince the others that he was just sad and that sadness would fade if we were kinder to him. But I remember he was impossible. He looked at us as though we meant nothing to him, and after that I was angry.

I did not try again.

The night Madame came for him he was sobbing mostly silently. We'd grown used to the sound and could sleep around it. I was a light sleeper, though. I heard Madame tiptoe into the room. "Come with me," she whispered to Solomon in his bunk bed. "Let's have a talk and see what we can do about sending you back." And they left together.

I followed them outside, thinking they were walking toward the shed, but they went farther than that. Farther and farther into the woods until I couldn't see the cottages behind me anymore and realized they were heading for the river. I remember wishing I'd worn my coat. They sat on the bank, and Solomon howled until Madame told him to tell her exactly how he was feeling.

"Heavy," he said, "like I can't breathe. I keep thinking about Lola. I keep thinking about Mom. She was screaming when they took me away. I know you say she wanted me to go, but she was screaming. Why would she be screaming if she wanted me to go?"

Madame did not answer any of his questions, though she asked her own. "Do you think it might get better? Do you think you can try, just for a little while?"

"No, no, no," he said resolutely. "I'm sorry, but I wanna go home. I just wanna go home." He dissolved into incoherence again.

Madame sighed heavily. "All right, then," she said, "come here." She hugged him, ran her hand down his back like a mother soothing her babies, and a wave of jealousy washed over me. As it was, most of us were clamoring for Madame's attention and barely got any, not in the right ways at least. "But we're going to miss you, little Solomon," she said, and then she said something else about this river's being special at a certain point and how it could carry a little boy like him back home. "It's like before," she said. "You just swim and swim until you reach the point where the darkness turns into moonlight again, and then you're on the other side." And Solomon entered the water.

Madame had strong arms.

And she never changed her mind about anything, even if the little boy did.

It was only a dream. Purely a figment of my imagination. I told myself that afterward, even as I ran back to the bunkers, even as I pulled the blanket over my head and shook and cried and was afraid. All nothing. Because when you lived in the cottages, there were some things you should tell yourself you didn't see—like a woman digging a small grave among the trees in the dark.

When the tree incident happened years later, Madame threatened me with those words: "Lirael, never again. Do you understand me? The things you think you know, the things you think you should do, always ask yourself: Am I following protocol? At the end of the day, it is the only thing that will save your life."

But that's not true. Sometimes three simple words—I *hate you*—work just as hard and just as well on the right people. Friends, real friends, the kind that shape your bones and claim little pieces of your soul, are liabilities, even if only for the fact that you are constantly worrying about them. Because when Madame said those words to me that night, I knew she could just as easily walk over to Edith's bed, Gray's bed, Alex's bed the following night and ask them to come with her. She would say, "Do you think you can stop being friends with one another, the four of you?" Edith would probably shake her head like Solomon. I wasn't sure, but it was a possibility, and I was afraid of it. That we might end up dying for one another.

I was ten years old then.

I blink out of that haze now and find Edith staring at me oddly. I want to say: *Do you remember what I told you that night? The night you told me Gray was suspicious of the way Alex and Margot died?* I know she does. I clutched her arm until she winced with pain and leaned in close and whispered urgently in her ear: "Tell him never to tell anyone. Never to let them know he knows. Tell him to always follow protocol." I made her promise to tell him this. I never once suggested that he might be wrong; the thought did not occur to me. I knew we lived with a woman who was capable of anything.

But I don't ask.

Instead I say, "We? Who is we?" She doesn't understand, so I add, "You said 'we'. You said 'I and the others.' Who are the others?" She doesn't answer; she just blinks at me, but it's too late. I already understand what she isn't yet sure she wants me to know. Here we are, paranoid and afraid we are being followed or watched. "You're all still friends," I whisper. The shock of it makes my voice hoarse.

"She remembered an appointment and couldn't stay," I tell Cecily, who looks disappointed to see Edith waving at her before leaving the café.

"Oh," she says. I can almost see her mind turning. She bites her bottom lip. "Who was that girl, Lira?"

I sit at our table and set down both of our mugs and a croissant. "You think you're the only one who has friends?"

She gives me a look and then looks toward the exit Edith disappeared through. "Please. I *know* I'm the only one who has friends. So, who was she, already?"

I am still thinking about the look on Edith's face. The fact that she didn't deny my accusation. I reach inside my pocket and feel around for whatever she dropped inside. I find a a silver watch, but before I can study it, Cecily nudges me, and I force myself to refocus on her. "You've started with the questions again," I say. "If I had a dime for every question you asked, my head would have exploded by now. And that's not really something to be proud of."

"Well, if I don't ask them, how will I ever learn?" And then a stream of liquid shoots from her mouth and across the table at me. She sniffs her mug, scans the menu again. "What?" she says, outraged. "This isn't coffee."

CHAPTER 21

"Hello? Anyone there?"

Every few weeks I knock on the flower shop door, and no one answers. The man does not unlock it, and there are no signs of life inside. I press my face to the glass for several minutes and wait. Sometimes another cottage girl or boy, man or woman I do not know will be there already or will arrive just after me. The older they are, the less friendly. I remind myself that not everyone has a grandfather who insists on frequent laughter like mine does, or a little sister who will tug on your lips early in the morning until you wake because you *were sleeping all wrong*. We all have different roles.

But the guy I am standing with at the flower shop door today defies the norm. He is wearing a suit and shiny leather shoes that make him seem like an old rich guy even though he can't be that much older than I am. In one hand, he is holding a skateboard, but he looks uncomfortable. As if he doesn't even know what to do with it. I stare down at those shoes and think that Da has never owned anything so expensive. We do not live in gutters or shelters, but we are not rich either, especially this season with the orchards. Sometimes the wind blows the wrong way or it doesn't rain and our fortunes are set for that season. This season the ratty sweater I am wearing, the old jeans, Da's old coat all reflect that.

The guy has a scowl on his face that I don't think can be removed even with surgery. He tries to force the flower shop door open in my wake, apparently thinking it hasn't opened because I was not strong enough. And then, when I softly say, "Hello," he turns to look at me as if I were crazy.

He has bags underneath his eyes; he obviously doesn't sleep much. I take a step back because of the way he looks over my old clothes, my frayed scarf, the woolen gloves Gigi gave me last year. I can tell that he finds me unimpressive, yet still I force myself to make conversation. "I guess it's an evaluation day."

"Look, please stop talking, okay," he snaps. His breath is laced with whiskey; his voice reminds me of scraping sandpaper.

"Okay." I don't take it personally. I walk around to the back of the shop, where weeds and thistles grow side by side and on occasion a rat scurries past my foot. There is what I think could have been a garden at some point, but it is overrun now. A large metal shed sits right behind the building; it's even more crowded with plants than the flower shop itself. They cover every inch of the shed, including the windows. Anyone who did not know what they were looking for would assume that this was all there was. But I push past the plants, can feel the man following me to the back, where underneath a small wooden table I feel around for the lever of a hatch. The first time I came here I could not find it. Today I yank it open and enter. There is a ladder to climb, but it is so dark. At some point you have to let go and hope that you're as close to the ground as possible.

The air inside the hatch is dank, depressing. It is different from with the plants. Down here every breath seems to echo infinitely, and yet there is no air at all. Each time you hit the ground you wait for some midnight monster to pounce, to devour you. It never happens, but I find myself holding still all the same, wishing we could do this upstairs instead. Wishing that we did not belong in the dark so much.

After a moment a flashlight flickers on to reveal a dark hallway and the man standing next to me. I open my mouth to say thank you, but he shoves me out of the way. My elbow slams into the wall so hard that for a moment I can't feel my arm. Angry Guy doesn't apologize, but now I am so mad I want to kick him. He walks past me, and I yell after him. "I'm sure everyone you meet cowers in front of you like some baby, idiot," I say. "You and your cardboard face. But I'm not one of those people." I cover my mouth, horrified. Normally I would never say anything like that.

"What?" asks the man, sounding surprised and annoyed to hear me still talking to him, but it is already over. I am walking away from him.

At the end of the hallway there is an office, and inside it sits Miss Odette Abernathy, my handler. She is behind a desk, but she has large headphones over her ears, and her eyes are closed. She smokes her cigarette halfheartedly, and her head bobs to the music. When I tap on her desk, she jumps. "Oh, Lirael," she squeaks. "I've done it again, haven't I? Gone and lost track of the time." She scrambles to rearrange her desk, but all this means is that her papers go flying. The room is already littered with all sorts of things—papers, empty soda cans, half-eaten chocolates. I do not know where the man in the suit disappears to. I imagine that he has his own handler to see, though I have never seen the person inside the office next door.

I sit on the chair in front of Miss Odette. She is not the old woman I had imagined she would be. All my life, at the orphanage, in the woods, all the people who have watched over me have been alternating versions of Madame—the strong, calculating types. I was shaking in my boots my first time here. But Miss Odette is tall and bubbly, with red hair and a pale, freckled face. She is not much older than thirty. She seems like the kind of person who could not hurt a fly, but then again, that is what we are meant to think. When she smiles and says, "You can tell me anything," I almost believe her. She hands me a blank piece of paper to fill out while she does other things. Checks my blood pressure, takes a sample of my blood, makes me step out of my clothes and spin around for her. On the piece of paper I answer the same questions about my life: the most significant things that have happened this month, how they have made me feel, how they have not made me feel. About the fishing trip with Da, the way Gigi's bones seem to be shriveling right inside her skin. Afterward Miss Odette flutters back to her desk, fumbles around for her glasses. She slides them only halfway up her nose as she reads my answers. She says nothing for so long that I rest my chin on her desk.

Finally: "Well. You certainly have a very interesting family, Lirael. I just *love* reading about them." Her voice is high-pitched when she says this. Her eyes twinkle, and the smile on her face is huge, like a teacher compensating for being older than her student. She asks me more questions about my life. Some of them are hypothetical questions like: What would you do if Da died today? How would you feel if Gigi was killed? What about Cecily? To all these the answer is the same: *nothing*. Secretly I think about what I said to the guy in the suit. I think about how out of character it was for me. But when the tests and questions are over, Miss Odette reaches beside her desk and retrieves a freshly printed page. On it, a graph and more numbers than I can understand. "You are doing well this month, Lirael," she says. "Keep up the good work."

"Thank you," I say.

She retrieves a black bag from underneath her desk and

hands it to me. When I open it, there are weapons inside: three guns, a few more knives, some rope, some wire. "They will become necessary in the coming months," she says. "I am also advising my sleepers to train whenever they can. I understand that it is more difficult now than it was at the cottages, but we need our sleepers to be especially strong now."

She means now that the Silence has ended.

"Yes, miss," I say, and stuff the weapons inside my messenger bag.

She also gives me a small plastic case with enough blue and white pills to last me another month. The blue pills, I know from the cottages, is why she can print those graphs out. Madame told us that we were taking them only so that she, and one day our handlers, could print out these graphs and "monitor our levels."

"There must always be a perfect balance," she said, "in order for every sleeper to be at their optimal."

It is the white pills that keep us at our optimal. That is why Miss Odette takes my blood sample. To make sure they are working well. Miss Odette smiles. "I will see you next month, Lirael," she tells me.

I breathe a sigh of relief when I am out of her office.

I was not punished. Despite what I said to the man in the

suit. Despite stepping out of the character of Lirael for that moment and becoming someone I did not recognize. Maybe there are limits, but they are pushable limits. I think about the watch Edith slipped into my pocket at the café. About her breaking the rules by staying friends with other sleepers.

There must be small ways in which I can rebel.

But this is not a dangerous thought for me to have; unlike Edith, I have no intentions.

CHAPTER 22

The following week it is time for a flower shop visit, but Da is taking forever putting his fruit together. By the time he has the basket ready for me, it is late afternoon, and he forbids Cecily from going. I am wearing my coat when he changes his mind and forbids me as well. "Leave it till tomorrow," he says. "They can bake their pies then."

I blink at him in surprise. It is almost dark. The flower shop man will be expecting me. But Da is in one of his overprotective moods, and there is nothing I can say to change his mind. I try everything. "But we can't disappoint them," I say. "You always say they're counting on us."

"And they'll still be counting on us tomorrow, Lira," he says, flipping through his newspaper.

So I decide to make everyone a cup of tea. I go upstairs and run my fingers underneath my mattress until I find the hole inside it. From there I retrieve the sleeping pills. I sit with Da until he announces that he is going to bed, and then I help him upstairs to where Gigi is already fast asleep. I wait until the house is quiet; then I wear my dress, my only good dress, on what has to be the coldest evening of summer and bike all the way to the flower shop, shivering. *Of course the dress was a bad idea,* I tell myself. Seeing Edith looking so put together inspired an improvement, but tonight I'd rather be warm. The sidewalks are sleek and shiny, an illusionary pool. Twice my bike skids out from beneath me and into the road, and I pick myself up as a car swerves and honks. By the second time there are wet patches on my dress, my hair is matted to the side of my face with mud, and my skin is covered in goose bumps. Only then do I become aware of the emptiness of the sky. No stars, no moon, an uncomfortable blackness, the kind that comes before something explodes. Now that I think of it, I wish I could remember the weatherman's words on the radio in the kitchen this morning. I had been distracted by Cecily, by Aunt Imogen on the telephone.

The slinky silver watch Edith slipped into my pocket before she left the café is still with me one week later. I don't know why I have not thrown it away. When I got home after the café, I was planning to drop it in the trash can, but when I reached inside my pocket, I found a piece of paper there as well, with an address written on it in Edith's neat handwriting. "If you're coming, turn this on, make sure the second hand is moving," the note said. "It throws the trackers, and they won't know where in the city you are. Please come (any night this week). XO, E."

Now the watch is in my pocket, and the address has stayed in my memory. It is the perfect time. Da, Gigi, and Cecily are all fast asleep.

But I am not going.

I said this immediately when I read the note and then again when I reread it tonight. I said it when Aunt Imogen called us all into the kitchen this morning to tell us her big news: that she'd found a man to take her traveling all around Europe for the next year and she was leaving in a week. It was going to work this time because her standards were much higher and her expectations much lower. She wasn't expecting much of the world, she said, but she'd heard someone say at a church that life happens only once. But then she could not recall whether she'd read it in a book instead, because she suddenly did not remember ever setting foot in a church, unless being in love with someone who had counted. While she spoke, Gigi sobbed, and Da glared at her, but Aunt Imogen barely noticed either of them.

I am not going.

I said it again this evening as I slid the dress on, thinking of how silly it looked on me, frumpy in places it shouldn't be because I am not the right height, not the right size, not the right anything. A green dress with an intricate lace design that is lost in all the material catching on the wheel of my bike. I told myself that I owed the flower shop man a visit, but that was it. That was the only place I would go.

I stare now at my reflection in front of the glass of a boutique store after I've just picked myself up from the pavement, and my answer is firm this time.

Even if I was planning on going to Edith's address after the flower shop, I cannot go now. Not looking like this.

It is completely dark. I ride to the flower shop, expecting to find no one there, but the man opens the door and frowns at me. "You didn't turn up today," he says. "I was beginning to think that you were dead."

He does not ask for an explanation, and I do not offer him one. I follow him to the counter, pretend not to care about the flat tone of his voice. Why should it bother me that the flower shop man would not care if I was dead? Why should it bother me that I can think of only three people who would, and it is only because they are either too old or too young and innocent and do not know any better?

I read the instructions on the piece of paper and open my mouth, but the flower shop man beats me to it. "Tonight," he grunts, pushing an envelope my way. "You're usually here earlier. Was about to call it in." And then he starts to shut down his store right there in front of me. I have no choice but to leave. I go to the nearest grocer's and buy everything on the shopping list. I load it all onto my bicycle and pedal to the warehouse, but even before I reach it, I can already tell there is going to be a problem. A group of angry-looking kids stand in front of the building, smoking and drinking around a garbage can fire. They spot me just as I am turning around, but before I can pedal far, someone catches up to me: someone with cold, dry hands, who lifts me right off the bike and throws me. This time when I hit the ground, it really hurts. I stare up at the black sky, gasping for breath. Forever seems to pass this way.

Sometimes I forget that there is bad in this world. I mean,

I know there is, but when I think of bad things, I think of us. The cottages, the sleepers. I picture us with horns, with blood dripping down our faces like vampires, with our knives and guns and porcelain smiles. I do not think of them. Wanting things they cannot have. Taking things they do not want.

Two boys tug at my clothes, ripping the fabric until it doesn't cover me, while their friends watch and laugh. They promise that it's only a little fun, they won't hurt me. *Only a little fun*, and they *surprise* me all over again.

Why do the biggest mistakes of our lives always look so small before they are made? Why isn't a poisoned road lined with dead bodies or the stench of corpses until you're standing right at the place that will kill you?

The rain starts to fall. It is quiet. My head must have hit the ground hard because a fourteen-year-old girl who looks just like me drops to the ground next to me. I can see right through her like she is layers of nothing but water. She's dead. She's inside my head, but she watches me outside, too. The old man is also here, standing over me, and he says, *Fight. Fight, dammit*, but he is softer in the real world.

"Pretty little thing, ain't ya?" a large boy rasps, and then he sits right on my chest, heavy enough that it's hard to breathe. Everything is spinning. *Come on, come on*, I think. *Get up,*

Lira. All I need is for my head to stop spinning, my body to start functioning again. But the boy sits heavily on me as his friends cheer him on, and I cannot move. Can barely breathe.

This might be what I deserve, I think tiredly. *For who I am. For what I have done. For all the things I will still do.*

Get up, Lira. I must speak the words out loud because for a moment the boy glances at me. His eyes are blacker than any I have ever seen in this world, their world. The other boys even seem a little afraid of him. He's holding me down, looking me over and smiling as if he has a terrible plan. Then he leans away to put out his cigarette and reach for his zipper, and the pressure on my chest eases. My lungs fill with air, my head clears, and I am me. I am a soldier again.

If I were anyone else, this would be an unfair game. An unfair fight.

But here is the thing:

For all his darkness, my eyes hold no light, none at all.

The feeling returns to my hands, my feet, as if I willed it so. I push the boy, and he tumbles off me in surprise. I am on my feet. We stare at each other, one monster to another. I have lost my green dress, but I know that I will win this.

I am going to kill him.

He must see something of this in my face because he

lunges first. I don't have time to think. My hands scramble around for the first weapon I can find. I pick up the rock and throw it hard without hesitating. The boy howls. There is a gash leaking blood down his forehead.

He stumbles to his feet again and charges at me. He is furious now, and he uses his weight to throw me back down on the ground, but I am ready. When he's close enough, my knees lock around his neck and squeeze until his face is first red, then purple, until he is lying there soundless, and then I stand, ready for the rest of them. Wearing only my underclothes.

For a long moment everyone is silent. And then they make the mistake of thinking that my ability to kill is a fluke. Of thinking that every evil thing in the world looks like them: burly and mean and drunk.

There're more of them than me. But I do the best I can to be quick about it, to keep them from drawing any attention to us. I am strategic about positioning myself in the dark so that there will be no memory of me. The ones who remember this will remember only the shadow of a girl.

All this lasts less than a minute. It feels longer. It would be longer, but Edith's brother, Gray, turns up and twists their hands and knees until they scream. As he does this, I put the pieces together inside my head. He is meant to be the receiver of whatever is delivered to the warehouse today, and I am late. Very late. He must have been waiting. And now he's going to be in trouble because of me.

Afterward he says something, but my ears have stopped working. The words sounds something like "You're usually here on time," which makes me think that he knows what days I deliver and has been looking out for me. He does a quick sweep of our surroundings, to make sure no one saw us. I am still in my underwear.

"I can, um, carry you so you don't have to—" he says, gesturing with his hands to the wet ground and looking embarrassed.

The look on my face stops him from finishing. "Right," he says, still not looking at me, and starts walking. "This way."

I follow him into his truck, where he turns up the heat and rummages around inside the back until he finds something. An oversize sweatshirt, a pair of jeans. "I sleep in here sometimes," he says, answering a question I did not ask. I pull the clothes on over my frozen body while I stare out the window, not even embarrassed, just numb. My own green dress is lying in tatters somewhere back there by the garbage bin, by the bodies that are no longer moving.

"Are you okay?" he asks. "Are you hurt?"

I shake my head.

He stares at me. "Are you sure? Do you want to talk about it?"

I shake my head again.

He gestures down, and when I look, I notice that there is blood seeping through his shirt, just a drop, so close to my breast.

"Lira," he says.

"Don't," I whisper without finishing. *Don't be this person. I don't want you to be.*

He understands somehow.

Gray and I sit in silence. "I think we missed one," he says after a moment, his hands fisted on the steering wheel. My head whirls back to the bin, and I see it. A dark lump, crawling across the ground, possibly going for help. Before Gray can say or do anything, I am out of the car. I walk toward the boy without any feeling or sentiment inside me. I am all monster now, and I do not know whether my fist connecting with the boy's face twice will kill him. But at the very least I owe him a concussion.

When I am finished, I see the watch Edith gave me lying on the ground. I pick it up, hold it tight inside my hand as I walk away.

I climb back into the truck. I know that I should say this is my fault, say I will take full responsibility, say that everything will be all right, but instead I say, "The food. The kids at your cottage will starve." My voice is barely more than an empty whisper, and Gray looks startled that I spoke at all. He clenches his jaw and leaves the truck again, starts picking up the food. A smashed loaf of bread here. A dented bottle of milk there. But with each thing he picks up he seems to be getting angrier. "Fuck it," I hear him say eventually. "We'll go buy more tomorrow."

But I come out and help him put the food together again. The ones that are still good, that are not broken or spoiled. I remember the days we starved. I remember the days Madame would say, "It's not safe for me to go into the city," and all we would have was a cup of flour. We would sit at the river all day, drinking water until our bellies hurt, pretending that our mouths tasted of apple pie instead. Character building, Madame called it. When we were young, those days—when our characters were still in their infancy—were the worst of our lives.

We do not speak as we load up the truck, but it is understood that we must take the food. There will be no character building, not tonight, not if we can stop it.

We step over the bodies and all the blood. We step over the ones who look like they're only sleeping and the ones who might never wake again. Once I trip over myself in his clothes, which are bigger than I am, but eventually we're back in the truck. And in my hand, covered in dirt and blood, I hold on to the watch Edith gave me more tightly than ever. I know that tonight is supposed to turn me the other way. Make me think that staying out of trouble is the smartest thing, that sticking to routines and protocols are the only things that keep us from breaking. And maybe I will think so tomorrow. But tonight, when Gray asks quietly, "Do you want to turn on the watch?" I know it means I can disappear from this city, from this world for tonight, and so in response I open my hand. I turn on the watch.

And then he puts the truck into gear.

We do not speak to each other. I do not ask where we're going. We drive out of the city and toward the trees. It is always toward the trees. Somewhere deep inside a forest Gray stops the truck. "Do you want to come in?" he asks, gathering the food in his arms.

"I'll wait here," I say, and wrap my arms around myself. Somewhere in the distance a light flickers on and I hear children squealing. I imagine how excited they are about the smallest things—the bags of tea, the biscuits, the bread rolls that are just as important to inhale as to eat.

Some of them, a few boys who want to pretend to drive Gray's truck while he is not looking, wander this way. I think about cowering and pretending not to be here, but in the end we're all just staring at one another through Gray's open door. "Oh," one boy says eventually, backing away, disappointment written all over his face. "Sorry, ma'am."

I force myself to smile and wave them inside. "Hurry up. I won't say a word about this to anyone," I say. "Not even him." I'm sure he knows already.

They give me Cecily's grin and climb inside. A tubby boy with red hair and freckles flashes his gapped teeth at me. He stutters when he talks. "Do you know how to play ISA, miss?"

His friends nudge him. "Don't be stupid, Frederich. Of course she doesn't *know* how to play ISA. It's for boys." And then they talk over one another, trying to teach me the game. ISA stands for International Space Adventure. Another boy named Gavin, who isn't here, came up with it.

That is all I hear.

The steering wheel turns to the left and to the right. I cannot picture all the places we're going to. From imaginary adventures in London to the forests of Brazil, driving against the wind. The good guys chasing the bad guys turn into the bad guys chasing the good. I must fall asleep in the middle of their game, because when I wake up, three faces are peering over me and they do not belong to children. Edith's is one of them, but Gray's isn't.

"He dropped you off. Said you fell and bumped your head," Edith says. I can tell from her voice that she does not believe it. I stand up and pretend that my head does not hurt, that I am swaying because I want to.

We are still on the edge of the city. In a small lonely house on a dark road that has all its windows barred. It is their weekly film night, and there are seven of us altogether. Gray (who isn't here), Edith, a boy and a girl both named Robbie. The girl explains that her name is Roberta, but everyone calls her Robbie. Better that, she says, than Robin, and makes a face. I am surprised to see Julia, though she feels like a stranger to me now, as though we never really knew each other. I didn't realize Edith was her friend. Her skin is still pale, her face still soft and shy, and there is almost something frailer about her blue-green eyes. Because of this, everyone bet against her ever making it onto the yellow bus, but she did. I remember Davis, too, who steps forward and holds out his hand for mine. "Oh, *you*," I say in a voice that makes everyone laugh.

He clutches his chest and sighs. "Thirty seconds into this, and you've already hurt my feelings. If it's your math victories you're thinking of, don't worry. I haven't even learned to spell properly yet. Madame would be horrified if she knew the kind of life I was leading, grammatically, that is."

"I doubt she'd be impressed if she knew anything about your life, Davis," Edith says.

He shrugs. And then he does the strangest thing. He hugs me. This is so unlike Davis that I don't know what to do with it. Especially because before I opened my eyes, I heard him ask Edith, "So, this is who you meant? Are you sure we can trust her?"

"Yes," Edith said.

The group disperses back to a small couch in front of the television. I stare at them. We assumed as children that we were the only cottage in this region. That there was one Madame, one set of examinations. But the world must be peppered with cottages like ours and with others who trained at the same time as we did—perhaps even in the very same woods as we did—and were released into our world, too. It is strange to be standing in the same room as them—the two Robbies.

I clutch my side until I see Edith watching me. "What happened?"

"It's nothing," I tell her, and drop my hand.

I look around. It's not a very nice house. A small heater blasts at full force, but even then it is freezing cold. There are things that need fixing and smells that have no real origin; they just make up the air. Dirty cups fill the kitchen sink; food brims over in the fridge; even the toilet croaks. There are two bedrooms, the kitchen, and the living room. Outside, I find a garden that grows tall and appears untended except for a vegetable patch in the corner. We are on a large farm, and somewhere in the near distance there is a chicken coop and somewhere else, a cow. Edith points everything out proudly and holds my hand. Everyone's even wearing varying shades of gray—gray shirts and shorts, jeans, some of the girls even with their hair in ponytails. It is like a regression to the things that made us feel safe, the old things of comfort. But even so there is fear here. I hear it in the things that are not said and in the things that are. Fear of being found and all kinds of attempts to disguise that fear. The cherry red curtains hung up against the boarded windows that will never see sunlight. A vase of fresh flowers on the table. A pile of magazines in a corner of the room. A radio underneath the couch. A large collection of books, of games and even a small typewriter. But there is no telephone, and it is dark, and they only ever come here at night or early in the morning when no one will notice.

We're safe here for now, but eventually there will be another house or farm, another secret meeting place.

I sit down in front of the television.

Edith passes me the bowl of popcorn. She smiles at the look on my face and whispers, "We only do normal things here. No sleeper stuff." I grab a handful of the food, cross my legs, and lean back against the couch, thinking, *We have never done normal things in our lives. We are not normal. We could die for this, this small, small moment, and that's not normal. We are supposed to be soldiers. All seven of us.*

I eye the door. I count the steps it would take to reach it. Six, maybe seven. Seven steps to walk away.

"Okay, girls," Davis says, pushing his hair back over his forehead, "I need your honest opinion here." He tilts his head toward the television. "If I got a perm exactly like his, would you date me?"

I laugh.

CHAPTER 23

I go back to the farmhouse three more times before I manage to convince Edith to tell me exactly how their technology works. I am mastering the art of sneaking over after completing a mission. Tonight there was no mission; I just snuck out. My family is already asleep from the concoction I gave them. "It's not enough to tell me that this is safe," I tell Edith. "I need to know *why* I'm safe. How do we know nothing bad is going to happen to us?"

She hesitates, as if she has to choose her words carefully. We are washing pots and dishes in a bucket outside, pretending that we are at the river again. That we are younger and it is the old days. The pots are the results of Edith's latest cookbook recipe. It looked good on paper, but when we actually tried to make it, bad things happened. As if to prove the point, Davis leans out the window, holding a chicken leg that is so black it looks painted. He tries to bite into it, but the thing is rock hard. "Mmm, so good," Davis says, still trying to bite into it. "So, so good."

"Geez, Davis, we get it," I say. "You do the cooking next time, okay?"

His eyebrows go up. "You're getting feisty, Lira. I like it." And then he quickly shuts the window before I can spray him with water.

I can see that Edith is hoping I have forgotten about my question, but I haven't. "I need to know," I say.

"Okay. There are two types of watches," she says. She nods toward my wrist. "The one you're wearing is basic. It just scrambles the signal of your tracker so they can't figure out exactly where you are."

"What's the other type?" I ask.

She reaches inside her pocket and pulls out a small black button. "Put this underneath your mattress when you get home," she says. "Whenever it's on, the tracker will always say that you are home, no matter where you are. But remember to turn it off whenever you're actually somewhere you should be. You don't want to overuse it."

I take the black button. It feels cool against my fingers, like some kind of metal. There is a switch at the back. I drop it gently inside the pocket of my sweater. "I'm supposed to trust that tiny thing with my life?" I ask her, not sure that I am convinced. "What if I forget to turn on the watch? Or the black button stops working?"

She hesitates again.

I frown. "Edith."

"Lira," she says, and then she meets my eyes with a reassuring smile. "We have thought of everything. We wouldn't be here, doing this, if we hadn't. Honestly the watches are just our backup method in case things go wrong. We have more secure ways, but they're complicated. And I would tell you everything right now, but the others want to be able to trust you first. So I can't tell you. First you have to trust us."

I turn back to the dishes, trying to decide whether to leave or not. Does Edith understand what she is asking me to do? Trust goes against everything we believe in.

"What?" I ask when I notice the look she is giving me. "Why are you smiling like that?"

"Do you still have those dreams?" she asks.

I know exactly what she is talking about, but I stare at her as blankly as I can. I don't like how quickly she wants to change the subject. Makes me wonder what she is keeping from me.

"That was how we became friends, remember? You told us you thought you were sick because you could dream when the rest of us couldn't. And you were going to tell Madame in case there was a cure."

I remember.

Edith talked me out of it.

It was as if all the carriers had arrived in this world and stopped dreaming exactly when I started. They dreamed about nothing but blackness. The old man holding my memories is all I have ever dreamed about.

We were still in our rebellious phase then, still new to this world, still defying Madame. "It'll be our little secret," Edith said, squeezing my hand. "And anyway, it'll probably go away one day."

By the time we became the obedient children Madame wanted, we'd also become scared. Of her. Of what she would do to me if she knew. Once we weren't friends anymore, I spent my time at the cottages frightened of what Alex, Gray, or Edith might decide to say about me to Madame.

But they never said a word.

"You still dream, don't you?" Edith asks me again later when I am leaving for home.

I shrug noncommittally.

She pulls me into a hug.

"Good," she says with a smile. "It's official then. You're the most normal one of us all. Welcome to the group."

CHAPTER 24

Sometimes I'm good. I bake bread just the way Gigi likes it. She smiles at me to show me that she approves, but most afternoons I am too busy looking down to notice. I bite my bottom lip, put all my concentration into it. I knead the dough until my palms hurt, until my fingers are two steps away from becoming bloodied. I tell myself that the bread will be just right because of how much conscientious effort I put into it. And then afterward I come away and realize how small that was, how unremarkable, and how by evening it will already be gone.

Da leaves for the orchards before any of us are awake today. He only ever does this when he is sad about Gigi, and most days I don't blame him.

I help Gigi into the bath and wash her back like I do every day. The very first time I did it, about six months ago, she cried. She said she was sorry, and I said it was okay, so many times that I started to cry myself. She said that she wished her disease would take her quickly. "Death is not," she whispered, "the worst thing in the world. It's the slow progression of it, the drawing out, that hurts. You're still here, but you're missing out on everything already, cooking the way you used to, baking peach cobblers, sewing new dresses for your grandchildren. Suddenly fingers don't work right, eyes don't see, breathing becomes nearly impossible. The death is simple, but the dying part is like a volcano, simmering quietly underneath the surface for years." She cries still sometimes. I've never told Da.

Today I tie my hair out of my face and put on the radio, to a channel that plays music all the time. I remember that just a year ago, Gigi was this small, bubbly woman saying "Don't slouch like that, Lira" and "Don't eat that." And "This is how you make apricot jam" and "Goodness, child, do you intend to brush your hair today? You look like a rascal. Tell her, Thomas." Everyone in town knows who Gigi is, tales of her baked goods and her jams spreading like wildfire every summer, people pushing wheelbarrows of the stuff away some hot Sunday afternoons. But nobody knows about this part yet, about what has happened, about the last six months. That's the way Da prefers it, I think, but also Gigi. "Not everything needs to happen in front of the window," she says.

Downstairs Cecily and her friend, Mathieu, are playing with our neighbor's children, Freddie and Rachel. Their mother has dropped them off at our house to be baby-sat while she is in the city. Gigi has that reputation of eleventh-hour kindness, but I answered the door because Aunt Imogen and her suitcases left yesterday. "Gigi's actually in the bath at the moment," I said.

"Oh," our neighbor said, holding on to her hat, fighting the wind. "I hope she doesn't mind two more."

No one notices that Gigi rarely goes out anymore. Nobody knows how bad things are. And that is how my grandmother likes it.

It makes me feel better.

In a way, every one of us, in every world, is a liar. It is what we are built on.

Now Gigi touches my cheek when her coughing fit has subsided. "You're beautiful, you know," she whispers, and her eyes are glassy. "As beautiful as my Rosie ever was."

I grit my teeth because I hate it when she talks like this. When her touch is full of sentimentality and her voice is weak. It means she thinks she's closer to the end than ever. It means she thinks that she will finally leave us, end this burden that she has become. Every day with Gigi is full of sentimentalities now. No more of that toughness, of that meanness I could handle so much better. Still, I try. "You're the one who said that beauty is not the most important thing in the world," I mutter.

"No, it is not. But when one has it, it is useful."

She holds my chin, and I see my eyes reflected in hers. Pale gray as hers. "Beautiful or not, don't ever waste who you are, Lira," she whispers fiercely. "Promise me." And then just as quickly the moment is lost as her wheezing resumes. I can see her fighting for it, that moment, but I don't help her find it again. I can't. When a loud crash reverberates in the walls, I run downstairs, soapsuds still on my arms. I find Cecily sitting at the piano, pressing the same key over and over again, eyebrows furrowed, as if she were concentrating. I know better. Mostly because her friend, Mathieu, has picked up a book and is pretending to read it. Upside down. Rachel and Freddie sit next to him, trying to look innocent.

"What did you break?" I ask.

"We didn't break nothing, honest," Mathieu says, eyes wide as coins.

I frown. "Cecily, you're supposed to be the responsible one. You're supposed to be the good example."

My sister shrugs. Her tone is solemn. "I don't know why. He's the one who's older. He's the one who broke the vase. He's the guest, and he's behaving pretty badly. When I behave badly, I get punished."

Mathieu gapes at her. "But you told me . . . but you said . . ."

"Don't be *stupid*, Mathieu," Cecily says, rolling her eyes.

The room is silent for a long moment before chaos erupts and they both are suddenly gone, out of the house. I do not know who chases whom, but I hear them both screaming, making deals about who can fight whom, who is wrong and who is right, who should live and who should die. Mathieu tells Cecily that everyone at school thinks she's strange because she's always talking about *the trees* and all the things Da does to keep them alive, that she should be grateful he even bothers with her. And then they're running again because Cecily says she will break his ears off and he's laughing at her. Rachel and Freddie chase after them, making a game of it.

I go back upstairs. I help Gigi with her dress, with her makeup, and then she insists she sit outside today, underneath the shade of a tree, breathing in the fresh air. She knits her sweater while I lie on a mat, reading a book, pretending that I am not fascinated by the game that Cecily, Mathieu, Rachel, and Freddie are playing. Pretending that I am not quietly laughing at their jokes, as if I were still a child myself. Fifteen suddenly feels very old. This is how the summer passes away, the same as every other summer and yet different.

Tonight is one of those summer nights when Da does not turn up for dinner. Cecily, Gigi, and I sit around the table and pretend that there isn't an empty chair. "He's not in the orchards, is he?" Cecily sighs. "He's gone to that place *again*."

"Of course he's in the orchards," I say automatically.

"Time to brush your teeth," Gigi says at exactly the same time. And then, as soon as Cecily is upstairs, she throws me the truck keys. She does not meet my eyes when she says, "Go bring your grandfather home, Lirael."

These are the blue moon days.

I have never told her where I find him. Have never mentioned the pub or the men he drinks with. Have never said anything about how I rarely have to help him into the car because he's hardly ever drunk. I don't know whether he walks or finds someone to give him a ride. Each time I come he looks deep into my eyes, waiting to hear the news: Is she dead yet? As if some unspoken force whispered in his ear suddenly this morning: "Today is your wife's last day. Run, hide." I don't know what sort of answer he wants, the good or the bad kind, but he always breathes a sigh of relief.

I do not make him come with me immediately. I find my own booth in the pub and pull out my sketchbook. I am not sure whether this is something I would have liked without the original Lira's liking it first. I just know that it has become a part of me. Sometimes my fingers itch to draw something I do not recognize until it is finished. Today, though, all I want to capture is the way the people in the pub sit, relaxed and laughing, without a care in the world. This feeling of freedom, of choice. That is what I draw.

"That's not how I look," Gary, the bartender, says. He taps my grandfather on the shoulder. "Thomas, you ought to get this girl a proper drawing job in the city. She'd make you a fortune."

"Thanks, Gary," I say, smiling at the bartender. He's good at being kind.

But my grandfather ignores me and I him until he is ready to go. And then we climb into the truck in perfect silence. Except it's not perfect because my mind is spinning with words the dead Lirael would have wanted to say. Words like, *It doesn't count, your telling me that family is important if you run from yours the first moment you become afraid.* And, *Wait until she's dead before you fall apart; why can't you do that?* That's the worst one. The thing I can never say. I rarely ever see my—*her*—grandfather so small, and as we drive back home, he begins to force his shoulders back up, clear his throat as if he has forgotten where he is, but it's almost always too late. He lights a cigarette and smokes it in silence. As we drive back home, he'll usually point at the orchards and say, "That's going to be yours one day," as if I have forgotten.

Tonight I don't answer. Gigi is waiting for him in the kitchen when we arrive, and I know to go upstairs immediately. "Thomas," she says softly. All the lights are out, but she looks tough in candlelight. Tougher than I've seen her look in months; I almost believe that a miracle has happened. That she is well again, but she doesn't move from the chair she is sitting patiently in, and I know it's not because she doesn't want to. I can't help stopping at the top of the stairs, can't help pressing my body against the wall and listening. I do not know what Da says. Probably something like "If we had more money for doctors . . . if I had done better . . ." his voice cracking, weak.

Because Gigi snorts. I hear her say, "You dumb, dumb man. You think it's your money and your medicines I want on the last days of my life? You think they're the most important thing in the world? When I was without those things, was I dead? Have we ever been unhappy?"

I sit down with my back against the wall. I listen to them cry. For *practice*, I tell myself, *it's all for practice*.

Just before dawn every morning, I sneak out of the house. I practice throwing my knives at the tree trunks in the orchards. I pretend an invisible Ezra is sparring with me, and I break his bones with my hands. I disassemble my guns, clean them, and reassemble them again.

I take my pills, and then I train for about an hour. Then I go home, climb back into my bed.

There isn't anything that I am not ready for.

The birds poke incessantly at the ripe apricots through the tree nets. The really dedicated ones manage to eat a few, but for the most part they are unsuccessful. It is that time of the year when everything is out in full force, from birds to worms to mischief-seeking squirrels. The fruit pickers are here, too: little boys sent from our neighbors for the few coins they will earn while their brothers are in the city. They come after school and climb the trees and crowd the ladders with small arms and full baskets. Lately they come also for Da's stories, the things he says about when he was a little boy, adventure stories involving ships and wicked pirates that almost certainly could never have happened. But the little boys don't notice. Even the ones who are too young to help, who listen from the base of the trees, stomping fallen fruit with their boots. "Tell us the one about the swordfight," they yell up, and Da begins his story.

"Well, once upon a time . . ."

"God, if I have to hear that story again," Philip says, climbing down his ladder with a basket of fruits. We are working on the same tree.

"We can't both go," I tell him solemnly. "And you're the one who has to stick around. You're taller."

He laughs. "See you later, Lira." He loads up the truck with the baskets, and then he drives to the city to see how much he can sell at the fresh food market. There are also orders to be filled locally, houses to make calls on. Mrs. Eckles wanted two boxes of peaches; Mr. Danon wanted four. Normally I go with him, but I am renetting the trees to keep the birds away. When the day is over, Da drives us home with several boxes of fruit.

My bones are so tired they hurt. I am shrugging out of my clothes and halfway up the stairs when I realize that we have company. That the voices speaking in the living room belong to Gigi and someone else. Someone who cannot be here. In my shock I forget all about my half-buttoned clothes. I enter the room just as Julia stands, shy smile on her face. She looks relieved to see me, but when my mouth falls open and stays that way, her smile fades. She shuffles her feet and says, "Um, hi."

"Why are you being rude?" Gigi chastises me after too long a moment. "Your friend has been waiting hours to see you."

I say nothing. Sometimes, when I am extremely tired, I see things, shadows in the corners of my eye, tricks of light that turn into a girl or boy shape, that laugh and play hide-and-seek on the walls. But Julia's shadow does not fade away. The look of irritation on Gigi's face does not dissolve, and so I have to face the truth: there is another sleeper in this house. Another person like me, and that makes me more uneasy than I can say.

My *friend*, I think.

Hours, I think.

It occurs to me to be embarrassed, especially when Da enters the house and begins making a fool of me. "You say you are Lira's friend?" he asks, for the second time in the span of a minute, and when Julia nods, his face breaks out into a smile.

"We don't get to see too many of her friends," Gigi explains, making things worse.

"Lira works too hard," Da says. "Doesn't do much of the things a girl her age should be doing."

Julia laughs. There is sympathy all over her face when she finally turns to look at me. I understand that the expression on her face is saying, "I have come to save you from these crazy people." "That's actually why I'm here," she tells my grandparents. "I was wondering whether Lira might be interested in coming on a hiking trip with my family tomorrow. Just for the weekend."

"A hiking trip?" Da says, pretending to think about it. He actually looks like he wants to come, too. To make sure I go, to make sure it happens. He doesn't bother to ask me before offering his consent.

"But I haven't finished the netting," I remind him.

"Philip will do it."

I finally have the calm of mind to scowl at him like I should.

Julia can never be my friend, not in public. She cannot be some random girl I met in the city; it's too dangerous. Someone would recognize us together, but in front of my grandparents we pretend that is exactly what we're going to do. Walk around in public together like normal teenagers. Her "family" is everyone at the farmhouse. This invitation is from them, too, not just her. Still, I find use of my legs only when it's time to escort her outside. We both pretend not to notice the way Da moves to the window and gently opens it.

"Lighten up," Julia says. "If I'd known you'd look like that—"

"You wouldn't have come?" I ask.

"I would have brought a camera," she says.

"Is this really possible?" I ask. "A whole weekend?" It's one thing to disappear for a night without our handlers finding out. Two seems impossible.

"Gray and Robbie are taking care of it," Julia says.

I want to ask about this secret protection Edith refused to tell me about, but Julia shakes her head in warning. I remember that Da is listening.

"Don't worry, Lira." Julia hugs me. "Dress warm, and come prepared to do crazy things." She lowers her voice so Da won't hear and pulls me away from the window. "We're making a list," she says, "of all the things that people our age do that seem to make them the happiest. I've been investigating, and after it's finished, we'll do everything on the list. We have been planning this weekend for ages."

She hesitates, glances back at my house. "You trust us,

right? I mean, you trust me? You know that I am your friend? I know we were never close, but . . . well, I hope you don't hate me."

She's talking about the way I just reacted.

"I'm glad you came," I say, and wave when she drives away.

I am lying.

"Don't you want to know where I met her?" I ask Da at the dinner table.

"A *friend*, Lira," he says, ignoring my question.

"Maybe she can finally talk some sense into you and change those clothes you insist on wearing," Gigi says.

I don't ask: "What's wrong with what I'm wearing?"

"She's probably going to be a terrible influence on me," I warn instead.

Gigi beams at Da. Cecily is the one who asks the question I know they are thinking: "So, when can she come for dinner?"

I roll my eyes at how normal we are being.

I ride my bike into the city early the following day because Edith and Julia want to go to a movie together before we go hiking. It is not about what we see but the act of doing it. This is the first thing on our list. The cinema is small and musty, and the film we've chosen interests no one. At first we are disappointed by the emptiness of the room, but then we begin to see the bright side. We yell things at the characters from the front row and predict how the movie will end.

The movie does not match our mood at all. It is a quiet, somber film, but for once we can't afford to be those things, not today. We whisper-shout out our opinions during the really poignant moments of the film. "Okay, I know they're about to kiss and everything," Edith says, "but I really think she should think about dating his brother for a minute."

Julia and I turn to look at her. "But his brother is responsible for the deaths of half the people in the movie."

Edith stuffs her mouth with popcorn. "I just don't see the relevance in all that. The way I see it, only one thing really matters when a girl has to choose between two guys, and it is this: Does he have good teeth or does he not? Only one brother in this movie is even *remotely* worth considering, and I can't believe they're trying to sell the other one to us because he's a nice guy."

Edith delivers all this in a deadpanned way that makes our eyes water.

We eventually lower our voices but only because

the usher walks into the room and eyes us suspiciously. Whenever the movie lights up his face, he looks like some kind of bogey monster. Julia keeps making noises like she's deeply affected by the movie. Small gasps, with her hands clutching at her throat. Edith and I copy her until our shoulders shake with laughter.

A man dies; we laugh. His wife breaks down at the funeral; we laugh larder.

The usher frowns at us a moment longer before he leaves. He cannot do anything about the fact that we all are clearly mad.

When he is gone, we laugh until everything hurts. We are not laughing for any good reasons. We just laugh because we can. It tastes like rebellion in my mouth, and I am afraid of it. The fact that I can laugh. That I choose to be here doing these things, terrified of what might happen if we are caught, yet still laughing. I hold a shaking hand to my chest and feel how fast my heart beats. "Stupid, stupid," it says.

Afterward I cannot even remember what the film was about.

The others are more carefree. They laugh as though they've known this game a long time. I will never fit in, not in the way they want me to. It doesn't help that I am the youngest, that I know the least about life, that I do not go out to clubs or parties like they do. I do not have rich parents or an expensive school. In a way I am less than they are, but then Edith links her arm through mine and whispers, "I'm glad you came," and I can tell she means it in a way I still do not understand. I do not question it. It is hard but not impossible to turn my mind off just this once.

The three of us agree to ride separately and meet up with the others. I ride my bike, and Edith catches one bus while Julia catches another, yet we're all headed for the same destination.

But when we reach the farmhouse, the others are waiting, quiet. Roberta stares down at the ground, as if there were something interesting there. "What's wrong?" Julia asks, her eyes wide.

It's Robbie who answers. "I had an assignment today," he says, and his voice actually sounds shaky. He clears his throat a couple of times. "A bunch of sleepers."

I frown at him, then at Roberta, Gray, Davis. I realize that they all are afraid of something. This makes me so terrified I cannot move. Edith opens her mouth to make an argument. "But, Robbie," she says carefully, "this isn't your first time—"

Robbie shakes his head. "You don't understand. The address I was given. It was right where they were staying. It was a place like ours. They were . . . meeting there. Like us. Some apartment in the city."

It's as if he is slapping us in the face with icy water. The idea that there are others like us, bending the rules like us, that they died for it. I can barely stay standing, and Julia actually collapses onto a chair. This is our warning. Probably the only one we will get. We have to stop this now. We have to say good-bye.

Miss Odette said that all sleepers needed to be ready. What if they are checking on us all, to make sure we are? What if the end of the Silence means more for sleepers like us than just more missions?

They could be watching us right now.

It's a long time before I find my voice. "What should we do?" I half whisper, and I am hoping, *hoping*, that someone says this is over. The farmhouse, the meetings. Someone else, not me. Because now we know for sure that meeting like this is the most dangerous thing we could be doing. Any second now the door could burst open. Any second now a round of bullets that will erase us.

All it takes is one moment of carelessness. That moment might even have happened already.

But no one says it.

Not a single one of us.

Instead Robbie says, "But those kids were not Safes. They had a lot of surveillance on them." It sounds like something heavy is pressing down on his throat.

"Okay," Edith says. "Okay." She sounds even worse than Robbie. "Then they were nothing like us. So we have nothing to be worried about. Right?"

We all nod our heads without actually looking at one another.

We tell ourselves that we are much more careful.

In the end the most frightening thing isn't the fact that we might die from this. It's the fact that we know it. And yet we blow that knowledge away from ourselves like feathers.

What weight will this choice carry?

I am terrified of the answer.

In the end maybe the brave ones are also the foolish ones. Maybe only fools are ever truly brave.

At first our list consists of silly things. We sit outside in the trees and spin bottles and plant kisses on each other. Me on Julia. Julia on Davis, and he acts like he has died and gone to heaven.

"Does this mean we're in a relationship now?" Davis asks,

fluttering his eyelashes. "Me, you, Lira, what do you say?"

"You watch way too much television," Julia says, laughing.

Robbie and Gray are a lot more reserved than the rest of us. That makes sense; they have seen and done worse things as Safes than we can imagine. Instead they watch over us like sentinels. They scare me a little with how serious they are. Once, I offer Gray a small smile, just to see if he will return it, and when he does, he looks as though he doesn't smile often. It's one of those dark, miserable looks. Davis is the opposite. We have to beg Davis to put his clothes back on. We have to beg Davis to stop drinking.

Then we have chocolate milk shake contests that cause brain freezes, laced with some special ingredient Julia won't reveal. We run back into the house and make them, and then I hold my head and whisper, "Oh, God, it's almost worse than dying."

"Almost?" Davis slurs, milk shake all over his shirt. "What do you mean almost? Are we standing in the same room right now?"

"Um," Julia squeaks, "is it also supposed to cause temporary blindness?"

My eyes snap open, and we're all squinting at Julia. "Wait," I say. "We don't know the consequences of what all these things we're going to do are? I thought you did the research."

She nods, but she's rubbing her eyes like they're about to fall out.

I laugh, but Roberta doesn't find it so funny. "What exactly is next on your list, Julia?"

"Well," Julia says, blushing, "the bridge is—"

"Okay, I'm gonna stop you right there," Roberta says, holding up her hand. "It's dangerous enough that we're meeting like this. Am I the only one who thinks we shouldn't be doing things that involve blindness and bridges and possibly never waking up again tomorrow morning?"

We all raise our hands, and Julia coughs. "But that's the whole point." She sounds young and mousy as she looks around the room at each of us, as if we're back at the cottages and she's trying to become one of us again. I want to hug her, and this surprises me. I want to tell her that there is no us, or if there is, she is more of a member than I will ever be. When Roberta suggests rethinking the list altogether, Julia's shoulders fall, but she hasn't given up yet, and underneath her breath she adds, "Gray found us some motorcycles. They're outside."

The motorcycles. That's how Roberta loses her battle. One by one we make our excuses and shuffle outside as quickly as we can, heels clicking in excitement. I have never ridden a motorcycle before, and the rule is this: one of us rides the thing while the other tries to stand on it without falling. "You're being really stupid," Roberta hisses when she hears this plan. "Let's say we find out that we're not invincible tonight. Then what?" She doesn't wait for an answer; she storms back inside the house and from the window watches us put on our helmets. I stare after her. It's strange because she seems like a tough sort of girl, with her cropped hair and the stud in her nose, but she looks horrified at the prospect of riding with us. We leave her at the farmhouse, and although we don't go far, we go far enough that the noise of motorcycles and raucous teenagers will not wake anybody up.

Nothing is more terrifying than standing unprotected, willing your body to stay upright, to defy gravity. Nothing more than staring danger right in the eye; it makes my cheeks hot and my palms sweaty. But in this moment, standing here on the motorcycle, I do not feel any more afraid than I do on a daily basis. Robbie is driving, and at first he goes slowly, but I say, "Faster," and then again. Faster, faster, but still nothing. It is the same as waiting to die in those bunkers when we were children, not knowing which ones of us would disappear before we could become our alternates. Still, I fight for it, shutting my eyes and holding my hands up. I am trying to muster the feelings I'm sure a normal teenager would have. I am trying to prepare myself, trying to miss someone, anyone, but I am still me. I am me, and I can tell when the others are done that they feel the same.

Julia's list hasn't made us normal. It hasn't made us forget, and it's only when we're on our way back that Robbie tells us about Roberta. "You don't know this," he says, "but her alternate had a brother who died in a motorcycle accident a few months ago. That's why she's being this way."

"Dammit, Robbie," Edith says, slapping his arm. "This is something you tell us before we leave her behind. I thought she was just being her usual controlling self. We have to go get her."

"We have to figure out something else that she can do with us," Julia says.

I am the one who comes up with the plan. I lead the group to the train tracks near the city where we can hear the howling noise getting closer. The game is this: to come close to something, to that thing, that ending, without letting it touch us. So we press our bodies to the ground in a line, holding hands. Edith on my left, Gray on my right, both of their hands warm and dry in mine. The only part of us missing is Alex. We're lying there for so long that I've almost fallen asleep.

When the train comes, it will crush me. It will tear me up into a thousand tiny pieces that can never come back together again. It is this feeling I am counting on. I fill my head with it until someone swears and we all scramble out of the way with only a hair's worth of time to spare.

But afterward I put a hand to my chest, and it's beating at its usual steady pace. As if I am not frightened enough. Nothing. Nothing is enough. *Why?* We ask this question all night. When we think of Madame, we are afraid. When we think of the cottages and all our training, and even now when we remember our examinations. But standing unprotected on a moving bike, waiting for a passing train, all the things that would frighten a normal teenager . . .

We are desperate now. I know this because just a few hours later Roberta leads us to the bridge. It is a small thing in the middle of nowhere. A crossover landmark, half broken down, with a large river underneath that must run all the way through our orchards. We have to drive nearly an hour from the farmhouse just to reach it, but the drive is worth the isolation it affords us. For a while there is silence as we stare down over the railing.

It's terrible because of what the water means to us, because of how much we hate it. Because of what it did to us, all of us, growing up. Being dropped into the ocean as children was bad enough, but after Solomon, and after our living through Madame's method of conditioning, it is hard to overcome the idea that water leads to death and near-death experiences. Someone tries to estimate how deep the water might be, but the words are just noise in my ears.

I am not sure at exactly what moment this stops being a contest. I am not sure when it becomes important. I am only aware of my fingers on the buttons of my shirt. I let it fall to the ground, and then I stand there with the others, all of us half naked and shivering. We're supposed to count to ten and jump together. That is the plan. Edith and Gray are on either side of me. I count, "One, two . . ." but I close my eyes and jump on "three." We all do.

Ten seconds are too long to wait to find out, to be afraid, to feel normal.

I fall too fast to do anything but scream. The moment I hit the water I lose track of everyone else. The river is cold as ice as it envelops my body, but I tell myself that all I have to do to survive it is swim. It is that simple. *Swim*, and the water will become nothing. I flap my hands until my body begins to move toward the bank. Next to me the others are doing the same, frantically. This is not the same as the train.

It is nothing like standing on the motorcycles.

This is Madame we are fighting against.

I am relieved when I reach Davis where he crouches and retches on the bank. I lie down on my back and try to catch my breath. My arms and legs are numb, but I don't care. My heart is beating so hard it might find a way out of my chest. I hear it. I *feel* it.

This is what we have been looking for.

The water will always be terrible. But I am relieved that there was something, that frantic feeling, that loss of calm. It became a different kind of game there for a while, but we have conquered the cottages. Not completely, but enough.

We stumble back to our farmhouse, collapse inside. We sleep the day away, and then we agree to spend our second night underneath the stars. We toast marshmallows around a fire and make up songs. And now our list consists of books we want to read, of films we want to see, of schools we want to go to. Mostly we're joking, happy to be around one another. Davis does the naked thing again, and Roberta threatens to cut off all the parts that are offensive to her. Davis swears, not sure whether she is serious, and stumbles back into his clothes, and for a little while all we can do is laugh.

At some point it stops being so funny. It becomes a little

sad, but that just means that we try harder to laugh over it. To pretend that nothing is wrong. *Robbie wants to be a dentist one day? Okay, ha-ha. Julia wants to teach kindergarten, ha-ha-ha.* The worst part is Edith. "I want children when I'm older," she announces suddenly. "And a husband and a nice job and a pretty house."

I immediately stop laughing. Julia and the others still try, almost desperately now, but Edith will not let go of her sudden melancholy. And without knowing what exactly she is sad about, I am suddenly sad, too. She stares down into the flames, watches her marshmallow burn without retrieving it, and says softly, "Do you remember when we girls had the procedure when we first arrived at the cottages, Lira?"

Everyone looks at me, and I blush. "Yes," I say.

"We had it, too, in our cottages," Roberta says. "Madame said it was a new procedure they'd just started doing. For a special kind of sickness that only affects girls. A sickness we could only get from being around boys."

"The boys had an injection," Davis says. "For some secret disease, too. We figured it out later."

Edith touches a hand to her belly. Her eyes are glazed, and I have never seen her like this. "Is there anything they didn't do to us?" she whispers. She suddenly seems older. Infinitely older, as if there is no touching her and all the wrinkles in the world are not enough to catch up. It is dangerous to be so sad, to be so angry. And it is easy to jump from a small thing like clenched fists to questioning our cause. She continues. "Do you remember Madame said to each of us, 'Do you want to get better?' Every single one of us. And we had to say yes or she wouldn't do it? As if yes means anything to a kid. As if yes counts when you don't know what you're saying yes to."

"Stop it," Gray says quietly. I've almost forgotten he is here, but then he takes Edith's marshmallow stick from her and puts the flame out. "Let's talk about something else."

No one says anything for a while. We can't think of anything to say.

In the end Edith attempts to make a joke of it. "It's just as well, I suppose," she says. "With how much fooling around went on at the cottages, the world would be overpopulated by now."

She forces herself to laugh harder. She acts drunk, but I know for a fact that she hasn't had anything to drink. Gray keeps frowning at her, and eventually she stands. They walk toward the farmhouse together. Davis tries to follow them, but I stick my foot out as he passes, and he falls. "What did you do that for?"

"It's none of our business," Roberta says, though she has

her head cocked to the side, trying to listen.

Davis sits up and rubs his elbows. "You're such a bloody spoilsport sometimes, Harrison."

I smile. "Thanks."

We cannot hear their exact words, but they are arguing. They glare at each other when they return and sit on opposite sides of me. I hold my hands out in front of the fire. I am not cold, but it is something to do while the silence festers.

Nobody, not even Davis, knows what to say to fix the mood.

I nudge Edith with my leg. "What's the silliest thing you've had to do since you became a sleeper?"

My question works. She sits up straighter. "Oh, God," she says. "That would have to be the time I had to let some idiot mug me. I was fifteen, we were at the farmers' market, and I couldn't exactly break his nose. So I had to stand there screaming like I was the weak pathetic human she used to be."

We laugh. Davis gives his own exaggerated version of something that happened when he first left the cottages. An incident with a tractor that was harder to drive on their farm than it had been to simulate at the cottages, and all the crops he destroyed in one afternoon.

Eventually Edith is smiling, really smiling again.

Still.

One day we will look back and hate this night.

More and more I get the sense that we think our lives will be short. Shorter at least than they're meant to be. That whole children thing. There isn't going to be anybody in the world like me or Edith or any of us ever again. Right now we are a necessity, but one day they won't need us anymore. I think about the words Edith did not say. I think about all the Madames in all the cottages.

I don't think they expect us to live long at all. I don't think they want us to.

But how long past the war do we have?

CHAPTER 26

When I step out of Miss Odette's office a few days later, he is waiting for me. The rude guy from before. I almost do not see him in the dark and curse the fact that I never remember to bring a light despite the fact that the hallway has been dark for months. "What cardboard face?" he asks, and I jump.

When his flashlight comes on, I hold up my hand to shield my eyes. "What cardboard face?" he asks again, in that same barking voice.

This time I do not hesitate. "Well, I'd imagine that it's cardboard since it only has the one angry look. I figured it was either that or plastic surgery." He splutters. I take the opportunity to add: "If you were a person on the street I was walking past, I would still greet you. I don't know why you had to be such an asshole."

I leave him standing there, gaping at me, and think that I will never see him again. But a few weeks later we're in front of the shop at the same time again. This time he pulls an apple out of his bag. "Here," he says without meeting my eyes. "I've got this if you're hungry."

I feel the confusion flood my face. "You're trying to feed me?" I ask after a moment, holding the apple as if it were poisoned.

The guy shrugs. He looks embarrassed all of a sudden. "You look like you need it."

I recognize an insult when I hear it. I throw his apple onto the road. I pull my patched-up coat tighter around my body, and I walk away without looking back.

The next time, a box of biscuits. Which I actually don't mind, but they meet the same fate as the apple. Though this time he walks with me. He is still holding the skateboard in his hand, and I shake my head. "You're a very confusing person, you know."

"I know," he says, staring at me, and then he sighs

dramatically. "This is me trying to apologize here. I realize I was rude when we first met."

"Okay," I say, taken aback. When there doesn't seem to be a catch, I add, "Apology accepted."

He holds out his hand, and when I shake it, he smiles. "Great. See? And now we'll get along."

"Oh, I doubt it," I say, pulling my hand back. "Anyway, why do you have that?"

He follows my eyes to his skateboard. "This? I'd never had one before. You ever wake up and have one of those days when you think, *Oh, crap, I'm twenty-three, and I've never even been on a skateboard.* Or a bike. Or a horse. And you're shocked because you always *thought* you were more interesting?"

I give him a blank look. He shrugs and runs his hand down the skateboard. "It seemed like something I should have, so I just walked into a store and bought the first one I saw. You see, I've decided to renovate my life. I quit my job, got a haircut, bought a skateboard, started writing a play."

We walk until the flower shop is out of view. I glance skeptically at the skateboard again and then at his shiny leather shoes. "So, how good are you?"

"Good?" he asks, and then he understands that I am still talking about the skateboard. He makes a face. "Oh, I'm not actually going to get on it. God. I would never do that."

A smile escapes my lips, unbidden. Who buys a skateboard just so he can carry it around while wearing a suit and expensive shoes? "I can't decide whether you're fifty or ten," I say.

He laughs. "That's good," he says. "It means you're wondering about me. Which means that I'm already more interesting than I used to be." Before I can say anything to contradict him, he turns off onto a different street. "See you later." When he walks away, he limps a little and grimaces, as if he's in pain. He might be wearing an expensive suit and holding a skateboard, but he's toothpick thin underneath. I suddenly understand that this might be more than friendliness. He might be a sick sleeper looking for someone to care for him, one of the jobs Miss Odette told me would be a possibility. And I've probably failed his test.

Good.

I stare until he rounds a corner and then decide to forget about him.

I ride my bicycle toward the orchards and pick Cecily up from school. "I'm in the mood for some crazy," she says gravely the moment she sees me. I have no idea where she comes up with these things. We spend half the ride home trying to come up with her *crazy*, with me fending off everything that crosses over from crazy to suicidal. Finally Cecily is sitting on my shoulders while I ride my bicycle, and she tells me it makes her feel like a flying bird. "Faster, faster," she shrieks. "Lira, why are you going so *slow*? This is basically nothing."

"Oh, well, I'm sorry that you're *basically* about to break my neck," I say. Her schoolbag swings into my cheek. "What's your problem anyway?"

"I live for the thrills, Lira," she says slowly, superiorly. "You wouldn't understand. Mathieu says his brother is going to jump from a plane tomorrow afternoon and land on his feet. Because that's what people do in the city. They live for the thrills."

I squint at her. "Yeah, you know, most people who say that never get the chance to say that they shouldn't have."

She is quiet for a while, and I make the mistake of thinking that it's because we're almost home. But just as we reach the orchards, she begs me to put her down. Suddenly I'm chasing her past the trees. I know where she is going even before we reach it. The river breaks off into a stream that has formed a small lake behind our house, that we sometimes sit by in the summer. "Just one quick swim," Cecily pleads, even as I argue with her. "Just one. Philip, tell her."

I turn around and find Philip standing there, frowning at the water. He has a bucket of soil in his hands, which means he has been helping Da all day. Then he looks at me. Cecily has him wrapped around her little finger like thread, so I know even before he does that he will grab my little sister and jump into the water with her. I resign myself to it and sit by the lake, watching Cecily wade in. But Philip doesn't join her; he joins me. Sits beside me and yells to Cecily, "We'll watch you from here." She waves, and he waves back, laughs when she does a somersault. He grimaces when the water splashes him, but then he jumps up and applauds Cecily wildly, and she laughs. But he doesn't go anywhere near her. Or the lake.

I try not to let my hands shake. I force a smile and look away, pull a fresh blade of grass from its sheath.

Because I know the boy *she* loved is dead.

What would you do if Da died today?

How would you feel if Gigi was killed?

What about Cecily?

That time is coming. Are you still ready to do what you must, soldier?

Yes.

At any moment?

I have not changed, miss.

Today I am wearing a dress that Julia brought from her house. A simple blue cotton dress that she saw, that made her think of me. I am offended as I strip out of my clothes, but she laughs. "I just mean," she says, "that you *like* simple things. And the color makes your eyes stand out. There's no boy in his right mind who won't go mad, and yet there is nothing to it. It's just a plain blue dress. The next time we go to the movies you *have* to wear this."

I stare at myself in the mirror after I am dressed. I have no idea what she is talking about. My eyes are exactly the same. But I humor her. She is trying to have something in common with me, and it is not her fault that I am as boring as I look. "Thank you," I say, running my hands over the dress. It is open and low at the back, with a large bow that cinches it to my waist. The front might be plain, but the back is the opposite. Aunt Imogen would approve.

"I've got some earrings and makeup here, too," Julia says, clapping her hands. But she must see the way my shoulders droop because she hesitates. The others—Davis and the two Robbies—leave me alone for the most part, but it is different with Julia. She plays the part of a typical teenager too well, and it is hard for me to keep up. Tomorrow she might bring a board game she wants to play with me or ask me to braid her hair like we did in the cottages.

I am trying, but being her friend is exhausting.

Edith walks into the bedroom with a fresh pot of tea to refill the mugs the three of us have been drinking from. She takes one look at me, eyeing Julia's makeup bag with horror, and laughs because somehow she understands the things I cannot say. She sets the teapot on the dresser. "Poor Lira. I don't think there's anything she hates more than getting dressed up."

"Oh," Julia says sadly, and puts her bag away. Tomorrow

she might try again but today gives up on me. "Well, I should go home, I guess. My parents are probably expecting me."

"Maybe we can go see a movie . . . soon." I croak the words out. "So I'll wear this dress."

Julia smiles at me. "Okay," she says, and I feel bad. I don't know what she wants from me.

"I invited her into the group because of you," Edith says when she's gone.

"Me?"

She smiles at my surprise. "You were so good at protecting her at the cottages. I'm sure you were hoping no one would notice, but I did."

"I don't know what you mean," I say.

"No? My mistake, I guess." But she doesn't sound as if she believes her own words. I don't want to disappoint this flawed memory of me she has, so I say nothing else. I listen instead to her talking about how she and Julia live in the city near each other and how they accidentally run into each other sometimes. At the same supermarket or on a walk. It has become a game for them. They have special signals— secret winks and hand gestures and coughs. "There was a time," Edith says, her eyes glowing, "months ago when we were standing on opposite ends of an aisle making plans for a movie with our special gestures. Some little boy walked by, saw us, and ran off screaming to fetch his mother. I guess he thought we were crazy or something. Julia was so shocked she knocked a stack of cans over and landed on top of them."

"And you?" I ask.

She waves me off nonchalantly. "I left her there, of course. I heard the boy's mother yelling at her for making obscene gestures at her son while I was hightailing it out. Julia pretended she was deaf and couldn't understand a thing."

We both laugh.

It has been six weeks since my first time at the farmhouse and only two weeks since our night of dares. I have been back every chance I could get. Most days there is no Robbie (girl or boy), there is no Gray or even Davis. They are usually out completing their missions, especially Robbie and Gray, who always seem to have the most work.

Edith and I are now lying on the bed with our feet hanging over. We're staring up at the cracks in the roof, lazy and wordless. We do this sometimes. Julia cannot understand it when we do this. I get the sense that she does not appreciate her friend being stolen away, and I wonder what Edith is like without me. But each time I try to find out, she'll pull up a chair or ask my opinion on a book or song.

When Gray walks into the room, we are playing a game like one we played when we were at the cottages. Madame would divide us into groups and then write a list of things on a piece of paper. On bad days the list consisted of horrible things like punches, no dinners, sleeping outside, no shoes for a week, washing duties for a month. And then Madame would pass the list around and make us assign each thing to someone in our group, right to her face. And the people with the most votes had to do whatever they'd been assigned. I was no longer friends with Alex, Gray, and Edith at this point, but Madame felt there were other friendships that needed to end. To break. Most of us had caught on to this by then. We would see that Jenna and Annie still talked to each other, so we would give Jenna the punches (from Annie), and Annie would sleep outside.

It was a horrible game, but over time it became one we liked. A way to settle any differences, especially among the boys. We would play it even when Madame was not around. The skeleton game, we called it. The boys would have physical fights with one another, but with us girls it was all about how cruel we could be: Martha was not allowed to brush her hair for a week, no matter what, and for ten days I could not bathe with soap. I looked homeless, smelled worse. But one of the meanest things we ever did was to a girl named Naomi. A group of us held her down while each one of her former friends wrote down what they really thought of her on her skin with black markers. She tried to wash it off afterward—the word U*gly*—but it was there for days, and it is entirely possible that it is still there now, hidden underneath her skin.

But Madame was pleased with us. Her game worked well, and we were no longer friends. For us, though, we liked the game because being hurt by the other cottage girls and not letting it break us was our way of showing strength.

In our modified version of the game, Edith and I trade in pinches. It is not horrible, but it hurts. She tells me a single thing about what she's done in her life that I do not know about, and I decide whether it is worth a pinch or not. A pinch means I don't find it interesting. Then I tell her something about mine. The longer the game progresses, the harder the pinches, until either one of us manages to draw blood or begs to stop.

"My alternate has been taking riding classes since she was eleven," she says. "I have a horse named Barnacle, but we've never won any races together. I love him anyway."

I consider this for a moment. The cracks in the ceiling seem to grow bigger. I turn and pinch her hard and for as long as possible, until she howls and shoves me away. We've both got red welts along our arms, but when Gray comes in, we stop. The room is dark, and we pretend to be part of the lumpy bed. He shrugs out of his jacket, shirt, tosses them on the floor, and finds another clean shirt in the cupboard. His arms are covered in bruises. Then, without even looking at us, he says, "I can see you, you know."

Edith and I giggle. The sound is so strange it makes me giggle even harder. We're like little girls. The kind of little girls we never got to be. "Is that the shirt you're planning on wearing?" I ask Gray. "Wait, I've got something better." I stand and twirl in my dress. "It'll bring out your eyes, and you won't understand why because it's so simple. All the boys will come running. Or is it girls? I think Julia said it only works on the boys, so if you're looking for a girl . . ." I shrug.

He doesn't seem all that interested in any of it. I tell myself that that's Gray being Gray, but it suddenly seems a lot harder to reach the bed in the dark. I don't realize just how hard it is until he is catching me just before I hit the floor.

"Don't," he says softly, eyes on mine in the dark, as though I might have any control over gravity. His fingers are wrapped tightly around my waist, but he lets me go almost as quickly. As if the skin underneath my dress were made of fire. Edith is watching us with interest. My cheeks heat up, and I look away. I must be full of imagination today. Gray squints at us both, and then he sniffs the air, walking right over to the mugs sitting on the dresser. "Have you been drinking?"

"No," I say, straightening. "We've only had tea."

But he's frowning at his sister. "Did you get her drunk, Edith?"

Edith doesn't meet either of our eyes. "Don't look at me like that. She's less wound up."

Gray shakes his head. "Did you ever think that she might be wound up for a reason? She's got a family, a kid at home, for crying out loud. What's she supposed to tell them?"

"Sister, not kid." I correct him, but I am suddenly distrustful of everything I am saying, everything I have said in the past hour. Gray is right: I do not get drunk. The whole staying-on-guard thing does not work otherwise. I sit back down on the bed, saying nothing to Edith, hands clenched at my sides. I listen to Gray and Edith argue for a few moments before I stumble into the kitchen and put a pot on the stove for coffee. Even from here I can hear them.

"You can't do things like that to her," Gray is saying. "You're supposed to be getting her to trust you."

"It's not that easy," Edith replies, and her voice fades out.

I clench my fists at my sides again. They are talking about

me like I am a game. Like I am something they have to accomplish. I'm going to leave the moment the alcohol wears off.

I am standing at the stove when I hear muffled laughter coming through the wall on the other side of the kitchen. Which is strange because Edith, Gray, and I are the only ones here. Julia left, and the two Robbies and Davis don't come until evening. I follow the sound and wind up at the bathroom, but it's empty.

I return to the kitchen, vowing never to drink again.

By the time my coffee is ready the fight is over. Edith convinces Gray to play the skeleton game with us.

He is sitting on the bed, waiting, when I enter the room. "But I can't stay long," he says, watching me.

I sit on the dresser. My hands are still in fists, but I say, "I never throw out my old paintbrushes. I initial them with the last date I ever used them, and then I save them in a box without washing the color off the brush so I remember the last thing I painted with them. My grandfather says they are like commas instead of full stops." I take a huge gulp of my coffee, even though it's too hot.

Edith still isn't meeting my eyes. "My father wants me to apply to medical school next year."

"That's not a thing," I say automatically. What her father

wants tells me nothing about what she wants.

She scowls. "Yes, it is. Gray, what's yours?"

Her brother pretends not to notice the tension between us. "I really like my truck," he says. "It's not new, but it has yet to disappoint me."

I put my coffee mug down. I climb off the dresser and walk over. We both pinch Gray. For every single one of his responses, which are small, superficial things about his truck, his boots. He gives nothing about himself away. The less he says, the more intrigued I am. Who is this boy? "This was never going to be a fair game, was it?" he says afterward, clutching his side and pretending we ripped his skin right off. "Come on, I'll give you and your bike a ride back into the city."

I stand, scan the room for my boots and other things. I climb back into my normal clothes once Gray is gone. Edith and I do not say a single word to each other. It is my own fault for not paying attention to what I was drinking. But I hate the fact that I trusted her. I hate the fact that it's what you're supposed to be able to do—trust your friend—because of how quickly I've done it. I should have known better.

"Bye," I say quietly when I'm done.

Edith is standing by the door, looking miserable. "Don't be mad, okay?" she says, and hugs me.

"Okay," I lie.

I walk down the hallway toward the door. Someone laughs again, the sound reverberating in the walls, and this time I stop. Either I am going mad or there are ghosts here. "I thought we were alone," I say, and wait for Edith to tell me the truth.

She nods. "The house is old. Sometimes it creaks."

But she doesn't meet my eyes. She is lying to me again.

There is someone else in the farmhouse with us.

I think this as I enter Gray's truck. I don't know what it means, and I should probably leave it alone. Trust them. But the moment I shut the door I know I can't. Gray is already turning the truck around, headed for the road. I say, "Can we go back? I forgot something. The dress Julia gave me."

He says okay at first. He stops the truck, and I climb out. Walk back toward the farmhouse.

Then he must grasp what I am banking on. That Edith has gone off in search of company. "Hey, Lira, wait," he calls, climbing out of the truck and coming after me. But I am already running.

When I enter the house, there is a gap in the wall of the living room that was not there before. A door. It is open, and I run down the stairs, hearing Gray call my name and ignoring him. When I reach the bottom, the two Robbies are cuddled up together on a couch, but they pull apart guiltily. Edith is sitting across from them. Her head snaps toward mine in shock.

For a long moment there is silence. Gray reaches the bottom of the stairs and says nothing, just watches me walk around the room.

The television screens are like the ones at the cottages, the ones we used to learn about our alternates. On them now, there are different people, different faces. I do not recognize any of them. And then I see Miss Odette, but she is not sitting in her office. She is in an apartment, and she's sitting with a little girl no older than two or three, and she's singing to her and laughing. I know adult sleepers did not have the procedure, but I am surprised that Miss Odette has a daughter. I don't think she knows she is being watched. I don't think any of these people do.

My heart stops when I see the mess Cecily left on our kitchen table this morning.

My hands grip my coat. "I don't understand," I say. My voice is empty. "What is this place? What are you doing?"

The two Robbies look at each other and then at Gray. Edith looks down at the ground.

CHAPTER 29

I step toward the screens and then step back again. The room is filled with them. All these faces. But only one house, one image, matters to me. I scrutinize it until I am certain that it is mine and that it is not in my imagination. When I speak, I am surprised that my voice does not waver, that it is firmer than I feel.

"Take my house off the screen," I say.

Robbie holds his hands up in protest. "This isn't about us," he says. "This is about them. We've only hacked into their system, to see the things that they're seeing. To know the things they know and, if we need to, manipulate their systems. We can remove your image from a place it's not supposed to be. It's keeping you safe. How are we supposed to know when you're in trouble if—"

"Take my house off the screen," I say again, except this time I have turned to look at Gray. He understands that I mean it. He ignores Robbie's words and walks slowly over. He turns a small knob and the screen goes black, and once it is, I push past him. I start back up the stairs. *This was a mistake. Everything was a mistake.* Those words are clear even without my saying them. Suddenly every single moment since I met Edith is playing in my mind. From the moment I ran into her with Cecily up until now. The fact that we happened to meet in town. The fact that she put a piece of paper in my pocket with a note and an address I didn't watch her write. Which means she had written it beforehand and knew she would run into me.

They've been watching me.

They all follow me up. And when I turn around, Roberta is holding a gun pointed right at my chest. I'm not surprised. "You have to understand, Lira," she says, "that we have to sort this out."

I shake my head. I am dangerously close to crying; that

makes me even angrier. "I have no idea what you people are doing, and I don't care. I won't tell anyone."

Roberta steps closer. There is apology in her tone. "Look, once you're a part of the group, you're a part of the group. It isn't safe for us any other way. We know that Cecily and your grandparents matter to you in some capacity. We have seen that, and I'm sure you understand what I am going to say now."

Menace flickers in her eyes. I think I have the same look in mine. I cross my arms and stand there, waiting. There are four of them against me, and I cannot win. Roberta knows it, too, because she puts the gun down as a show of good faith. "We just want to talk to you," she says. "We were waiting until we knew one another better, and now we do. We trust you. And we want to share our ideas with you, that's all."

She pauses. If she is waiting for me to reciprocate with my own declarations of trust, she will wait forever.

"But before we talk," she continues, "let's get one thing clear: If you ever tell anyone about us and this place or what you have seen here, I will kill you myself. Right after I kill your sister."

I'm not really sure how I manage to reach her, how my hand wraps around her neck. Suddenly my arms are bruised, and my lips taste like blood, but I do not remember fighting her, do not remember winning. Don't know how my hands got to her neck. Gray and Robbie pry us apart, but Edith wraps her arms around herself, stays where she is. I shout, "Why did you bring me here?"

And Edith says, sobbing, "I don't remember anymore. I'm sorry, Lira."

"You told me I was here to be your friend," I remind her.

"You are my friend," she insists.

Robbie holds me back. He is twice my size.

"You're right," Roberta says to Edith, rubbing her throat. "She's good."

My head snaps back up.

"I'm good at what?" I ask. "I'm good at what, Edith?"

Edith doesn't look at me. "Lira," she pleads, but she doesn't say anything else to me. To Robbie, she says, "Let her go. And give us a few minutes. I'll talk to her." When Robbie lets go of me, I think about running. But there is nowhere to run to. I'd be found in moments. Edith tells them we'll talk in Gray's truck. He keeps the keys.

I am cold now. As cold as I can possibly be.

I follow her into his truck. I do it with every intention of killing her if I get a chance.

"Don't tell me," I say once I'm inside, because I already

understand that this whole thing—the farmhouse, the friendship—was her doing. "Don't say it." I stare out the window and wonder how I can be so angry and yet sit so still. There's a knife in my boot. That's what I have to reach.

Edith takes a deep breath. "Have you thought," she says, "about what would happen if we could stop people coming through the portals?"

My head snaps in her direction. "What?" I whisper. I am afraid I didn't hear her correctly. At the same time I'm not sure I want to hear her again.

"The cottages would stop, Lira," she says. "We wouldn't have to do this anymore. We could be free. If people knew we were here . . ."

My voice croaks. "Knew *who* was here?" I ask.

"Sleepers," she says. "If people knew what we were doing, if we went public with everything—" Her lips move, but I am barely listening. Her plan is to find as many cottages as possible. To take pictures of the children. Of the Madames and Sirs. "They would have to believe us," she says, "because of the trackers in our wrists. Because of the pills we take that make us healthier than nonsleeper children. They would believe us because of what we know and how we've been trained. And when we show them the portals . . ."

I am staring at her with my mouth wide open. "You want to tell the world about us," I say, still hoping I am wrong.

Her voice is soft, almost nonexistent. "We would be careful, of course. We could start by leaking the story to a newspaper. We could start a rumor. Even if they don't believe us, at the very least, it would make someone think. Make someone wonder. Then the cottages will end. Even if they don't, telling the people of this Earth about us would give them a fighting chance against us."

I look away from her. I stare forward again.

Why? It is the question on the tip of my tongue, but it never leaves my lips. Edith must hear it anyway because she answers me in her still soft voice. "Look at what they have made us into, Lira. Look at what we have become for them. All the things we have had to do. All the guilt we must carry with us. And Gray."

"What about Gray?" I ask.

She drops her eyes. "You have no idea what they make him do. Every single day. He was different before, we all were, but I am afraid of what he will become at the end."

Her words make no sense to me. We are Safes. Whatever missions they send Gray on, they are for the good of our people. If Gray did not have the ability to kill, I would not be here today. I would have died in that orchard when I was fourteen years old.

I try to understand the emotions running through me. I am first shocked and confused. Then I am scared, because in the furthest corner of my mind there is a voice that is saying absolutely nothing. That does not agree or disagree. Finally there is only one right reaction, and it is the one that sticks. I can feel my face twist with it. Horror, revulsion. Who are these people? Who am I sitting with? "Traitor," I spit at her the way Madame would do. The way we've been trained to do, except we've been trained to do much worse. My voice shakes when I speak. "You're supposed to be loyal to *us*, to our cause, Edith, not this. I know Alex's death did something to you, scared you, but this . . . this is wrong."

"That's not—" she begins.

I cut her off. "I thought you'd grown up when I saw you. I thought we all had, but you're all exactly the same. All of you. You think being nice to people is going to get you somewhere? You think that you can be a murderer today but that it makes it better if you warn them? Do you think they will forgive us for the people we've already killed if we tell them we're sleepers? For the ones that we have already replaced?"

Edith flinches. "Lira . . ." I'm surprised to see that I have the power to hurt her this badly with my words. She sniffs and looks sadder than I've ever seen her. As though she already knows how this conversation is going to end. Julia, Roberta and Robbie, Gray . . . I cannot believe she has managed to convince all these people to agree with her, to turn on Madame and our whole lives and our whole cause. She wants to kill us all.

"What about these people?" she says finally. "The ones we are killing?"

"What about the ones we left at home?" I say. "What about us? What about everything and everyone that're going to disappear from our Earth in the next few years? I might not agree with you, but that doesn't mean I don't care. I care about different people than you do." I shake my head. "You're not asking to be my friend. You're asking me to be a part of this. Why should I die for you? Why should I die for them?"

"Why should they die for us?"

I stare at her, waiting for her to laugh. Waiting to hear her say this is a joke. But I can see it in her eyes. She wants to tell the truth. She's hoping it will absolve us of what we have done.

But it is a suicide mission. It will cost our lives.

"Lira . . ."

"I'm done here," I hear myself say. I do not recognize my voice. "Either kill me or let me go, but I won't come back."

Edith sniffs. "We can live with you not being a part of things. That doesn't mean you have to go. I'll talk to them. It's all my fault, and I'll fix this."

I say nothing. We both know she is lying. It is impossible for me to remain here with them as nothing but their friend. We sit in silence for a long time. I stare out the window and watch it grow darker. How swiftly is this world being taken over? How many of our people are here, and how much longer before the war starts? There are too many questions with few answers. It's this part that is killing us. This waiting. Turning our own minds against us.

"I could never survive like that," I tell Edith finally, my voice so small it is almost a whisper. "Being your friend and still being a sleeper at the same time. I'll fall apart. I'm weak, not like the rest of you."

Edith reaches for my hand. I bunch it in a fist, but she holds it anyway. "So stay here, and if you do fall apart, we'll be the only ones who know. Go back out there and you're lost, and there'll be no one to mind your back. You think you're the only one falling apart? We all have our doubts. It's how we let it define us that matters."

"I can take care of myself."

Edith lets go of my hand. She shakes her head at me.

"We're all mad, Lirael. All of us. And the maddest ones of all are the ones who think they are sane."

I don't look at her, but I say, "You're making a mistake. You're all going to die for this." It matters that she know this, that I tell her this. And if I thought begging on my knees would change her mind, I would do it, too. How did we become so different so quickly? How did our paths diverge? All the Madames in all the cottages failed six people. And if there are these six, how many more? How many people on our Earth are counting on us to pull through for them only to have this happen?

"My brother did you a favor once," Edith says, "or have you forgotten already?"

I swallow, shake my head. We've never talked about it, but I know what she means. "I'll find a way to pay him back. But not like this."

"I guess he knew you would say that." She removes a set of keys from her pocket and tells me where to leave the truck. Then she climbs out. She does not look back at me, but I will have an impression of her eyes forever. They will haunt me. I start the truck before she can change her mind. In the rearview mirror all the others except Gray are running, trying to catch up to me. They look mad. I don't care.

Just because it is difficult being a sleeper does not mean I have lost faith in our cause. In our Earth. I have not. I never will.

I should go to Miss Odette now, tonight. I should tell her what they are planning.

But I tell myself that it is enough if I don't see them again, if I do every single thing in my power not to think about them, not ever.

CHAPTER 30

He doesn't have the skateboard the next time I see him. I leave the flower shop, and he walks up to me, introduces himself, saying, "I'm Jack." And when I say, "Good for you," he walks alongside me. I am on my way back to the bakery. I walk faster. Jack falls behind. I am about to breathe a sigh of relief when I hear a thump.

I turn around. Jack is lying on the ground, in the middle of the street. He has tripped over a small rock. "For goodness' sake," I say. "Did you fake that?"

"Sure," he says, sitting up. He is a bad liar. When he tries

262 .

to stand, he is in pain. He looks even weaker today than the last time I saw him.

"I've got it," he says when he sees my outstretched hand. But he lets me hold his arm.

I see this moment when I help him up and hate it because it is the moment when I start to feel sorry for him. You cannot truly hate a person you feel sorry for; it's one or the other. I don't want to be friends with this sickly man. But then I let him walk beside me as I head to the bus stop. I even go the long way for his benefit, through the park where children play and their mothers chase after them. I do not introduce myself. I do not answer any questions. I just walk.

Finally Jack hobbles over to a park bench.

He sits and rubs his knees while trying to pretend he is doing something else. "That stupid rock," he mutters.

I want to tell him that it's too late for me not to know that he is sick, that I know what sickness looks like, smells like. I breathe it in every day. Instead I stand next to him, shifting my weight from the one foot to the other.

"I'm just going to sit right here for a second, okay," he grits out. When I don't join him, he squints up at me. "How old are you?"

"What if something happens to us?" I ask, instead of

answering him. "What if we're breaking some mortal rule? What if talking to each other is so far out of character for our alternates that we're marked because of this?"

"Then we're about to find out," he says. "Because they'll kill us."

I scuff my boot against the ground. "Are you nervous?" he asks.

I look up and say, "If your question is whether or not I want to die here in a dirty park with some stranger, then you know the answer."

He ignores my jab, looks me over again. "How do you feel about tuna sandwiches?"

"I don't need taking care of."

He's not done talking. "I tried to kill myself two summers ago," he blurts out. "I figured there was something wrong with me. I wasn't a very good sleeper. I was always asking too many questions. Handlers don't like us asking questions, and I had all these doubts. They don't tell you about that part. The part where it gets too hard." He laughs. "I guess it doesn't happen often. Their training is pretty effective, isn't it?"

"I don't have any doubts, Jack."

"Yes, you do. And they're only going to get worse."

"Okay," I say. I want to leave. This is not what I need. Not after leaving Edith and Gray and the farmhouse behind.

"Have you ever been back?"

I'm not really sure what I am asking. W*here?* I am asking, but he shakes his head.

"After a while," he says, "the two sides of a coin start to look exactly the same. You can't tell whether you're looking at two heads or two tails. You accept whichever side you're standing on."

I sit on the bench and pull my legs up against my chest, stare off into the distance, watching the children play. I am convinced now that it's not a good idea to have this much time to think during a war, to ask questions, to witness the world. Look at what happened with Edith. The best kind of war is one fought with one's eyes closed. A war where you hold a gun and you don't know where you are shooting.

But no. That's not right either. There is nothing brave about that kind of war. Only cowards fight it.

"You should try to eat more," he says quietly. "You should try to . . . hide the way you feel. Do everything you can to keep it from them. If you seem weak in any way, it's only a matter of time before they kill you, no matter what your handler says."

I *know*, I think, which surprises me. Even still, I hear Madame's whispered threat every night before I fall asleep.

"Weak, weak little girl." Maybe I have never stood a chance. I picture Miss Odette behind her desk. What do her smiles really mean?

Nobody lies better than a handler, not even a sleeper.

"I don't even know the way I feel," I confess.

"Tell me," Jack says. "Did you stop eating after you killed her?"

I don't meet his eyes. "I'm just thin, is all, Jack. There's no crime against that. Leave me alone."

"It's strange," he says, "who we become when we're not being who we're supposed to be. Sometimes you're walking along on your merry way, and you think you're happy until you meet someone. And suddenly it occurs to you, for the first time, how lonely you are. How you don't want to die alone after all. Suddenly all your plans are shot to hell."

I shake my head. "I don't know what you're talking about. Please don't go getting any ideas."

I hate how carefully he watches me. I hate how transparent I apparently am. I feel like I am standing outside my skin. "I'll bet you weren't always this sad," he says to the ground after a while. "You were probably very different before they brought us here."

"You don't know anything about me."

"Maybe not. But I'd like a friend at the end, and I haven't got much time left. Just a friend, nothing more. So, if I can get clearance from both our handlers, will I see you again?"

"No," I say, and stand abruptly. The last thing I need is another friend problem, and a dying one at that.

"Thank you," he says.

"I said no."

He rubs his knees again. "Meet me at the café down the street this time next week. There's more hope than you think. I'll tell you all about it."

I walk away, but then I come back because I have left my scarf behind. I snatch it out of his hand, but I suspect my fury doesn't even reach my eyes, that my eyes are as blank as they ever are.

"I have a feeling that we are meant to save each other," he says softly, letting the scarf go. "That's all."

"From what?" I say.

I don't look at him as I walk away. I don't wait for his answer.

Nothing is ever that simple.

CHAPTER 31

At my next meeting with Miss Odette she beams at me. "Good news," she says. "I have an assignment for you."

I flinch even before she elaborates. When I first became a Safe and she explained assignments to me, I secretly hoped that I would never have one. I prefer my life the way it is, but I cannot tell her that. Instead I force myself to return her smile. I sit in my chair stiffly while she explains that whenever sleepers are sick or need assistance in some way, another sleeper is assigned to them. "For however long you are needed, of course," she says, and an invisible noose tightens around my neck.

It's like I've switched one terrible friendship for an even worse, mandatory one.

I arrive at the café early the following day. I sit by a window so I'll see when he's coming and I can show him: *You cannot force someone to be your friend.* I have it all planned out. I won't smile; he'll say things I will not respond to. I cannot imagine what he might have said to Miss Odette to convince her that someone like me should be assigned to him.

When he finally hobbles inside the café, I have ordered my second cup of coffee and a brioche. The brioche is only half eaten, and he notices that. I imagine he thinks he knows me from that half-eaten brioche, can feel his judgment leaving marks on my skin.

He offers me a smile as he sits. "Thank you for coming," he says. As if I had any choice in the matter. When he takes off his hat, his hair sticks up at odd angles. He orders a bowl of soup from the waitress and stares out the window. "Where did you just come from?"

I cross my arms and lean back. My voice is monotonic. "I delivered a bottle of poison to a man who lives with his wife and his three children in an apartment a few blocks from here. Last week I delivered a gun to the same guy. I assume he is not using the poison on the same people."

"You don't like me, do you?" he asks.

I shrug.

He leans forward, fascinated. "Why don't you like me?"

I sigh and make a show of looking at the time. "I can tell you'll get me in some kind of trouble."

"So you think if you're mean, I'll leave you alone? Is that your tactic?"

I tap my fingers on the table without answering.

He stares at my face for a moment, as if I were an open book that he was reading. Then he leans forward, his tone conspiratorial. "Do you want to know who we're killing when we deliver whatever they send us?"

I meet him halfway. My eyes bore into his, and I will myself not to blink, not to seem as insignificant as I feel. "What I want to know, Jack," I say with venom in my voice, "is why they allow people like you to exist when a war is coming. Weakness is such a nonsleeper quality. Honestly I'm surprised you've managed to skate by this long."

After I've said this, I wait. But he doesn't leave like he's supposed to. He looks at me steadily.

My shoulders deflate. Now what am I supposed to do?

"Let me tell you a secret, Lirael," he whispers, leaning in even closer. " I don't care about the war or the world."

"That's treason," I warn him.

"Of course it is. That's why I'm saying it. Because no one can stop me now."

"Of course they can stop you," I say, frowning. "You're still alive." I hate that word, *they*. It implies somehow that we are apart from them. The truth is that if I were ordered to kill Jack at this moment, I would not hesitate, nor he for me. *They* is really only *we*.

We sit in silence for a while longer, and then Jack says, "I was trying to think of something we could do together, and I decided to write that play. Or maybe a short story. Something interesting anyway. That's better than learning to skateboard, right? I figure we could meet here once a week. I'll write; you'll edit. Does that sound good?"

A man strums a guitar in a corner of the room and sings a wistful song about birds and the color of the sky. "What sounds good," I mutter, "is you finding another sleeper for this."

He ignores my lack of enthusiasm. And when we both leave the café, he still hasn't changed his mind. The next time I see him, he's carrying a typewriter that he says he's owned forever and some notebooks. Inside the books are stories he started a few years ago but never finished. Now that he's had time to think about it, he tells me, he is enamored with the idea of writing something down.

"You can never print it," I say.

"I don't need to print it. But it would be mine, you know? Not something they made me do."

I watch him speak, hands waving about animatedly. I have never heard of anyone having a midlife crisis so young. But even as I think that, I remember the farmhouse and realize that I know the feeling. Of wanting to be someone else, somewhere else, for a little while.

I begin to feel sorry for Jack again. But feeling sorry for him and enjoying sitting here with him are two different things. He hands me the notebooks. Tells me to flick through them. "Which idea do you think I should work on?"

I flick to a random page with as little interest as I can muster, and eventually he has to select a story without me. He chooses one about a man who transforms into a dog. He turns to his typewriter, eyes narrowed with concentration, and I look away. I don't have the strength to tell him that it's the trying—trying to be different, trying to change what we are—that eventually hurts us.

Somehow time passes like this. One week becomes two, becomes a month, without my being aware of it. One month of listening, of pretending not to care.

***

"So. The next time you see me, I'll probably be in a chair," Jack says suddenly one day. I blink to find him sitting across from me, holding a walking cane this time because his legs hurt. He has told me things I have not heard, asked me questions I have not answered. I have to calculate in my head to realize that I have been assigned to him for three months now. Three months of insults, of eye rolls, of cafés. My coldness is nothing like how the real Lirael should be; we both know it. I am the crueler version of her, but Jack bears it. Smiles despite it.

His persistence makes me sad. And it makes me tired of ignoring him. "What do you say about me in your reports?" I ask, cutting him off in mid-sentence.

"That you're doing a spectacular job," he says.

I rest my chin on the cushion of my palm. "Why?"

He looks embarrassed for a moment before offering me a wry smile. It almost makes him handsome. "I'm a bit of a masochist, I suppose."

"I'll bring my sketchpad next time," I say. His eyes widen in surprise. He was in the middle of telling me something about the latest chapter of his great book. "I paint better, but I think I can draw a couple of dog pictures. To go with the finished product. Okay?"

This is as close to an apology as I can manage.

He nods.

I ride my bicycle home with a few pages from his story. Since the cottages I've hardly read any books. I hide his story inside the mattress of my bed where I keep my pills and pore over it by flashlight when everyone has gone to bed until my hands are stained with red ink.

"What did you think?" he asks the next time I see him.

I hand back the pages. "That you should never have quit your day job. And that maybe you'd be better at the skateboarding thing than this."

"I was thinking the same thing," he says, and then he laughs and continues typing.

Frost coats the leaves at night even though spring was supposed to have begun weeks ago. Gigi says this does not bode well for the trees, that it is a bad omen, the promise of a short summer, a long, cold winter. Da reasons that dooming things with words is the omen, and so they spend the morning arguing about who is right. This is nothing new. I eat as much toast as I can manage before I'm outside in the sun, apron drawn over my clothes. Since we cannot afford more, I use my paints sparingly. This is nothing like the cottages, when we were encouraged to engage in as many hobbies of alternates as we could. When some mornings my brushes would be dripping with paint long before anyone was awake.

I sit on the veranda. Cecily is at school, and it is just me, hours after I have finished my own schoolwork. When I dip my brushes in the paint, my fingers itch in a way they haven't in a long time, but today nothing comes out right. No proportions, no colors, no slant of light can explain whatever it is I am trying to say.

I do not know what I am trying to say.

In the afternoon Cecily sits next to me, her legs crossed. She is drawing her own things, too, although she keeps looking at mine for cues, frowning because a certain blob of red does not make sense where I put it. For a moment I watch her, and I am suddenly overcome with something. I don't know what. A feeling that should not be inside me. It is uncomfortable, and so I try to get it out. "Hey, Ceilie," I say softly, "I'm not dying, okay? You don't have to take over anything for me. You can just you can relax, okay?"

She nods, but I can tell she's not convinced. "Da says you got skinny because you wanted to die. I heard him telling Gigi. I heard him say that something made you sad. Was it us?"

"That's not . . ." I turn back to my drawing, suddenly

afraid. It's like I am waking up from the wrong dream. I did not realize they had noticed. The difference between me and my alternate. The fact that I arrived with no appetite.

"Why then?" my sister asks; her shoulders slump from carrying the weight I put there.

And I fail her without the answer, without the correct words. But the truth is written up there in the sky for everyone to see. *Our war.* And it is written in the ground, where no one can hear its screams. *Her sister.* The watery ghost girl who sits by me every single day, who follows me around, still fourteen. Still wearing that green dress, those black rain boots. There when I sleep, when I wake, when I am in the orchards pretending that I am all alone, when I sit at the table with my family. I think of her, and sometimes I cannot keep the food down, and it shows. For every moment she is here, I waste away just a little bit more.

But no one was supposed to carry the weight of that but me.

Sometimes I feel broken. I feel like *them.* Heavy, weighed down by the world. Jack tells me that the secret of living isn't feeling light but being able to carry that weight and to understand that it was worth it and why. *Every time you see her ghost, remember why you had to do what you did.* "But once you lose that," he tells me, "once you forget the meaning of who you are, then you are lost, and there is no hope."

When I give him a skeptical look, he adds, "I couldn't care less about the war. I just care about helping you survive it."

Sketching in the café is hard. Everything on the page plays out in black and white; there are no colors to hide behind. But I start to look forward to it every week.

This, I have decided, is my purpose after all. This, him—not Edith and her friends, not farmhouses and dare lists. I almost drive myself mad sometimes. Afraid that their screens are focused on me in the farmhouse. That they are watching me again, except this time like they would any other subject. In the end I have to let it go and hope that they are not. I have made my choice; I cannot change it. For all his complaining about the world, Jack would never ask me to risk my life the way they did.

I have reluctantly given up on the idea of being alone. It seems that every time I think, *Okay, I am going to try to be alone now*, it never works. I never had a father or a brother. I had no mother. No family but Madame. No life but the cottages. I always thought it was something I didn't care about. Sometimes I think that loneliness is just another word for fear.

At the café Jack sits at the back with an old chunky typewriter his father gave him, keys clacking away. He prefers this to a laptop. I sit across from him, my fingers bruised from holding my pencil for so long. The first dog I finish makes Jack laugh hard because it looks a little deformed. "If a horse and a bear had a baby," he begins, but changes his mind.

Once I get over the insults, I understand his point. I pick up my pencil and try again.

He sends me home with his pages, and each time I come back with more red marks. For weeks we sit at the café, and neither of us has finished anything.

"You have an imagination, Lira," Jack says one afternoon, laughing. "You imagine that I'm going to live forever. You think my hands are going to keep working, but in truth I'm losing feeling in them already."

I push his chair out of the café and into the world. I lean down and whisper in his ear, "Stop making excuses, Jack." We eventually agree that he is going to live for at least a century.

We have known each other for nearly four months when Jack tricks me into visiting a funeral parlor with him. Something about the idea of being handled by someone who does not even know his name, of being put in the ground by someone like that, frightens him. He would rather choose how he goes and when. He doesn't tell me this in advance, of course. He just asks me to meet him at a "new café" he has discovered on a different street. I am still standing outside the building that says EXQUISITE FUNERALS, in letters far too exquisite for such a gray affair, when he arrives in the taxi.

"I don't like this," I tell him, helping him out. He leans heavily on me for a moment before finding his balance.

He's frowning at the building, too. "I don't like it either. But we'll do it as quickly as possible, and then we'll never talk about it again."

He chooses a black coffin. He tells the salesman that he wants a simple box, the simplest they can find, and even that is surprisingly harder to find than we can imagine. It seems that people don't want simplicity when they die. They want something more, something extravagant, *exquisite*. I don't understand it. *Why?* I want to ask the salesman, a round man with long feet, who waddles about the room, waving his hands to the left and to the right. Why, *when it is already over, when after a little while only the ground will remember you and even that only for a short time?*

As we walk around the room, I cannot help the feeling

that crawls out of my throat and down my neck, down my spine. I shake my head, trying to clear it, but I cannot stop thinking about my life as a sleeper. Is this it? Is this all we get from them, after everything we will give to this war? We fight for them, and then they pay for our coffins?

It is not enough. To be a sleeper and then to die with nothing, no one. I want more than this.

And that frightens me.

The look on my face must linger long after we leave because Jack snaps his fingers in front of my eyes suddenly, and I realize that somehow we have caught the bus back to the café. I don't know how long we have been here. Jack is squinting at me with concern as we get off. "I asked whether you wanted to go with me to a party."

"Party?" I ask.

"Oh, I promise," he says. "This one is going to cheer you up. It'll be the most interesting thing about me you'll ever learn."

I call Gigi at a pay phone to tell her that an imaginary Julia and I are going to see a movie and that I'll be home a little later. Then Jack and I get on another bus. I do not want to go to a party, neither of us is really dressed for it, but curiosity gets the better of me. It's the twinkle in Jack's eyes. It's not often that he forgets his pain. During the ride I reach for his hand when his teeth grit together. He takes his pills, and then when the bus has stopped he says, "Are you ready?"

And before I can change my mind, I follow him down the street and into a tall office building. We ride the elevator to a floor where nearly every inch of the carpet is filled with cubicles, but in the center of it all, there is music playing and snacks being passed around. There are hundreds of computers, but people maneuver around them. Pale-skinned, pimply people who look like they never leave this room. We are at a technology company. "I used to work here," Jack says under his breath. "As one of them. I quit just before we met. I figured I couldn't die sitting behind a damn computer, not writing program codes at least. Where's the fun in that?"

A man walks past us with the strangest head of broccoli hair I have ever seen. Jack laughs. "I used to look exactly like that. Aren't you glad you know me now, not before?"

I shudder. "I can understand why you quit."

"Being an artist sounds so much better, doesn't it?"

He introduces me to his friends. "She's thinking about going into the tech business," he says. "I figured I'd bring her here and show her what she's missing out on."

They don't understand that he is kidding. Two of his

coworkers actually give me a tour of the place. "These are what our cubicles look like. And these are our telephones and computers." They are so enthusiastic that I wonder whether there's gold hidden underneath the shabby carpet.

I nod, pretending to be interested and trying not to laugh.

Jack must have been the life of the party when he worked here. Everyone likes him, fights to share all the latest gossip with him. He tells me that they have this party just once a year. It's supposed to happen at a bar, but very few are willing to leave their work behind, so they bring the party here. It's not much of a party at all, but this is as good as it gets for these people. I understand what he is telling me without the words: at the end it is not only sleepers who are dissatisfied with their lives, who feel as though nothing was ever enough. It is never enough.

"Shit, Jack." A woman walks over and hugs him. "I can't believe you quit. And who is this you've brought with you?"

I hold out my hand and smile. "Lirael," I say. Even though she is Jack's age, she is eyeing me as competition. I want to laugh because I cannot imagine Jack, the one I know, being competed over by a group of women in ill-fitted suits. As everyone chats, they treat me like one of them. They think I am older, eighteen or nineteen. I accept the bottle of beer offered to me, and when everyone starts dancing—some strange strangled sort of dance—I kick off my shoes and join them. And then, when Jack finds me, we form a circle with everyone in the office and do a strange dance that makes me giggle. This is what I have learned about myself: that I giggle when I am drunk. "Maybe this is who I'll be when I grow up, after the war," I tell Jack, standing on my tiptoes to reach his ear afterward. "It's nice. It's simple, to wake up every day and know what is expected of us, to be predictable."

"Some people in this world are too good for simple."

I sigh, knowing he's right. We cannot go back to being simple after the life we have led.

"What?" Jack says, seeing the way I am looking at him.

"It's just," I say, grinning, "absolutely nobody in this room knows how to dance."

Neither of us is surprised the next time we meet when Jack says, somberly, that he has been chastened by his handler for our appearance at the party. "We're probably going to have to tone it down," he says, eyes twinkling over his mug of coffee. "We're apparently giving people the wrong idea about us. They think I want to date you."

I laugh so hard that I choke on my coffee, and Jack has to

lean over and pat my back, but then he makes a show of taking his hand away. "No touching," he says in a high-pitched voice. "Absolutely no touching."

I wipe my eyes and lean back on my chair. My lips are still twitching. We did not wind up together because of the cottages; we chose each other, and if I had to, I might even admit that I am a little in love with the idea of that. Of someone who likes me for me, who knew me with my eyes black as night, with my shaky morals and questioning character and chose me anyway.

"What are you thinking about?" Jack asks.

"That you're too young to be my father. Too annoying to be my neighbor. Too tall to be my friend. I don't know how to classify you."

He pretends to consider this. "Brother," he says finally.

I nod. "We can come up with a story about our lives."

We decide that there was a secret affair somewhere along the line within our families, and he is an illegitimate child, cast out because he would have inherited the family fortune and Da would not have stood for it. He wanted those orchards all to himself.

"Your grandfather is a very scary man."

"Very," I agree. "You're lucky. He wanted to have you

killed, but my grandmother talked him out of it. Even when you took the DNA test, he had you tested three more times just to be sure. And your real name is Lucien, not Jack."

He wrinkles his nose. "I was thinking Christopher."

"Stanford," I say.

"Ernest?"

"Nathaniel."

"It's Augustus for sure," he tells me.

"Hmm." I cock my head to the side and study his face carefully, the shape of his eyes, the curve of his lips. "I suppose you could be my brother. Lucien Stanford Augustus the Third."

"Christ, and does it come with a crown, too?"

I start laughing again.

This was one week ago.

I did not know yet that it would be the last time I would be that way with Jack.

CHAPTER 32

Today, when I think of an omen, it might be the blackbird that flew by my window this morning. I have not seen a blackbird since the cottages. But I have not been this optimistic since the cottages, so I ignore it. Even when I wake Cecily and she grumbles, "Today's gonna be a bad day," which she always manages to say just before it starts to rain, as if she knew it was coming.

It doesn't rain.

I stuff myself full of zucchini bread until Gigi smiles and pinches my cheeks, as she used to when the real Lirael was younger.

If it did not visibly cost her so much, I would pretend to hate it. Instead I smile with pieces of food poking out of my teeth. Da comes home early from the orchards, irritated. He feels he is being followed, he says. "Those damn thieves, stealing the apples from my trees, laughing at me behind my back. I've had enough. I'm calling the police this afternoon."

He does, and they promise to come tomorrow. But in the evening, when darkness has fallen and we are getting ready for bed, Cecily spots an orange flame somewhere in the trees. Looters brazen enough to start a fire infuriate Da. He picks up his gun before any of us can stop him. "Stay inside," he growls, "and lock the doors. Enough is enough."

I do not know what he intends to do. But the moment he leaves, I find my coat and boots and follow him, leaving Cecily with the same warning: "Lock the doors and keep Gigi company. I'll be right back."

Cecily makes a face, but I stop her at the door. "This isn't one of the times when you get to be like me," I tell her, and kiss her forehead. "This is important, Ceilie."

"Okay," she says with a sigh.

I grab a flashlight before I leave, but I don't turn it on. I walk slowly through the trees, so Da won't know I am there. It makes no sense. We have so much space in our orchards, so many trees to hide behind. Why would looters start a fire this close to our house? Why not deep inside the orchards? Something about this doesn't feel right.

"Hey," Da yells somewhere ahead of me. I want to tell him that's a really bad idea, even with his gun, but he is too angry. "Come out of there, nice and slow," he says.

I pick up my pace. But before I reach them, the fire flickers out and everything is pitch black. I cannot see my hand in front of me.

"Da?" I whisper.

I hear him scrambling around. "Lirael? What are you doing here?"

He starts to say something else, probably ordering me to go home, but he lets out a yell instead. Too late, I remember my flashlight and turn it on. I bend for the blade in my boot and move toward the sound of fighting. Of grunts, and bones breaking. But they seem to be moving farther away from me. The looters that steal from us are usually pretty harmless. Da's shouting is usually enough to scare them away, at least for a few weeks. But not tonight.

"Da?" I call again, but this time there is no answer.

It is the single gunshot that finally snaps my thoughts into place. If I had been thinking like a sleeper, I would have figured this out much sooner. I would have walked much faster.

The fire was not an accident.

They *wanted* us to see. Whoever started it wanted to lure Da out here.

Because we are not dealing with a looter.

My heart stops. I run in the direction of noise, but as I get closer, I slow down. Even before I see, before I know, my body goes cold, as if a winter wind has blown in. It is too quiet. It's far, far too quiet, and I know exactly what I will find. When I finally reach the place, they both are there, exactly as I expected. My head begins to spin; my vision blurs.

I don't know how long I stand there or if I am even standing. Nothing feels real. There are two bodies on the ground, not just one. They both are lying there unmoving, eyes staring blankly up at the sky. Da and his alternate. I am still holding my blade in my hand, uselessly. A low, guttural moan pushes me toward my grandfather, and I shake him, start to beg him to wake up, to hurry, before I realize that the sound is coming from me. Me, not Da.

I cover my mouth with both hands, but it doesn't stop. Doesn't lessen. Continues like an animal dying inside me.

And then I find myself crawling over to the alternate's

side, trying to wake him instead. Because I do not know which one of them is which. I do not recognize Da, not the way that I am supposed to. Not the way that his true granddaughter would have.

Either of these men could have been Da, to me.

The gun lies on the ground between them. I sit there shaking for a long moment, my hands covered in their blood. Our cleaners, the ones who get rid of alternate bodies, will arrive here in just a few minutes to hide the mess. When I hear the rumble of tires, I force myself to stand on shaky feet. To step away from the bodies. I cannot be caught here, not with their blood all over me. Not with the way I cannot stop shaking.

Sleepers do not cry over people they don't love.

My body moves on automatic. The closer the noise gets, the farther back I step into the trees until I am a part of them. A black van stops in front of the mess. The cleaners wear gray suits and carry small silver suitcases. One man says, "I'll take care of this. You search the area."

The remaining cleaners spread out. I gauge my distance from the house. No. They'll see me before I can reach it. I head toward the lake instead, my feet moving as fast as they can, and I don't have time to think, don't have time to be afraid.

I lower myself into the water until only my head is exposed.

One of the sleepers walks past the lake. I hold my breath and dunk my head for nearly a minute. I keep my eyes closed. I *am somewhere else*, I tell myself, but it doesn't help. When they are gone, I climb out of the water. I have lost my knife somewhere in the lake, but I leave it behind.

As I reach the house, a policeman is climbing out of his car. Gigi called him as soon as she heard the gunshot. She takes one look at me and begins to cry. I am wearing my blank face, but Da's death must have poked holes in it. Or perhaps it is simply because he isn't right behind me. Gigi wants to go find Da, but the officer tells her to stay with me. He disappears in the direction of the orchards.

While he's gone, Gigi pulls me into her arms, holds me there. She's crying so hard my body rocks with her every breath.

"Where's Da?" Cecily asks, frightened.

Gigi lets go of me and hugs Cecily instead. I stand there, watching them, with nothing to say. No idea of what my job is right now.

When he returns, the officer stares at me carefully. He is one of us. A sleeper. He pulls out a chair for me at the dining table, and I sit in it. He takes out his pencil and notebook.

"Can you please tell us what happened, Miss Harrison," he says, a false kindness in his voice.

I nod. Gigi sits at the table as well. "Lira?" she whispers.

My stomach begins to turn. With only a few seconds to spare I bolt from my seat and into the bathroom. I throw up my dinner and clutch my belly. Everything hurts and feels numb at exactly the same time. Foggily, the sound of Cecily's voice echoes as she tries to help me hold my head up over the toilet.

Afterward I let her put her arms around me. My own arms are heavy at my sides, but that doesn't seem to matter to her. She's crying as she whispers, "Don't leave me, Lirael. Please don't leave me, too." As if she can see something in me, something I cannot.

But I start to think that it is my imagination, that the words never leave her small watery eyes. Seven, I have to remind myself. She is only seven.

"Go stay with Gigi," I tell her after a few minutes. "Tell the officer I'll be right out."

After she is gone, I look into the mirror. Will myself to be calm.

Gigi wants answers. The officer wants answers.

But they are not the only ones.

Why did they send me a new grandfather? The question bites into my skin. All my life all I have been told is that the young are better than the old. We were the ones who were made for this. Few cottages even house carriers older than eighteen. What use is an old man to the cause?

Why didn't Miss Odette tell me he was going to be replaced tonight?

Perhaps protocol changed because the Silence is over, or perhaps this is something else.

I think about the farmhouse. About my friendship with Jack and the kinds of things he talks about. The way the war no longer matters to him. If they knew, any one of those things would be enough.

Am I no longer a Safe?

I want to tell myself that I am. But my teeth chatter violently as I stumble over to the loose brick underneath the bathroom sink. It is a hiding place no one but me knows about. I remove the brick and reach inside the hole in the wall for the small blade I keep there. I drop it inside the pocket of my dress, and then I stand.

If the officer is here to take me, he will have to do it by force. He will have to kill me here, in front of my family. I will not make it easy. It will cost him something—his right eye or his left ear or all the meat inside his belly. I stare at my reflection in the mirror and promise: Before I die, I will make it cost them *something*.

When I come back out, I have composed my story. I say it perfectly. Pause at the right moments. "There was a man. I didn't see his face. He attacked Da, and I was afraid. I ran, hid."

The officer nods. "You have no idea what he looked like? What he was wearing? How tall he was, perhaps?"

I shake my head.

"Thank you, Miss Harrison," the officer says when he has finished writing. "Will you walk me to the door?"

I fight the urge to hesitate.

I follow him outside. That is where I tell him my other story. Again I am a good actress. I am able to turn off my emotions when I speak. As if I don't care. As if the truth is that Da meant nothing to me.

"He killed the sleeper before I reached them," I say. "But the sleeper had already injured Da before he died."

"You got there just before your grandfather died?"

"Yes," I say. "I watched him die."

The officer nods, as if he believes me. "I'll report this to your handler," he says, "but you should be fine. Carry on as before."

I stare at him. I don't know whether he is lying.

He must be. People like us will always lie. Even when we

are telling the truth. I drop my hand inside my pocket, wrap my fingers around the cold steel, but he doesn't try to take me. No sleepers are waiting in the shadows.

"Good night, Miss Harrison," he says, and turns to leave.

I don't answer. Even if I am still a Safe, the fact that my replacement grandfather did not make it, and I was there, will reflect badly on me somewhere, on some page, in some file.

Lirael Harrison. Status: two dead grandfathers.

My fingers press against the blade in my pocket until there is blood.

The officer gets into his car and drives away, Da's body following in the ambulance behind him, but maybe not Da's body. Maybe it is Da the cleaners got rid of and some other man we will put in the ground. I lean against the wall and throw up again.

It is over this quickly. The life that I had. The family that I had. Miss Odette will tell me at our next session that although it is very uncommon, some sleepers cannot manage to take over their alternates' lives. That sometimes, alternates are stronger than anticipated. Sometimes they fight harder to live, to be with the ones they love. They never make it, regardless, but they don't know that, and a person who has hope will do anything to win. She will not answer any of my questions.

She will not tell me why they sent a new Da.

I go back into the house. Gigi is in her room crying, Cecily crying with her. I should go comfort them, but I shrug into my coat before I can think about what I am doing and how bad an idea it is. I leave the house, find my bicycle in the shed, and ride blindly into the city with only one destination in mind. I have never been there before, but I have the address because Jack said once, "I want you to know where I live," and "Aren't you going to write it down?" And I said, "I'll remember." But I was hoping I wouldn't have to remember. That he would die in his sleep one night and Miss Odette would tell me and I would never have to come here. He opens his door on my third knock.

"Lira?" he asks in surprise, and then, when he sees my tears, he holds his arms open, and I go into them. He asks me what has happened, but I cannot get the words out. Everything I try to say comes out muffled. While I was riding, I did not realize the rain had started. But I am soaked through, my hair matted to my forehead, and now Jack is wet, too. He shuts the door, and we sit on the floor. We sit there until I have run out of tears, until I can breathe again. "Tell me," Jack says softly. "What happened?"

I open my mouth, but even to my ears the words sound garbled, like I am underwater. "I'm . . . I was . . . ," I say. What I want to ask is: *How do I get over this?* Because I need to. It's one thing to pretend to care, but this is not what that feels like, and I don't know how that happened. When it could have happened. How do I stop feeling like this? How do I become a sleeper again?

"Did something happen at home?" Jack asks, and I meet his eyes. I'm not sure of why I am surprised by how worried he looks, but I am suddenly afraid for him. What have I done? Coming here has put us both in danger. But he's not even thinking about that. He's not worried that he could die because of me.

"I should go," I say, staring down at my hands. "I'm not supposed to be here."

"We can talk first," he says, and it's the wrong answer. I was hoping he would say something else. Be someone else for a moment. Say, "You have to go, Lira. This is too dangerous. You can't be this careless." But he didn't. Our friendship means more to Jack than our lives as sleepers.

I need this to end. The thought swirls about inside my head until it is all I can think.

When something bad happens, my first instinct cannot be to run to Jack.

I will not become weak. I will not turn into him.

"So, tell me," he is saying again, for the hundredth time, and, without thinking about it, I lean forward to close the space between us. I press my lips to his warm, dry ones. I stay there for a long moment. Jack pulls away from me, his arms stiff at his sides.

"Lira," he whispers.

He doesn't say anything else, but I understand the sad look in his eyes. I want to tell him that it was not real, that I only wanted to feel something else for a moment, but I get up instead. He stands, too, saying something about how young I am, how sick he is. "If things were different . . . ," he says, but I'm not really listening. "To never have a parent or sibling, to grow up completely on your own at the cottages, that's a really fucked-up thing, Lirael."

"It wasn't that bad," I say, opening the door and stepping out onto the other side.

"That's the problem. It was, and you just don't know it."

"You don't think I know how messed up I am, Jack?" My voice cracks in the middle of the question.

He opens his mouth, closes it again.

We stare at each other, and I know I have ruined it. Our friendship. Jack looks desperate but mostly sad.

"Look," he says, not quite meeting my eyes, "you're not thinking straight. You're going to wake up tomorrow and realize that you can do so much better, that I'm just some idiot, and then we're going to pretend this never happened. Why don't you come back in and I'll make some coffee and we can talk about whatever has happened?"

My grandfather is dead, I think.

And I broke protocol by coming to see you.

I shake my head. "Bye, Jack," I say, and leave him standing there.

As I ride back to the orchards, I don't even have it in me to be embarrassed. Part of me cannot believe I rode all the way to the city to kiss Jack. Part of me cannot believe I broke our friendship, but it is a small part. The rest of me, the part that makes sense, understands: I had to. I cannot have a father or brother or friend. I have to be alone.

When I'm home, I lock myself in the bathroom. I turn on the tap to wash my face, but all I can manage is to stare at myself.

It is almost dawn now, and there are bruises underneath my clothes. Every single one hurts when I touch it, and at first I flinch. At first I moan. But as I stand in front of the mirror, I can hear Madame whispering in my ear, now more than ever: "Weak, weak, little girl." But I add to her words: "This is what the world is going to feel like once you leave this place. This is how tough it is going to get. Like drowning. Like burning. But the only time that you should be worried is the moment when you start to find yourself caring about anything and anyone but yourself and your people." That day on the bus she saw this coming. She warned me, but I wasn't listening until now.

A switch flickers inside me. A switch I did not know was there. I hear it, feel it, and then I turn off the bathroom light and sit in the dark.

At different points all the cottage children become exactly the same way. More focused, less frivolous. The smilers will smile in a way that does not reach their eyes. The ones who have to love will love with emptiness, in a way that is no longer obligatory or all-consuming.

Is it brainwashing if we consent to it?

Madame.

We were always going to become like her. She has been inside us this whole time.

A part of me is sad about this. About the new reflection of my eyes in the mirror.

A bigger part of me, relieved.

Gigi dies two months later. There is nothing romantic about this, and no part of me thinks, At least they went close together, couldn't live without each other. We bury her in the orchards next to Da, and then Cecily never forgives me because I let Aunt Imogen sell the orchards to the very first man who offers for them. We pack our things and move to an apartment in the city. I don't have the energy to explain that we are too young—she and I—to have managed the place by ourselves, that no one ever imagined that Da would die so soon, before even Gigi. Aunt Imogen certainly had no interest in the orchards, and I did not know enough about the trees, about my legacy. It was better to leave them to someone who could take care of it than to watch the trees die.

On our last day at the orchards Aunt Imogen had this idea about floating lanterns. You light them and then release them at night and, with them, all your sadness. But she didn't turn up. She told us she was driving to the city to check on our apartment, but I knew she would look for the nearest bar, drink until she felt better. We were lucky to still have Da's truck. In the end it was just me and Cecily standing there. Cecily believed with all her heart that doing it was important. The lanterns floated above us as we drove away.

The next summer, when I ride back on my bicycle to look, the trees are tall, shriveled things with poked branches.

I carry that secret.

CHAPTER 33

A few weeks after we move to the city, there is a story in the newspaper of a couple who hanged themselves from the balcony of their apartment. Everyone is outraged because the newspaper managed to obtain pictures and had no qualms about printing them. A copy floats on the wind that afternoon and finally settles on the ground. It is covered in oil and dirt and what else, but when my boot grazes the edge of it, I pick it up and read it. They left no suicide note, but the police inspector insists no foul play was involved.

I recognize them as dead sleepers almost immediately.

It is something about the way they were found. So much like Margot and Alex. Even the clothes and shoes they wore. Gray clothes, brown leather shoes. Their hands, tied together with ribbons.

The same inspector quickly changes his tune when two more pairs are discovered in exactly the same way. A John and an Alice, a Jessica and an Eric. "None of them knew one another," the inspector says, baffled, during a news conference. "It is as if their killer found two random people and hanged them together. Anyone who may have seen or heard something that might help us needs to come forward."

Our sleepers are killing themselves?

Or is this something worse? Are they being killed?

"Stay vigilant," Miss Odette tells me with a firm smile when I see her next.

I remember Gray's theory. Madame killed Alex and Margot because they broke our rules. "Did they do something wrong?" I ask her. "Are we being sent some kind of message?"

The question surprises Miss Odette. Her eyes study mine for a long moment before she relaxes into a smile. She leans forward as though she is telling me a secret, one friend to another. But her words are not friendly, not to me. "Lirael, if we wanted to punish our own people, we have far more effective and less public methods of doing so."

I try not to flinch. "So, something is wrong?" I ask. "Someone is after us?"

But all she says is: "We're taking care of it as quickly as we possibly can."

But it keeps happening. Their hands are always tied together with small red ribbons.

Not that many people in the world know what happened to Alex and Margot and know what it means, but they don't have to. Even sleepers who did not live in our cottage will recognize the white shirts and gray bottoms and frumpy gray cardigans, the brown leather shoes, patched and repatched over and over again. Most of those things, we made ourselves.

And if Madame was only following protocol with Alex and Margot, then all the other Madames in the other cottages would have done the same with their traitors. So any sleeper who passed through the cottages recognizes that we are in danger. And they, like me, begin to check their apartments carefully before they leave or enter. They carry more blades inside their boots. Worried that they are being watched, they become self-conscious in every way. It is the beginning of the next stage after the Silence, at least for us: the Paranoia. The Fear. Someone knows something. Somebody is sending us a message. Somebody knows exactly who we are. Somebody who once lived in the cottages but, for some reason, is no longer on our side.

I remember Edith asking me to betray our cause. What does she think of all this?

Is *she capable of doing something like this?* The thought makes me shiver, but I cannot help it.

Did she decide that the red ribbons would send a more powerful message than gray ones? Is there a list of people who are going to die?

Am I *on it?*

I shake my head to clear it.

I have to be more careful. I can't keep thinking about the past. I have to be the perfect sleeper now.

If you want to live through this, the old man in my dreams warns me, *you'll never look back again.*

Part THREE

One and a Half Years Later . . .

CHAPTER 34

The bravest snowflakes stick heavily to the branches of trees, to the edges of buildings, hoping to stay there forever. But when one person passes or the gentlest wind blows, they rain down on us, glittering like diamonds in the sun. A refalling of the snow, a retelling of yesterday's winter's tale. The whole city is covered in it, and that is what I walk back into once I have delivered a package to a warehouse on the outskirts of the city. A gun and a name inside a paper bag.

The sentimental ones come out of their houses and offices to take pictures; the harried ones do not notice it at all. I could watch these people for hours, but I am supposed to meet Jack at the café. I pull the hood of my coat down over my eyes, stuff my gloved hands inside my pockets.

And then I walk past Gray.

I do a double take as he passes. I have not seen him or Edith in almost two years. He is looking elsewhere, looking away from me, and then he looks up. For a moment I swear our eyes meet, and even though we do not speak, do not acknowledge each other in the slightest way, I stay where I am. I cannot control it. I watch him walk into the warehouse, and he doesn't come back out, at least not the same way. Still, I wait and wait until it occurs to me that I don't know what I am waiting for.

I finally manage to shake him from my head as I enter the café, where Jack is already waiting for me. He is sitting in front of three empty coffee mugs, and papers that are neatly stacked all over the place. A small space is left for where I might set my things. But I have no things to set but my hands. I drum my fingers on the table. The silence between me and Jack is no longer awkward. We have just accepted that this is who we are now, and I have somehow grown used to it. It is easier now than it was when Da first died. Jack watches me for a moment, orders another coffee, and then asks politely, "How are you?"

"I'm fine," I say, just as politely, but I can feel the tightness of the smile on my face. Smiling has become even less natural over the past year and a half. Practice in the mirror does nothing for it.

"No sketchbook today?"

I flick a spot of lint from my coat. "Sorry, I forgot," I say. This has become my usual lie.

"That's all right," Jack says, trying to keep his smile from falling. I pretend not to notice.

We lost each other, stopped understanding each other, the night Da died. But the day things really changed was the first time I demanded payment from him, about six months ago. I don't know why I said it, but once the words were out, there was no taking them back.

"I can't be expected to sacrifice so many hours of my day for you without any compensation," I suddenly heard myself saying, in a voice I did not recognize. "That's not how all the others do it. That's not what it means to do a job and that's what this is, isn't it?"

Jack went quiet. Before this, all he knew was that my grandfather had died, and that I was a little sad, and that I had moved to the city with my sister. But sadness is a very different thing from callousness, and though some small part of me knew that, wanted to take it back, the part that mattered said nothing. Jack shook his head, reached inside his pocket, and retrieved a couple of bills and then tossed them at my face, as if they were poisoned. I didn't even flinch. I just counted the money and calmly put it inside my coat. It would buy our groceries that week.

"So, they did it," Jack muttered. "They always talked about creating perfect soldiers, but for a while then, you were the most imperfect little thing I had ever seen, and that was the best thing about you. Now you are this." I could tell he didn't like my ignoring him because he suddenly grabbed my hand, pressed his face right up against mine until I could smell everything he'd had for breakfast, laced with whatever medication he was taking for the pain. "But tell me," he snarled, "what happens after the war? What becomes of their perfect little soldiers then?" Everyone in the café turned to look at us, at the scene we were making.

I snatched my hand from his. "See you next week," I said, and left.

Now I sit across from him as he types, but my eyes are lost somewhere past the window, somewhere in the snow that has become brown and tired. After only a little while Jack puts his typewriter in its case. "I'm done for the day," he tells me tiredly, and when I stand and push him to the bus station, he says nothing, not even good-bye. He tells me I can leave him there, but the moment he thinks I'm gone he turns around and wheels back to the café, retrieves his typewriter, and continues whatever he was doing. As if he could no longer do it properly with me in front of him. I watch from the window until he looks up and sees me, until we're staring at each other. But there is no remorse on his face. He turns away from me, carries on as if I no longer exist. The way I've done to him. He says nothing, but I hear his imaginary words anyway: "I don't have time for you to stop being a child about life."

I was supposed to be his friend.

He was supposed to undo the thing Edith and her farmhouse did to me.

But he doesn't invite me back in, and I do not offer. I am not good for anyone.

Even with his wheelchair and the way his fingers ache, Jack is better without me.

I leave him to it and go home. I stumble over a basket of dirty laundry right inside the apartment when I enter. The curtains are still closed, and even though it's well past noon, Cecily is sitting in front of the television in the dark with a bowl of milk and cereal. She should be in school, but she ignores me when I ask what happened. I kick the basket aside, trip over a pair of heels that definitely do not belong to me.

"Where is she?" I ask, gritting my teeth.

Cecily gestures to my bedroom without taking her eyes off the television. "We both know she's only here for the money," she says knowingly. "Maybe if we give her some more, she'll go."

"I did give her more," I answer in a mumble meant only for my ears as I make my way to my bedroom.

On my bed and half naked lies Aunt Imogen. Half naked is a major understatement since the only thing she's got on is a pair of panties that I'm pretty sure are mine. My bed, my panties, my clothes on the floor. Aunt Imogen turned up at the orchards one day after Da's funeral. "I've heard the bad news," she said, hand pressed against the doorjamb to keep her from falling down. She was drunk, but Gigi didn't seem to notice; she was happy to see her, she said. Her and Da's only living child. The person who would help protect me and Cecily from the world. I think Gigi thought that it was okay to die then. That Aunt Imogen would take care of us.

I grab her shoulders now and try to shake her awake, ignoring the way she groans, the way she asks for a few more minutes like a child. Cecily is right: she is here for whatever money we might have left. She arrived a week ago, promising change. I assume the dirty laundry left by the door was her best attempt.

"How was work?" she finally groans, opening just one eye. She thinks I'm a waitress at a café.

I ignore her question. "I thought we agreed that you would sleep on the couch and I would sleep here. In my room. And I thought we said that you would drop Cecily at school today."

She stares at me, as if she has no idea what I am talking about. And then she jumps up from my bed and rushes into the bathroom, where she stays for an hour. Cecily, who does not hide her hatred, turns up the volume on the television to drown out the retching sounds. "I have bad ears," she explains apologetically when Aunt Imogen screams for the noise to stop. "My teacher says that you might need to take me to the doctor to get me checked. You know what a teacher is, right? It's that person at that place called school that I'm supposed to go to every day."

"Lirael, make her stop," Aunt Imogen says.

I shake my head. "But it's really not that loud, not for me at least." I frown. "Are you feeling okay, Aunt Imogen?"

The bathroom door slams again, and Cecily pretends to walk past me, but our hands meet in the air in a secret high five. Our aunt is predictable. She dresses quickly and storms out of the apartment. We don't know where she goes. "Thank the Lord!" Cecily shrieks, and bolts the door quickly behind her and turns down the television and opens the curtains. We both know, though, that later tonight our aunt will return with tears, with promises and that eventually it will be Cecily who breaks first, who says, "Gigi said she was family," as if that means something. Da is gone. This is the best we get now.

I go to the flower shop more frequently than ever before. I told Miss Odette that I wanted more and more jobs, and she was only too happy to give them to me. Now, no matter when I go, there is always a mission, always a delivery. Today I stand in front of a knitting shop until a man I do not know walks up to me and says, "It's a pretty day, isn't it?" He gestures around to all the melted slush, which contradicts him, and I pass him the piece of paper with a name on it. These Safes are the worst ones, the ones who kill anything and anyone without blinking. I can see it in his hollow eyes. If I pick up tomorrow's newspaper or maybe the one the day after or listen to the radio, I will hear of someone who died or is in the hospital under strange circumstances, with the same name as on my paper. Some important politician, some lawyer or professor. But I never do. Those things matter even less with me now.

My only interest in newspapers is in the hangings. In the past year and a half there have been fourteen different instances, and those are just the ones reported. They are less frequent these days, once every few months, but I am still uneasy. Something is happening behind our backs. Something that even Miss Odette cannot explain to me. Whatever that thing is might one day get me killed.

I walk home feeling as though I am being followed. Once I walked around my block three times before entering my building. I train every night when Cecily is asleep. My gun is always ready, and then for weeks nothing happens. The newspapers are empty, and I think, *Maybe it's okay.*

Then the following day there is another story about two people and their red ribbons, found hanging.

The rest of the world believes in serial killers.

But what I believe is worse.

I see Gray again a few weeks later. I am sitting alone on a bench in a small park when he walks up to me, and this time he meets my eyes immediately. At first I think he's only here to say hello, but then he says the words: "It's a pretty day, isn't it?" As I pass him the note, I don't know why I am surprised. I knew this was his job. He stuffs the note inside his pocket, nods at me. He is eighteen now, closer to nineteen than not. Right away I start to notice things about him that I compare back with the cottages and with the last time I saw him: He is taller; his voice is deeper; his eyes have grown dimmer, no longer full of that fire from when Alex died. There is an underlying confidence about him, as if he understands the world perfectly now, and his place in it. I hope that I look exactly the same way.

"Thanks," he says, his voice a quiet rumble.

By the time I realize that he was waiting for me to say something, acknowledge him in some way, I am standing alone. I try to name the last look he gave me for days and for weeks. Shame. Shame was written all over Gray's face, and that baffles me. What is there to be ashamed of? Did we both not turn out the way we were meant to? Maybe there is a rule about the ones who take lives and the ones who only help do it, but then which one of us is the better person? The one who provides the knife and the name or the one who uses them?

In my mind, Gray leads to Edith. What happened to her plan after I left? Were they all part of it?

Worse than that, did she ask Gray and Robbie to carry out the hangings?

I told myself I wouldn't care, but I am suddenly terrified of the answer. I have to believe that this is the only reason why, the next time I see Gray, I follow him and watch him kill a person without so much as flinching. As if it has become second nature to him. Gray, with the eyes, with the emotions, the same little boy who was kind to animals once upon a time. Afterward he stands outside the building and smokes, staring down at the ground, one bloodied hand stuffed into his coat pocket, the other holding the cigarette.

Suddenly I understand his shame, although not why he offered it to me like that. Why he let me see.

No, I decide as I walk away.

Gray wouldn't hang sleepers.

Once I notice Gray, I start to recognize others from the cottages just like him whom I deliver packages to. I must have been seeing them for months without ever realizing it. A girl named Poppy, who had the worst giggling fits at the most inappropriate times. A boy named Bennett with dreadlocked hair. Another boy, named Dylan, who wet the bed until he was ten, who sat with the girls because the boys teased him so. And more, and more, and more. I am sure that there are other

Safes like me, who only deliver the names and the weapons, whom I will never know and never remember because we are careful not to be seen. Careful to remain invisible, but we all are here. An invisible network of seventeen- or eighteen-year-olds who grow older and colder and crueler every passing second. Two sides working together, each telling itself that it is better than the other.

But I *am* better. I am.

I think about whoever is out there hunting down sleepers.

I have to believe that somehow, somewhere there are worse monsters in the world than me.

CHAPTER 35

I go to the farmhouse to prove something to myself. It has been nearly two years since I have been there, since I have seen Edith. I go to the farmhouse because I want to know if it is in the same state I left it. If it is, then perhaps I was wrong. They were not found out. Nothing has changed. I am not sure why this matters, but I cannot talk myself out of it. I have to know. My bike takes me there and not the other way around. When I reach the place, I stand a little ways away and nod in relief. *Good*, I think. I *was right*. But then I stumble off my bike and run to the bushes. I crouch there for nearly a minute, retching, and I cannot look back. I cannot turn around again to the ruin that has made me right. I crawl backward until I find my bicycle. When I do, I climb onto it and ride back home, back to safety as fast as I can, without turning back once.

The image of the farmhouse burned to the ground, surrounded by nothing but charcoal, stays with me.

Seared scraps of clothes hung off broken glass. Shoes littered the ground. A broken pair of glasses. I did not even get close; these are just the things that had been blown by the wind. Closer, I do not know what I would have found. What the blackbirds could have been circling. The fire must have been recent. At most, a few weeks old.

I tell myself to forget it.

I tell myself it has been almost two years since Edith or any of them mattered to me.

But the next time I see Gray, I do not walk away. We stand in front of the bench, and I pretend to fiddle with my coat. I do not know what to ask, so I say, "I went to the farmhouse." I wait for him to tell me that the fire was their plan, that they'd moved their rendezvous to another place, but he simply stares at me. I look down at the ground, hating that I do not walk away. "What happened?" I say eventually. "Where is the new farmhouse?"

"There isn't one." He glances past me, as if he really wants to leave. "Everyone is dead, Lira."

I am not surprised, but it doesn't hurt any less. My hands clench, and I force them to unclench. I keep the emotion out of my voice. "Everyone?" I say.

"Julia is fine. I can't find Edith."

My head snaps up. My eyes are full of hope and questions.

"I think maybe she got away," Gray says, and he's still looking beyond me. My hope reflects in his voice. "Maybe she's hiding. I'm trying to find her."

"You weren't there?"

"I was working when they came. Julia was at her job, too."

"Oh." This is the longest conversation we have ever had without Edith. "You think this happened because of your plan?"

He finally meets my eyes. "It was never my plan," he says through gritted teeth. "I was helping her because she's my sister, but I didn't agree with her. I knew what she was doing was dangerous. I warned her."

I can imagine one of his arguments with Edith. Nothing could have changed her mind, not about this, not even her brother.

I take a deep breath of cold air. "How can I help you

find her?" I say it quickly before I can change my mind. Just because I did not choose Edith's side does not mean that I want her gone. And Gray does not look good. I have never seen him look so lost.

"You helped me once," I say.

He dismisses my words. "You don't owe me anything, Lirael."

"I know. After we find her, we'll go our separate ways."

CHAPTER 36

I sit at the café and wait for two hours. Aunt Imogen has vanished again, this time without coming back, and Cecily is alone at home. I order four cups of coffee and a brioche, the first two cups initially for Jack, but he never shows. Since the first time we met, this has never happened. I walk up to the counter and ask the waitress whether she has seen a man in a wheelchair with a typewriter. "He usually sits over there," I say, pointing, but she cuts me off.

"I remember him," she says with a smile. "I remember you, too, but no. Normally he comes two or three times a week. I haven't seen him for a couple of days."

I thank her and leave. Outside, everything is white, but it is not the kind of snow that decides a day. It is just cold enough that we can call winter beautiful, the best season and almost mean it. So Jack could get here. He could, but he probably just decided to stay home. I tell myself this and stuff my hands into my pockets and walk in the direction of the bus stop. Maybe he could no longer stand the sight of me. Dying with someone who does not want to be there is worse than dying alone. Dying in itself is bad enough.

My job is done.

So I am surprised when I am suddenly standing outside Jack's apartment building, out of breath, as if I have been running. What could I possibly be running for? Yet my feet carry me into the building and up the stairs. I find the right door, and then my fingers sting from knocking. My whole hand hurts, and I am thinking about what I should do next when the door opens. A woman stands there, frowning at me. She is wearing thick, square glasses and carrying a half-knitted sweater. "Yes?" she says, looking me over her glasses.

At first I think I have the address wrong. I back away and apologize, but then I smell the scent I have come to associate with Jack: the scent of medicines, of antiseptic cleaners, and, the worst one of all, of decay. He did not always smell like this. But suddenly this is all I can remember, and it makes me speechless.

"Yes?" the woman says again, this time less kindly. She pushes the door closed between us a little more.

I am afraid to ask. I am terrified of the answer and what it might mean. I ask anyway. "Is Jack here?"

"He doesn't want any company," the woman says gruffly. "He's resting. Who are you?"

"My name is Lirael. I'm seventeen," I hear myself answer. "I'm supposed to edit his book for him."

As if I were a robot. As if I were interviewing for a job.

"His book," the woman says, frowning. Jack did not tell her about me. I look her over. She is wearing socks and dirty sneakers underneath her skirt. Her lipstick is a bright fuchsia color that paints her ghostly. Her hair is as white as the snow outside, her face covered in wrinkles. Everything about her is severe. I wait patiently while she goes inside and asks a question. She comes back only a moment later with the same answer: "He's very tired."

"Okay," I say, but I don't leave. I just stand there.

The woman sighs and goes back inside. I hear voices.

"Come back tomorrow," she says when she returns. "He likes the mornings. He'll see you then, after— Hey!"

I push past her and enter the small apartment.

It is an open space. The kitchen, the bedroom, the sitting room; I can see them all right from the door. Almost every surface is covered with books and papers. Three typewriters sit in one corner; a couple of broken tables, in another. I look around and see stories I know. The stain on the wall from a bottle of ink that Jack decided to leave because it looked like a bird. The broken typewriters all happened during a particularly frustrating time of writer's block, after which Jack realized that they weren't exactly cheap to replace. So he moved on to tables. "I've broken about ten now," he told me once. "Tables are good for bad tempers and firewood, and that's about it." But I have never really seen his bad temper, not the kind that breaks anything.

He doesn't show it to me now from where, covered in a blanket, he is sitting in front of the television. He doesn't even look my way. I storm over, my hands fisting at my sides. "I thought you were dead," I say, embarrassed to hear the relief in my voice. "I waited and waited for you today."

The woman stands by the door, still trying to decide what to do with me.

Jack stares at the television without moving. "And you came all the way over here? I'm touched."

He is thinner, paler, skin drooping beneath his eyes.

"Look," the woman says, walking toward me. Her cheeks are splotchy. "You *cannot* just barge into other people's homes like this. This man needs his rest. If you do not leave now, I am going to have to call the police."

I look at Jack, waiting for him to tell her he knows me. Jack keeps watching the television, as if I am not here. It is only when the woman walks to the corner of the room and picks up the phone that he croaks out, "Brenda, it's fine. This is Lirael."

Brenda does not look happy as she hangs up the phone. She still eyes me with suspicion as she returns to the table and picks up her knitting again.

"Aren't you going to finish your story?" I ask, standing in front of the television screen. "What about the rest of it?"

"It's finished," he says.

"Good. Show it to me."

But he doesn't respond. I search for the pages myself. I know what I must look like, rummaging around a house that does not belong to me, papers flying about everywhere.

"Now, look here," Brenda begins again, picking up after me. "You cannot just come in here."

But I ignore her.

I find nothing. Not a single page. There is no story. Or maybe, after all his hard work, he burned them. It seems like the kind of foolish, poetic thing Jack would do. I am exhausted when I finally give up. Jack turns up the volume on the television and yawns. But all I can see is the way his hands shake. How long have they been that way? Why didn't I notice?

He balks when I make my way over to him, pushes my hand away, and says, "Look, this is unnecessary. I finally understand what I am to you. I picked the wrong girl. You can go now and I swear I won't hold it against you."

I swallow. "Jack," I say.

"Don't apologize. I don't want your lies. If you won't tell me the truth, then I don't want you here." I have never heard him like this, never seen him like this. All bones, all skin, nothing in between. No smile, no wise words, not even hurt. Just anger. Just coldness.

I rack my mind and search for a truth to offer him.

"You look terrible," I admit quietly. "Worse than you've ever been."

He nods, and I sit down next to him. I turn around and find Brenda still glaring at me. I cannot tell whether she is a sleeper or not, whether she will report this, but I don't care.

We watch the television for an hour. I don't know how I manage to close my eyes and fall asleep, but when I open them again, the woman is wearing her coat.

"Jack?" she says, coming to stand in front of him. Her voice is loud and no-nonsense.

"I haven't gone deaf yet, Brenda," Jack says, wincing.

She puts her knitting inside her bag. "I'll be back soon. I'm going to buy some more wool." She doesn't wait for an answer. It's probably the first chance she's had to leave today, and she has decided that I am good enough to look after him until she returns.

"Who is she?" I ask, once she is gone.

"Retired nurse," Jack says. "She lives on the floor below. She basically comes here every day and knits and makes my life hell, and I pay her a fortune for it."

I stretch out on Jack's sofa, pretend not to notice the way he frowns at me. "What brought you back?" he says finally.

I want to tell him a lie. But instead it's the simple truth that leaks from my lips. "I missed being your friend," I say.

Jack's eyes widen. I look down, and he fiddles with his hands. We don't talk like this; at least I don't. "That scare you?" he asks.

I shrug, try to seem careless. "Everyone that matters to me dies, it seems."

"Everyone dies anyway."

I look away, but he leans forward. At first, when he whispers, I think he's forgiving me, but the only word I catch is *bug*. My eyes scan the room, and Jack gestures to his cupboards and a large clock on the wall behind his television. *There are three of them,* he mouths. I nod to show that I understand. When sleepers die slowly, they have to be watched. The things they say to other people matter. The people they say them to matter. By unspoken agreement I help Jack into his wheelchair and take him into the bathroom. It is so small that there is barely any room. I turn on the taps, do a quick check, and find nothing, and then I settle in the bathtub.

He watches me in that horrible way he does when he's reading me. All the things I won't say.

"So, what's wrong with you?" he says finally.

"It's like you said," I say. "I can't feel anything."

"Bullshit. It is impossible to turn humanity off. They might have been able to program you to know how to care less, but you have to choose to do it. Only you can choose who you are. What happened with your grandfather, Lirael? That was the night you changed."

"He died."

"How?"

"I told you. He fought his alternate."

"And you loved him so much that you couldn't bear it, so you decided the best thing to do was to ignore me for a year? I thought we were friends."

He waits for an explanation I don't have. I shake Da's face away. More than anything in the world I suddenly want to make Jack happy, and talking about Da will do the opposite.

"There's something I've never told you about myself," I say, changing the subject. I lean back against the bathtub, make myself as comfortable as possible. "I used to have other friends. Just before I met you."

"Used to?" Jack says.

"I broke up with them."

He rolls his eyes. "Of course you did."

"They were sleepers. You would have liked them. They thought it was a good idea to do a bunch of stupid, dangerous things. All the things we shouldn't do."

Jack smiles for the first time today. "Is that so? Tell me everything."

So I tell him in the loosest terms I can manage. About the

friends I had well over a year ago. I do not mention traitors or fires or even the way I abandoned them after they told me their plans. I make up stories about the things we did together, but all of them based on some kind of truth. I tell him that we spent every secret moment we could doing silly things. Baking a cake that didn't rise because we forgot the baking powder, and then about another time we burned an entire box of waffles before we finally understood that our cooking skills were subpar at best.

In the evenings Edith and I would sometimes shrug out of our clothes and run around the backyard in our underthings, even in the freezing cold just because it felt good to go back inside and feel warm. The farm was so isolated no one could hear us when we screamed, but mostly we sang. Back at the cottages everyone knew Edith liked to sing, but in the farmhouse her voice had matured into something else. Something throaty and poignant. Julia and I were planning on secretly recording her one day. But then it ended. I left.

And now Edith is dead. But I don't say that.

Jack's face is wistful when I finish, and his cracked lips are starting to bleed. I climb out of the bathtub, put my cupped hands under the running tap, and hold them out to him quickly. He sips, and I do this three more times. "Do you miss them?" he asks.

"I don't want to talk about that part." I look down at my hands. "You said you wanted me to tell you the truth."

He hesitates, but he recovers quickly. "Do you want some advice on keeping friends? Since you don't seem to be any good at it?"

"Gee, thanks, Jack," I say, but this time I cover my mouth with my hands to hide the twitching of my lips. Right now, in this moment, I decide to let Jack become one of my mistakes. No matter what happens I won't run away, I won't ignore him, not ever again. I will be here until the day he dies, and when that happens, I will even let him break a heart I'm not sure I truly have.

Jack heaves an exaggerated sigh, presses his shaking hands to his knees. "It's just like you to take a dying man's best advice for granted, Lirael."

I say, "I don't know any such men."

CHAPTER 37

Sometimes my body goes numb, I tell the old man in my dreams, one night when we are sitting in the tree surrounded by water. My feet are small and they dangle from a branch, and somewhere underneath the water is orange like the sun. A flaming river, but its burn never reaches our tree. *I don't know why; it just happens. My mind keeps spinning, worse than ever, but my body holds still. I know what I have to do. I try to move, but I can't.*

He nods, stares down at our reflections in the water: a little girl barely five and an old man sitting in a water tree.

I dream less frequently now, ever since Da's death. What will I do if the dreams eventually go away? What will I be without them?

They are my comfort. The only sure thing I have ever had.

I *can't keep saving your life,* he says, a sadness in his voice. He holds my hand. I *mean, I want to, but I'm not always going to be there when you freeze. I can't hold you up forever.*

I shake my head and promise: *I'm not asking you to. But only leave me when you have to.*

CHAPTER 38

After walking Cecily to school, I go back to the apartment. I have no interest in the flower shop man and his missions today. Instead I search my room for the watch Edith gave me. I'll need it if Gray and I are going to look for her. I find it underneath my dresser, in a box that I did not unpack when we moved into the apartment. It feels heavy in my hand, but I hold on to it as I march out of the apartment again and down the street. I meet Gray at the same spot in the park as the last time. I can tell from the look on his face that he doesn't want my help. This whole thing is awkward. He is the one doing me a favor by letting me tag along. I force myself to smile, knowing it looks unnatural on me. That seems to make him feel better, and he stuffs his hands inside his pockets and says, "Follow me. Do you still have your watch?"

I nod and put my hand inside my pocket, turn it on.

We walk to the train station in silence. We wait separately, and when the train comes, we do not sit together. We do not even acknowledge each other. Still, I stand in a place where I can always see him. In a way he has not changed much at all since the cottages. Taller, much stronger, yes, but with the same short brown hair and brown eyes. Those eyes watch everything happening around them without ever seeming to. By the time you figure out how dangerous a boy like Gray is, it's too late for you. That is what I am supposed to be, too, but I will never be as good at being invisible as he is.

I am afraid that he will change his mind and leave me. That I will go back home and Edith will freeze to death somewhere. I do not take my eyes off him the entire train ride. I watch him move to his door as the train nears the station.

When the train stops, Gray gets off. I get off, too. I follow him out of the train station at a distance down some streets until we're standing outside an apartment building. It is one of those forgettable places with redbrick walls that seem to blend right into the scenery, nothing terrible and nothing extraordinary. Now Gray waits for me as he fishes his keys out of his pocket.

"Don't worry, the cameras around here are taken care of," he says.

I follow him onto an elevator and then down a hallway. *This is a bad idea.* The thought hits me suddenly. Edith managed to fool me once, and this is her brother. What if he is worse? What if this whole thing is a test and wherever he is taking me is where I will die? I left Cecily alone. Unprotected. Every step forward becomes harder, and I slow down. Gray must notice, but he does not stop. Does not even look at me. I could turn around, walk away right now, and he would let me go.

"Wouldn't they tell you what is happening?" I ask him. "I mean, about your sister being missing, wouldn't someone tell you, especially since you work for them like you do?"

He stops in front of an apartment door and holds it open. When I don't move, he enters ahead of me, but he doesn't close the door. It is not courage that eventually draws me inside. It is the mess of papers, of image drives and television screens that I can see from the threshold. I enter the apartment quickly and lock the door behind me.

"Gray?" I whisper.

He's sitting at a table and flicks a switch. A black-and-white image flickers on a large screen. "My handler says that he knows nothing about it and that he's looking into it, but it's been two weeks since I asked," he tells me without turning around. "He's lying. Take a seat."

"Oh, okay," I say, but there is nothing to sit on. This whole apartment is worse than the basement in the farmhouse. There are many more screens with people on them, and there are photographs that I do not recognize. In the strangest nooks there are dirty dishes, dirty clothes, muddy boots. I get the impression that Gray spends all his time here. Watching these cameras obsessively. I sidle closer to him, frown at the screen that he is frowning at, seeing nothing important. Only people going in and out of places, living normal lives.

"There are more monitors," he says, "and more footage to watch. We used to record everything at the farmhouse. All these are the ones I haven't watched yet. If you can't find anything that explains her disappearance, find something that explains how they could have known. I thought I kept her safe. But obviously I . . ." He doesn't finish. He crosses his arms and focuses on his screen.

This is not what I was expecting. I was expecting to scour

the streets. To yell Edith's name out in the woods. Instead I pick up a handful of image drives that I am standing in front of. I sit in one corner of the room and pretend not to notice the cockroaches. For hours I stare at my screen until my neck starts to hurt. There isn't much to see. I don't know what I am looking for. I glance at Gray, and I'm not sure he knows what he is searching for either. But we keep going in silence.

There are images of Edith working at a restaurant. She is tall and elegant, and the men stare at her, and sometimes she seems to notice. Sometimes she pushes her hair behind her ear and laughs at their jokes. A man hands her his phone number, and she smiles. Almost all the time she dumps it in the bin right after he is gone.

I come across footage from inside their house. I lean in. Neither Edith nor her brother ever talked about their family. The only thing I know is that they have money. But neither of them lives as though that money defines them. I am fascinated by the tall ceilings and large windows in their house. Their lives as sleepers are so different from mine.

One of the recordings is dated a month ago. I watch Edith, Gray, and two adults who must be their parents sit down for dinner. Servants appear with trays of food, and after they've been served, the family is left alone. The footage has no sound, but it doesn't look as if any of them are talking. Then I see their father stand, and he's pointing at Gray. Edith stands, too, but her mother pulls her away. They leave the room. Gray sits there with his father. He doesn't look up from his food. He doesn't ever look up, and that's probably why he doesn't see the first blow coming. I punch the stop button on that recording. I try another one, but it's more. It's worse.

I look over at Gray, who is oblivious. I can't tell, but his nose has probably been broken before. And his ribs . . .

I can't breathe.

Suddenly I'm looking through the image drives for just this one thing. Fast-forwarding until I'm there and then staring in horror, hand clutched to my throat, begging the bile to stay back.

There's an old one from before we took our alternates' lives. The real Gray is younger. Much younger, and he is lying on the floor, curled up in a fetal position. His father yells something and kicks him. Keeps kicking until Gray isn't moving anymore. The real Edith runs into the room. She sits with him until he wakes up, and then they just sit there, hugging each other and crying.

I blink at the screen.

"Wait," Gray says suddenly. He jumps up, realizing too

late and turns my screen toward him. "You're not watching—you—these ones." He hands me new image drives. "Watch these ones instead."

I say nothing. I don't move.

He is watching me, and I am staring at the blank screen.

"It's fine," he says dismissively. "It's old news. Focus on the important stuff."

But I can't. Every blow hurts, as if I were the one lying there. Bleeding, crying. That day in the truck when Edith talked about Gray. "You have no idea what they make him do." I thought she was talking about his missions as a Safe. I was wrong. "She was trying to save you," I say. "All that bullshit about wanting babies being why she was mad at the people who made us, mad enough to betray them. The whole time she was just trying to save you."

"She was trying to save us all." He won't meet my eyes. "Watch these, okay?"

I push a new image drive into the television. It shows the outside of the farmhouse, but I can't concentrate. All that time in the cottages that I was training to be an orchardist's granddaughter, he was training for this. Training to become the son of a monster. How do you train for something like that? And what about Edith?

"You knew, didn't you?" I croak.

Gray sighs and looks away from his screen. He studies my face before deciding I can handle the truth. "He thanked me," he says. "The old Gray. Right before I killed him, he thanked me. That's when I really knew I was in trouble. I'm older now; don't worry about it. I'm still here, and I'm stronger. It never happens anymore."

We stare at each other in silence.

I think about the date on one of the image drives. I think about the bruises I saw that one time when we were at the farmhouse. "Take off your jacket," I say. Because I want to believe him. Because I don't.

Gray doesn't move. Doesn't blink. Finally he looks away.

He could kill his father if he truly wanted to. He could, but he won't. As sleepers we blend in with our families; we don't destroy them.

"Where's the bathroom?" I ask after a few minutes of trying to concentrate. I walk in the direction he points. I sit in the bathtub and blink up at the ceiling. There are many cracks, a spiderweb of them. I sit in there, staring at the ceiling, until it's time to leave. Then I put on my coat. "See you tomorrow," I say, barely able to walk.

***

I find Edith on a Friday morning two weeks later. I find her on a recording of the day the farmhouse burned down. She is wearing a large, floppy hat and grinning at something Davis is saying. They stand together outside, at a corner of the house, and they are nothing more than shadow people. You have to be looking for them. You have to recognize the hat Roberta lets Edith borrow sometimes. Davis must say something else because Edith laughs again. She looks happy. Then she glances around to make sure no one is looking before she stands on her tiptoes and gives Davis a kiss. They stay there for a while, and then Davis goes back inside the house. Edith sits on the ground, head bowed, doing something until she finally gets up and leaves.

Every moment after that is fast and shocking.

Edith is there one moment and then gone. A flare comes from the exploding farmhouse. The aftermath.

I find it. But now that I have I don't know what to do. For hours I just sit on this information. If Gray asks, I'll tell him, but for the whole day I do nothing, just sit there. I set the television to replay and think about what Gigi said. Sometimes it's better to let people have their hope for as long as possible. I *am doing something kind*, I tell myself as I reach to turn off the screen. My hands are shaking.

"Are you all right?" Gray asks, frowning over at me suddenly.

"I'm fine," I lie, but my voice is too high. He gets a strange look on his face as he walks toward me. I back away automatically. For once he isn't wearing his jacket. Bruises are fading on his arms. Last week, when he got here, he was limping, but we didn't talk about it.

"That's the fire. I've seen this recording about a hundred times," he says, crouching down next to me.

I say nothing.

"Lirael?" And then he is grabbing my shoulders and gently shaking me. "Lirael," he says carefully, "show me. Tell me. Show me." He can't decide which he wants. "What am I not seeing?"

I meet his eyes, but I can't really see them. "You said Julia was at work," I say, and my throat hurts.

Gray frowns at the screen and then back at me again. "Okay." He looks like he's going to shake me again.

"Does she know about this apartment?" I ask. When he doesn't answer, I repeat myself: "It's important. Gray, does she know about this place?"

He shakes his head. He looks afraid. I show him the recording again. The image is grainy and hard to miss, but it is there. Just before the farmhouse explodes, there is a shadow, on the very edge of the screen. Edith is walking casually toward it. "She's talking to someone," I say, pressing my finger to the television. "Someone she knows. Someone who isn't in the farmhouse when it explodes."

I stop that recording and play one from the following day, except this one is of a tree a little ways from the farmhouse. Without seeing the shadow, there is no reason Gray would have looked for it. "This camera was turned off the day of the fire, but it was back on the day after. I couldn't figure out why. I thought it might be a typical maintenance thing but then—"

I hold up a shaky finger. "I remember this tree. But when I was there, there was no bump under—"

Gray doesn't even stay to the end; he's already running out of the apartment. I am running, too, but I never catch up. He has his truck today. He has his truck, and my bike cannot compete. Still, I try. I ride as fast as I can to the farmhouse, though my hands keep slipping off my handlebars. When I reach the tree, he is already digging. I find another shovel in his truck. We dig in silence.

As I stand there, I feel like somebody else. Somebody else watching Gray drop his shovel on the ground beside his sister's body. "No, no, no," he keeps saying. "Edie, no, no, no." And I keep throwing up. It's the moment when Edith gets up to leave and disappears off the recording that made me think.

She left because she was talking to someone. I couldn't see who, but it wasn't someone she was afraid of. And when the farmhouse exploded several minutes later, there was no sign of her coming back. If Edith was still somewhere close by, somewhere by this tree, then she would have seen the explosion. She would have run past the camera again, tried to save her friends, but she didn't. Because she didn't see the fire. She was dead already.

I just keep imagining Edith kissing Davis, then walking over to stand by Julia at the tree. I imagine that Julia says hello with that shy smile of hers. I imagine that Edith smiles back and does not see the exact moment when Julia wraps her arms around her friend's neck and snaps it. Except she wasn't anyone's friend, not really. Certainly not when she detonated the farmhouse.

Julia told. *Julia.*

Who else would have known exactly where to stand in order to lure Edith off-camera?

"Go," Gray says suddenly. He looks so angry I stumble backward. He looks almost as if he thinks . . .

I try to see things from his point of view. They all have been friends for years. I was the newest member of their group. I was the one who didn't agree with what they were doing and the one they couldn't trust. Nobody else knew. If I'd even hinted, just once, about the farmhouse to my handler, this would have happened. This would be my fault.

"I didn't—I wouldn't—" I stammer.

His voice is a shout now. I have never heard him shout before. "Get lost. Lirael, get the fuck out of here."

I go.

I retch again before I get on my bike, but nothing comes. My stomach hurts, and my head spins.

Edith, I think, and as I ride, *Edith, Edith, Edith*. It is all I can think. I swipe at my face whenever the road gets blurry.

This is why I don't trust anybody. This is why we can't trust anybody. None of us.

Julia will become a handler for this. She will not have to work for anyone anymore; it will be the other way around. I will sit in front of her, and she will smile at me, that same innocent smile. "Hi, I'm your new handler," she will say. She will wear expensive shoes and a suit. She will reek of expensive perfume. They only cost her four lives.

I learn an important lesson today.

About myself.

At the end that's the only person any of us is really looking out for.

CHAPTER 39

"Okay, I've done all the research," Cecily says when I pick her up from school. Even though she barely fits anymore, she climbs into the basket of my bicycle, sits at an odd angle, and squints up at me. "I think we should go shopping. I mean, mostly for you because you need an improvement, but if you want to buy me anything..." She pretends to consider it. "Actually," she says after a moment, her voice unnaturally squeaky, "I was thinking, and there's this album I want that all my friends—"

"Oh, God, not another album, Ceilie," I groan. "It's not happening."

"But Mathieu says—oh, fine. But can we at least get the dog? You know, the one I told you about *ages* ago."

I roll my eyes. "You know," I say, "you're supposed to start big and go small, not the other way around."

"Says who?"

"Also, it doesn't count when you whisper it in my ear when I'm sleeping."

"So, you did hear," she exclaims. "And do you also remember saying yes?"

"It's not happening," I say again. "But nice try."

I understand perfectly how this conversation will end before it has even started.

"Okay," Cecily says, and sighs. She hums under her breath, I ride. I feel uneasy. One of us is more powerful than the other today, and I am not sure which. I am careful on the roads, careful to pay extra attention as I pedal. The farther out of the city we go, the quieter we both become. The farther we go, the more I cannot believe that I am taking my sister back. Back to the orchards that I promised her she would never see again. "Past things have to stay past," I told her. But perhaps sometimes the past doesn't stay where it is supposed to.

The conversation is on replay inside my head. Cecily stomped around the apartment on one of her tantrum days.

"But everything's fine," I told her, always so perplexed whenever she got like this. "I told you. I've been there many times. The orchards look *great*."

"So, then why won't you take me?"

I shrugged. "There's never a good time."

It was a lie. All I have is time. But the trees are dead.

"I think you hate me," she said. "That's why you won't take me back. You just hate me."

I said nothing.

I am not her mother. I am not her sister. I was trained to be a sister, for years, but that doesn't make me one. I am sometimes so out of my element that we storm into separate rooms and stay there, I in the dark for hours, she with her latest toy. I shake my head clear now as the road grows bumpy and untarred. The side bushes have grown, and the path is muddy, but the sun flickers in a promising way. Maybe spring, maybe soon, it says. Cecily kneels in the basket and holds her hands up. A bird. She has not been a bird in a long time, and I have not been her wings.

The thing we're not talking about fades and stays back in the city air behind us. The nightmares. Last night she screamed so loudly I was afraid there was someone in her room. I came ready to fight off a sleeper. But Cecily's eyes were wide, as if she did not recognize me, her face red and bruised, as if she'd been clawing at herself.

It was a dream, she said. But she wouldn't tell me about it. She pressed her damp face against my chest. "You have to take me back," she said instead. "I have to see the orchards. They need me."

Now when we stop, I expect her to burst into tears. I brace myself as I let my bike fall to the ground. But my sister simply bends and straightens her school socks, and when I catch a glimpse, her eyes are made of steel. She walks purposefully through the trees, and I follow, wondering again about her dreams. About what frightens her. It is too quiet here, and the trees are completely void of fruit. The scents linger, though. Of betrayal. Of death. Of memory. Black and whites to contrast the green of my pea coat, the red of Cecily's rain boots.

"What does this tree need?" she asks me suddenly, stopping.

"I don't know," I say. The answer is automatic, and Cecily looks irritated. She stays quiet, though, her forehead puckered with concentration as she takes everything in. I know already that we will spend the evening here, and Cecily will do the only thing she remembers, the thing Gigi did when she was well. Walk through the orchards, both hands outstretched to touch a tree trunk. "A moment of warmth in case it has forgotten," Gigi said.

I am like Da. I do not believe that ghosts ride the wind, or that people can whisper goodwill to trees, or that trees can whisper happiness back into little children. I don't believe in magic or stardust that will rain down on the ones who wish hard enough. Those are pretty ideas, but they are not the science of a star, a bullet, or the things that make a person good or bad, or bleed.

When Cecily stops again, I walk into her.

"Is this one going to survive?" she says, pointing to a thin tree.

"I don't know."

This time she plants her hands on her hips. "Yes, you *do*. You just don't want to. If you tell me, I'll know it, too, and then you don't have to worry, I'll look after the trees for us."

I ignore her and keep walking, but she has more questions.

"If you take my half of the orchard money from the bank, will it be enough to buy it back?"

I pretend her question is a valid one. *This was a mistake; we're not coming back here*, I want to say. But I shrug. "Maybe for the house and a few acres of apple trees."

"Okay," she says, nodding. "Okay, that's good."

I watch her planning her future, and pity changes my mind. I want to give her something to hold on to. I walk over to the first tree she touched. "It takes years for a tree to realize it is dying," I tell her. "It will be here next year. They all will. There is time."

She nods at me, smiles this time. I return it.

There is money from the orchards, money to live on, but it won't last us forever. For Cecily, if she's still around years from now, it might last her awhile. She probably won't be. I cannot think about that. Sometimes, though, I wonder past eight-year-olds and think of fifteens, of seventeens, of twenty-fives. I am not sure whether these futures are mine or hers.

I think of the look on Gigi's face the morning after Da died, when she saw me putting on my coat. She didn't ask where I was going, but I could tell she wanted to. I said nothing to reassure her. When I got to the garden behind the flower shop, climbed down the ladder, I was afraid the office would be empty. I had no idea how to find Miss Odette any other way if I needed her. But she was there.

She did not seem surprised to see me.

It was the usual. The blood tests, the questions, the graphs. A refill on my pills, and then she said the thing I'd been expecting. The real reason I was here. "Lirael, I can make some arrangements for you, speed up the cottage training process. You can have a real sister. One of our own in Cecily's place as soon as you want."

I stared at her. *There is another Cecily,* I thought, but the words barely penetrated my mind. Of course there was another Cecily, born after my parents gave me up, after I was sent to the cottages. She didn't matter to me. I was thinking about the fact that I had been right. They didn't fully trust me. They'd sent Da's alternate to replace him, and that had failed. Now they wanted to send another one to keep an eye on me.

Why?

Maybe Julia had told them I'd been at the farmhouse with her. Or perhaps Madame had warned them about me, her weak little girl.

Miss Odette leaned across the table and held my hand like a friend, like a mentor. I let her.

This was a test, another one to see where my loyalties lay. The tests never end.

I tried to stay calm, but my hand shook in hers.

"Why do I need another sleeper?" I asked, meeting her eyes. "I thought I was fine on my own."

She didn't hesitate. "You can accomplish more missions

together," she said. "And with the hangings, it is safer this way. Two is better than one."

But she was lying. I didn't need another sleeper to protect me; if anything, an eight-year-old sleeper would be the one to need my protection.

My confusion turned into anger so quickly that I couldn't hide it. I removed my hand from Miss Odette's and reached down for my boot. I pulled out the knife I kept there and slid it across the table toward Miss Odette. "Here," I said, and I let the remaining words speak for themselves.

I was tired of all their tests. I was not Edith, who had been a traitor. I was nothing like Julia, either, but I was definitely not Edith. And if they could not trust me, then it should all end there, in that room. Better a knife I could see than a bullet in my back. Better then than later, when I would think I was safe again.

Miss Odette's eyes widened. I couldn't imagine what she was thinking. She picked the knife up, but she only turned it over in her hand; she didn't leave her seat. Minutes passed. When she still didn't use it, I stood and walked toward the door. I had my fingers on the doorknob when she finally spoke again, clearing her throat. "Lira, you haven't answered my question. About your sister. Would you like her replaced?"

I turned around and found her watching me.

I knew the wrong answer. And I knew the right one. I opened my mouth, knowing what I was going to say, already knowing before I'd ever come.

"Will you bring me here again?" Cecily asks, tugging on my arm as we ride home after our orchard visit.

I tell her the truth. "No."

She doesn't argue. Just pretends to be a bird, all the way back to the city. Then she rests her chin on the table and watches me paint.

I watch her back. Sometimes the sister who sits down across from me is actually too calm, too docile these days, the way children are when they pass through the cottages. Yes, she is younger than I was when I passed my examination, but that doesn't make it impossible.

Miss Odette does not need my permission to kill my sister.

A little girl with brown eyes might have washed up from the ocean. And she might be waiting somewhere now, or this might be her.

Nothing is more frightening than not knowing exactly who it is you are standing in front of. Sometimes you cannot trust your own family entirely.

Cecily laughs, and I open my eyes. "You've done it again," she says, pointing to my hand. I am holding a tube of blue paint upside down and have squeezed most of it out onto the floor. I jump up and run for the mop, trying to clean it up before it stains. Cecily helps me, and by the time we're finished, our hands and knees are blue. "You always waste all the paint," Cecily says with a sigh, but I am barely listening. I am still thinking about what I have to do, and I am not here.

"Lira?" Cecily says, after a while. There is concern in her voice, but I cannot snap out of it.

There is a delicate balance between a thought and memory. They both feel exactly the same, the way your fingers go sweaty and your heart races. You're standing on the edge of a railway track all over again and the train is coming and you're about to die. Then you open your eyes and realize that you're a sister, a daughter, a friend and that you are supposed to be breathing and that you are supposed to be here.

But I cannot be here. I cannot be a good sleeper and sister. One of those things has to suffer. Tonight, when we go to bed, Cecily waits an hour before she tiptoes to my door and pushes it open. She climbs into my bed and curls up next to me. She thinks I'm asleep. She whispers, "I am learning to be strong for you. For one day when you can't be strong and I can." And then she goes back to her room, not knowing what kind of damage she has just done.

Those words haunt me.

When I finally open my eyes, those words are still in the air, but I am alone in my room, lying in the dark, knife always underneath my pillow.

She may have been crying when she whispered them, but I don't go to her room to check on her.

This is harder than I ever thought it would be, I tell myself. *But I'm doing the best that I can.*

Yes. That was my answer.

I said it calmly, as if it meant nothing to me. I told Miss Odette that I wanted Cecily replaced with her alternate.

"But I'll kill her myself when the time is right," I said. Miss Odette smiled, nodded, but I could tell that she wasn't completely happy with me. I don't know why I said that last bit, about killing Cecily myself, why I didn't take it back. The last thing I needed was to give my handler fresh reasons to distrust me, but there it was. And here it still is now.

A whole year has passed.

Any day now I'll kill her.

Any day.

That is what I am supposed to say.

I hate the city. I hate the noise and the people. I miss the smell of apples and peaches and the calm in the country. But Cecily is safest here, where for the most part I hide her without her knowledge, where she thinks living in an apartment with five locks and being walked to school and back every day is something everyone does.

I do not trust the world with her.

She does not know this yet, but the world is not on her side.

I know what that feels like.

The afternoon after we visit the orchards it seems that chaos falls from the sky like a dead bird. Men and women crowd the streets as we walk home from her school. Fights are breaking out. I abandon my bike and pull Cecily close to me, pushing past people as carefully as I can. I ask a woman carrying her own child what is happening, and she points to the sky. "They're disappearing," she says breathily. Inside one of the shopwindows people are crowding around; a television flickers. On the screen is a world where all the streets have collapsed and the air is black with smoke and ashes. There are fires. Holes in the ground. There are people who have lost their entire families and have nothing else to do but wander the streets because they have gone mad with grief. A caption underneath the television has the word *Earth* II in large letters. I haven't seen my Earth in so long that I do not recognize it. I cover Cecily's eyes too late. She clutches my hand and starts to cry. Despite all this, I am calm. Until the woman next to me adds: "Some of them have managed to come here. Some of them are right here among us."

Someone else shouts: "We're going to find them. We're going to kill them all." And the crowd cheers.

CHAPTER 40

Of *course* this was going to happen. Of *course* people were going to murder each other in the streets, and gunshots would ring from morning to night, and hospitals would crowd with people who are afraid their sons or daughters are acting strange. They want to know if there is some kind of test for sleepers. Some way of checking, but they are disappointed at the answer. They find it hard to comprehend our world. The idea that we are not disappearing because of anything that can be explained or described; we are just disappearing. Because one of us, one version of us, has to.

In the meantime Cecily and I are running out of food. We've managed as best as we can so far, but if I don't get more, we will be in trouble soon.

"Don't go," Cecily says, holding my hand. She's barely let go of it since all this started two days ago. We follow each other on every bathroom break and sleep in the same bed. She screams when she wakes, louder than ever. In her dreams she says, "The trees, the trees."

I smile at her now, the brightest one I can manage. "It'll be fine," I say. "Don't open the door, no matter what. Not unless I do the knock I taught you, remember?" I do it again on the kitchen counter. "If someone comes, if they force the door open, lock yourself in the bathroom. Then climb out the window, Ceilie. Do you remember where the baker's shop is? Go there. Wait for me there."

"I'm not that hungry," she says.

"I know," I say, and shrug into my coat, pull the hood over my eyes. A gun that she does not see is tucked in behind my jeans. There are two knives in my boots. More guns and knives and poison are in a box under my mattress. Every sleeper has such a box, but I have never needed it until now. "I'll be right back," I tell her again before I'm gone.

* * *

It is for Edith that I go find Gray, but also for him. Because I know I will find him in that apartment. And he will be unshaven, empty, and racked with guilt. I go to him after I go see Jack. Jack has his own guns, and he promises me that he will be safe, but we both know that if something terrible happens, he will die. This is not how it is supposed to be. He is supposed to miss the war. "Well, I just can't catch a break, can I?" he wheezes.

I kiss his forehead. I pour him a cup of water. His nurse ran. The first moment she could, she ran, and she didn't look back. I promise to come back soon, and then I go to Gray. He doesn't come to the door for so long that I am afraid he is dead. Then he is standing there, blinking like he doesn't know who I am. He says nothing.

"Are you going to let me in?" I ask after too long.

"No," he says.

I nod. "I'm sorry you think that was a question." I point my gun at him. "Move." Even though I press the gun to his chest, he just stands there. That's when I'm truly frightened. I shouldn't have come. The devil is in his eyes. Finally it is my other hand, the one not holding the gun to him, that shoves gently at his chest and moves him.

The apartment is worse. It is dark, and there must be all kinds of creatures here now. Roaches, maggots, rats. The same dirty plates are still piled up. I expected all this but am at a loss for what to do. *Clean, I suppose,* a voice inside my head says. But I left Ceilie alone. Quickly I sweep and throw out the dirty dishes. Afterward I pull a loaf of bread, a piece of cheese, from my bag, though they were meant for me and Cecily. "Eat this," I say. "And in case you were wondering, that wasn't a question. Maybe shave, too, while you're at it."

He is watching me when I turn around. I pretend not to be afraid when he follows me to the door. I pretend not to care when he holds it closed with a single hand and stares into my eyes. I am not short, but Gray is taller. "Do you want to kill me, Gray?" I ask after a moment.

He drops his hand for a moment, looks upset, but his eyes go blank just as quickly. "Do you ever feel anything?" he asks, so softly I might have imagined the words.

I flinch. "What?"

Our faces are so close they're almost touching. I lean back.

He doesn't ask again, and I say, "You can't hurt me."

Gray shakes his head, as if I am stupid. "I'm not trying to hurt you. I just want to know what you're doing here."

"Edith would have wanted me to help you," I say.

"Edith is dead because of you," he says.

I flinch again. He is good at this. "You still think I did it."

"Julia was her friend," he says. "She was *my* friend. I *know* Julia."

Now it's my turn to shake my head. My turn to laugh cynically. "You know better than that. We all can pretend. *Pretend* to be your friend. *Pretend* to like you. *Pretend* to be anything that they have taught us to be."

"I quit the Safe team," he tells me, changing the subject. "I told my handler."

Our eyes meet. "You can't quit," I say after a moment. "You'll die."

"I quit," he says again, more adamant this time.

I shake my head. "So what are you going to do now?"

"Finish what she started. Find a way to close the portal. Find a way to stop anybody else from living like this." *And then die.* That is the part he doesn't say, but it hangs there between us like poison.

It's not something I can talk him out of. He is mad with grief. He shouldn't have loved her like this. He should have stopped the first chance he got. I turn and open the door. Before I leave, I say again, "I didn't kill your sister. I didn't turn you guys in. Don't trust me. But don't trust Julia either, Gray. It will be the dumbest thing you have ever done. I'll come see you again. If you're here."

CHAPTER 41

After school, a few days later, Cecily turns on the television. Instead of her favorite show, the screen is white. "Mathieu says his television is blank, too," she tells me, cradling the telephone against her ear. Our move has not affected their love-hate relationship, and she spends the next few minutes reminding Mathieu of the reasons why he's not allowed to have any other best friends at school even though she has left. "Because," she hisses. "You can't have one until I have one." Then after a short pause she yells, "Because I said so, that's why!"

She hangs up the phone with a slightly purple face. "Boys

are real stupid," she announces, sounding like Aunt Imogen.

I can't help my smile.

We fiddle with the buttons on the television for almost an hour. But it stays that way, so we give up. I am helping her with her homework when the screen begins to flicker, except that instead of Cecily's show, an automated voice says, "This is a special broadcast. Your regular programming will resume shortly," over and over again. After a full minute of this, we see a room filled with about twenty people—men and women and some teenagers about my age. It looks like some kind of news conference.

Then the first man steps forward. He is short and bald. "Hello. I am the alternate of Arthur Laurent."

He steps back, and a woman steps forward. "Hello. I am the alternate of Clara Dumas."

I *am the alternate of Sacha Denis.*

I *am the alternate of Zoé Masson.*

Peter Roche, Alan Gupta, Jama Elk . . .

They all introduce themselves, all twenty of them. They tell us they have something to confess, and I have forgotten how to breathe. Something hot pricks the back of my neck, but my hands hang at my sides. My mouth falls open and stays that way.

They are sleepers.

The moment they start introducing themselves, I know they believe the same things that Edith believed. Still, I am shocked when the first man who introduced himself, Arthur Laurent, steps forward again and says, "We are part of a group that we call the Resistance."

I am shocked when he tells everyone all we have managed to keep secret for years. "We are from the other Earth," he says. "We were sent here to replace your people."

Just like that. Just because he can.

The words are like fire around my ears.

"What's this?" Cecily says, "Some kind of television show?"

"Go and finish your homework in your room," I snap at her, grabbing the remote control and clicking it off. But as soon as she is gone, I turn it back on and collapse in front of the screen. My whole body begins to vibrate. From fear, from confusion, and from something else I do not recognize.

They sit in front of a long glass table. Behind them is a blank white wall. They do not hide their faces. Their message is clear: They are no longer afraid of the cottages, of their handlers, of what this will do to the world. They are willing to die for whatever they believe.

"There is a protocol in all the cottages," Arthur Laurent

says. He seems to be their leader. "If we believe that after all our training, sleepers will eventually betray our cause, we hang them before they can even take their final examinations. When they are dead, we tie a ribbon to their wrists as a symbol of their betrayal."

I wrap a hand around my mouth to keep from screaming. I listen to the man take responsibility for the hangings that have been happening the past few years. It was supposed to be a warning for our people, he says. To stop. To end the cottages. To return us to our world. But they didn't listen.

"It had to come to this," the man says, his voice never once wavering. "We had no other choice. We thought the hangings would work, but there are more hidden cottages now than ever before, and I am afraid that we have left things too late. That this is our last hope."

He retrieves a roll of paper and unfolds it into a map. The camera zooms in. The map is marked with several X's.

"There are nine portals around the world," he says, "all of them found in oceans and seas. We have pinpointed the exact locations of these portals, as well as all the cottages we know of." He points at the marks on his map; he is about to say more. Before he can, there is a commotion. Everyone on the screen begins to scatter. Something explodes, and there is screaming, smoke, smaller explosions that continue for several seconds.

The rest of the world might be confused about what is happening, but all sleepers watching are not.

We have found them. We have killed them.

"Oh my God," I whisper, holding my chest and trying to catch my breath. *Oh my God, oh my God.* We had protocol. We had a strategy.

The war was not supposed to begin like this.

The television screen goes gray for an hour. I can almost hear the chaos building inside that silence. When broadcasting resumes, sleepers are all anyone will talk about. Analysts voice their opinions, and presidents make speeches from all over the world. But what can they possibly say to reassure their people? They seem just as shell-shocked as the rest of the world.

Only hours after the announcement, soldiers flood the streets and begin rounding up as many "suspicious" people as they can find. Barely twenty-four hours after that, the Australian prime minister announces that they have found the first portal in the ocean.

By then I am sure it is too late. I am sure that every person who could have come from our planet is here now. I am sure that they are ready to fight. I can already hear the screaming, can already smell the blood. People in the streets begin killing one another aimlessly, senselessly, not ever sure who their true targets are. For hours all I can do is pace our apartment, check our locks, make sure my gun is loaded.

We lock ourselves away for over a week.

I make Cecily wear her headphones all the time, even when she is sleeping, listening to the same songs over and over again until it is her personal soundtrack. She is listening to her music, but I am listening to the world end.

I just don't know which one.

I finally gather the courage to leave the apartment and find that Gray has not eaten the bread or the cheese I left him. Since Cecily refuses to be alone, I bring her with me. All the schools are canceled, and the government is trying to maintain order with curfews, but I would be a fool to feel safe. I am exactly what they are looking for. Yet here we are at Gray's apartment.

I slam the door and set Cecily down at the table, as far from him as possible, and say, "Don't talk to him; don't look at him. Just wait and listen to your music, okay? I have to take care of some things."

She nods, and I start cleaning. She lasts about two seconds.

"I'm Cecily," I hear her say.

"Okay."

"Okay what?"

"Okay, your name is Cecily."

"Oh. But what's yours?"

"Don't have a name." And then to me: "Are you leaving anytime soon?"

I turn to Cecily and give her an apologetic look. "His sister died a short time ago," I say as softly as I can.

"Oh," Cecily whispers back. Her mouth is as round as each one of her eyes, and then she continues to stare at him. I work as quickly as I can, feet stomping on roaches, broom slapping the ones that get away.

When I turn around, my little sister is hugging him.

"Cecily—" I scream her name, but really I am looking at Gray, eyes boring into his. I am begging him not to hurt her. He can, and not even blink. She could be like any of his targets on those pieces of paper; only she is not. I bend and retrieve the knife in my boot and hold it up, as sure a promise as any. But Gray sits there perfectly still, as if she is the one hurting him with her hug. Before this he did not look eighteen, he looked forty-five. Now he is young again, younger even than me, and he gives me a pleading look. *Get her off me.*

He is afraid of her, I think afterward as we hurry home. Maybe she reminds him of Edith. Maybe he, too, cannot understand why she offers up hugs to strangers and says things like "I'm really sorry about your sister." Is it possible the little boy from the cottages who risked his life for broken animals is not gone? When we were leaving, Gray gave me a look, as if he knew what I was thinking. It was a worried look. It said: "Don't you dare."

I bring Cecily again. The next time we come he has shaved, his brown eyes are not nearly as dark. The apartment is cleaner. He doesn't say much, but he sits with her. He answers her questions in all the infuriating ways that make Cecily ask why. Why this, why that, forever why, and she forgets all about the world outside. Visiting his apartment becomes her favorite thing to do. Today, when we are leaving, Gray frowns at the ground. "Do you want to eat here?" he says gruffly. "And then maybe I'll just walk behind you. To make sure you get home safe."

"Okay," Cecily says, and sits with him. I am an afterthought. "We can, can't we, Lira?"

I look at him. *I knew it*, I think. I knew there was something about Cecily. Everyone falls under her spell somehow within just moments of meeting her. I stare at the two of them for days that become weeks. In the end Cecily, not I, saves his life.

"I'm sorry for what I said," he says, over burned toast one afternoon when Cecily is fast asleep on the couch. "I don't think you had anything to do with Edith."

I squint at him. "I'm not sorry for the gun business if that's what you're waiting for." He smiles, but I wait because this is not really the conversation we should be having. We have not visited the flower shop in weeks. We are not doing our jobs. And if the world were not so chaotic right now, we both would be dead.

"It's time, you know," Gray says as quietly as he can. "They'll want us out there slaughtering them soon. That's our job now. That's what we came here for. The big finale is about to happen."

"Yes," I say, but I look down at my hands. "I'm—I'm planning on getting out there. Soon."

"Me, too," he says. He drinks from his mug.

I hesitate before speaking again. "They've made a terrible mistake, haven't they?" I ask, not looking up. "They've given us a chance to think for ourselves all this time. What if what we're thinking isn't what they're thinking? What if they haven't created what they think they have?"

Gray says nothing. We sit in silence. I am afraid that he knows something more and he's just not saying it. "You should sleep," he says eventually. "There's a bed in there, I swear it's clean, and you should sleep because it's obvious you barely do. You'd have to trust me, though. You'd have to believe that I'm not going to hurt you or Cecily."

"I don't believe that," I say automatically.

Even though we have been coming here for two weeks now.

He holds out his hands. "Then handcuff me to the table or the sink or something, but sleep." He frowns. "You're not the only one who owes Edith something."

I can feel the coldness in my eyes. Can hear it creep into my voice when I stand. "If you hurt her, I will kill you," I tell him. "I swear it on any and everything worth swearing on."

"I won't hurt her, Lira," he says simply. "I won't hurt you, either."

I untie the laces of my boots but don't take them off.

"You know," Gray says, "that night at the cottages. You weren't the only one who went to the river. Did you think we would let you go off by yourself in the dark like that? All four of us watched what Madame did to Solomon that night."

"And yet you guys wanted to stay friends. I don't understand that. Why? Why are we still friends?"

He shrugs. "When we made that promise to be friends, we thought we were going to die. And of everyone there, we chose one another. That meant something."

"Temporarily," I say.

"Maybe." He drums his fingers on the table. "But, Lira, it's been ten years, and it still matters to me whether you're alive or not. It matters whether someone is going to hurt you. You are still my friend. You were Edith's friend, too. When we made that promise, it wasn't the kind of promise that normal people make. We decided on one another, and that was that. For life."

"I'm not sure I believe in friendships anymore," I say. "Short-term alliances, maybe."

He nods. I clench my fist.

I feel like a child trying to explain my stupid point of view to a grown-up who knows better. "If you hold your bleeding hand out in the water, a shark will come," I say. "It is a proven fact. That applies here. It is how we stay alive, how any world survives. If you put out your hand, someone is almost guaranteed to cut it off."

"I see. What about the person who might clean your wounds and give you a bandage? Isn't that person worth meeting?"

"Show me one good person who lives, who does it by staying good." He's silent, and I take this as my proof. "See? Altruism never wins. And I don't want to die, Gray. I have no idea what I want to be alive for, but I don't want to die today or tomorrow, not when I can live."

I leave him sitting there and curl up next to Cecily on the couch. It is many minutes later, just as I am falling asleep, when I think I hear him say, "I forgot you were from that orphanage in Paris where they groomed children just for this. You're not like the rest of us. You've been a cottage girl all your life." And I almost can't forgive him for saying it out loud. I hate the feeling of pity on my skin. I hate the sound and smell of it and the feel of the blanket that soon covers me and Cecily. But I sleep anyway. For the first time Cecily and I don't go home. I even forget to wake up more than once before morning.

The one time I do wake, Gray is standing at the sink, looking down at nothing. He doesn't hear any of my questions. He doesn't respond to any of the things I say. A single slippery strand of moonlight pushes past a crack into the room. I quietly step out of my boots for the first time since I've been coming here. I pad toward him, and the floor is cool, strange underneath my feet. "Is everything okay?" I ask when I'm close enough. Again, he doesn't respond.

So I do what Cecily would.

I wrap my arms around him. It is so strange and awkward to stand behind a boy in the dark and hug him. He startles at first, but then he relaxes. His bunched muscles loosen up under my arms. "I'm not exactly sure what this is," he says, and I can hear his smile. "Thank you."

"Yes. Well." I can't think of anything else to say. I might be blushing. I feel stupid. I drop my hands.

I am not a very good person, but does that mean that there isn't any good in me? I hope not.

I say, "You're welcome."

I go back to bed.

CHAPTER 42

"Is Gray our friend?" Cecily whispers, nudging me. I open my eyes and find the sun barely risen, the living room still half dark. We have spent the last four days in Gray's apartment. We haven't talked about going back to our place, and I don't know when we will. Cecily is sitting on the couch by my head, balancing a bowl of cereal on her lap. The handle of a wooden spoon pokes out of her mouth. "Is Gray our friend?" she asks again. "And how come he's our friend? How do we know him?"

I blink at her, trying to understand what she is talking

about, and more important, why we're talking about it. "It's barely six o'clock," I croak. "Did you have a bad dream again?"

She shakes her head. "I just want to know some things." When I say nothing, she tries again. "Where do you know him from?"

My brain fumbles, the wheels not turning quite right. "I don't know him from anywhere," I whisper. "I just—"

She rolls her eyes. "Right. How *else* do you know him?" She holds up her hand before I can answer and glares at me. "Don't tell me I'm asking too many questions."

So I don't.

I tell her Edith was his sister. After our first meeting at the café, I met her again in line at the pharmacy when I was buying Gigi's medicine. She was nice, and we became friends. The lies roll easily off my tongue. At the end I don't know whether Cecily buys it, but she turns back to her cereal. I turn back to my pillow, but the scent of shampoo perfumes the air. I turn to squint at her. "You bathed yourself?"

She shrugs. "It's scissors day," she says, and when I don't buy it, she bends in demonstration, so her hair is actually dipping into her cereal bowl.

She reaches underneath the couch, pulls out a pair of metal scissors and waves them at me.

"Okay," I say. I snuggle into the couch even more, though. "But give me one more hour."

An image of Cecily alone with a pair of scissors suddenly flashes across my mind. I reach out and grab the scissors from her before she can react. I put them under my pillow and close my eyes again.

"Older people"—she sighs, and I imagine her shaking her head—"are so stupid." Somehow I think what she really means to say is: "You're always lying to me. I don't believe you about Gray and Edith." Behind my eyelids, I imagine I get her killed by telling her about the cottages.

CHAPTER 43

"He shouldn't be alone," Gray says when I tell him about Jack. "It's better if we're all together, especially now. I'll go and bring him here." But he is gone for hours. In that time I do everything I can think of, twice. I clean (and break a plate). I cook (and burn two pots). I cut Cecily's hair perfectly with the scissors but then take to my own hair as if I were using shears. I tell myself nothing is wrong. I tell myself to stop pacing because it is making my sister afraid. At some point she turns on the radio and makes me twirl around the room with her. "It's our special dance," she says as I turn to find Gray entering the apartment, looking grim.

"You cut your hair," he says, shaking the snow from his coat.

I immediately feel self-conscious. I am surprised that it matters that he noticed. "Oh, yeah." I clench my hands at my sides to keep from touching it. "It grows too quickly."

"She cut mine, too," Cecily says, shaking her head. "And now I look like a boy."

"You look—" He pretends to search for just the right word, and then he says, "*Insanely* beautiful. I almost didn't recognize you." He lets her tackle him, but he turns back to look at me. "That's my sister's dress?"

My heart sinks. "I was doing the laundry. So. But I can take it off if you want."

"No, it's . . ." He shrugs. "I forgot I brought her boxes here, that's all. You can have them."

I look past him. "Gray, where is Jack?"

He hesitates, looks at Cecily. "I couldn't find him," he says. "I found this, though." He hands me a large envelope, but that's not what interests me. Gray's hands are muddy. I stare at them.

"Hey, Ceilie," he says. "I need to talk to Lira about something for a second."

"You can say it in front of me," she says, looking at me. "Right, Lira?"

I shake my head. "Oh," she says. She goes into his room but doesn't close the door. Gray steps closer. He whispers in my ear so Cecily won't hear, and then he covers my mouth to muffle my scream. I don't know how he knew I would scream when I didn't. I try to leave, reaching for the door.

"I have to go," I keep saying.

"There's nowhere to go, Lira," Gray tells me. "There's nowhere to go. It's done. It's over."

Jack is dead.

I wasn't there.

I couldn't do this one thing for him, this one thing he asked me for.

Later, when the tears have stopped, I am surprised to find that it is dark and that Gray is still sitting on the ground with me. Cecily is snoring softly on the couch next to us. The moon past the shades turns everything in the room silvery. "It doesn't matter to me that he's gone," I say.

"Stop it," he says.

"I don't care. Why should I care?"

"Lira—"

"Nothing works out the way we plan it." My voice breaks. "What are we supposed to do with that?"

"People die. We can't really change that."

I stand, walk away from him. "Is that supposed to make it okay?"

"Never," he says, standing, too.

I am so tired I feel like I am relearning how to walk. My bones creak; my knees clang against each other. Gray follows me around the room, and eventually I realize that somehow, at some point along the way, I started holding his hand. His hand is firm, warm in mine. Friends hold hands all the time. I tell myself this. But when our eyes meet in the dark, I know something is wrong. We both stop, and I am suddenly more terrified than I have ever been in my life. But I am not afraid of Gray. He is only Edith's brother. He is only a boy from the cottages. He is only my friend.

I am afraid of myself.

I snatch my hand out of his as if it were on fire. I wrap my arms around myself. "I don't know why I did that." My voice comes out a croak.

Gray says nothing, doesn't accept my apology. He stares at me for a long moment, and then he steps back. He turns around and goes to his room, the door clicking softly behind him.

I stand there.

I feel young. I feel as if something I don't fully understand is happening. Or has happened already.

CHAPTER 44

I keep imagining Jack's funeral. The things I might have said, the poetry I might have read as the coffin was lowered into the ground. I don't ask Gray for any of the details about what he found, how he found it or even how long it was there. Jack is gone. I will never see him again. I will never hear his stories or criticize the things he wears.

Sometimes I tell myself that this is okay. Other times I can't hear what I am telling myself.

His book sits inside the envelope, his note crumpled. "All this is missing are your illustrations," he wrote. "I'm sorry I'm not brave enough to wait for you, Lira." The words smudged, as if he'd been crying. And perhaps he held a gun in his other hand.

This, too, is okay, I tell myself, *at least as close as can be.*

But not really. Not at all.

Outside, spring has come, but you would not know it. Nobody remembers to wear color or extra-bright lipstick anymore. No one wears flowers in their hair, and very few people laugh. Despite the violence, which the police try desperately to contain, this city is not yet as bad as others. The bombs have not come here yet. The murders are not nearly as many as in Tokyo, Moscow, Abuja, New York. On the radio, we hear about a city where hundreds of citizens go door to door and kill anyone they find the least bit suspicious. The innocent and guilty alike, slaughtered. Paranoia has overcome the world. Our city is barricaded, a fence that also encloses some of the closest surrounding towns. No one can leave, and no one can enter. Gray and I console ourselves with the fact that the sleeper war hasn't actually started yet. That we have not yet been called to do what we were trained for. But we will be soon. The clock is ticking.

Right now all we have to worry about is staying hidden. It's too risky for any sleeper to complete any more missions.

So it's not so bad that we haven't been to the flower shop in a while. All we have to do is avoid the crazy citizens marching around with their knives and their rifles. Gray and I might be safe. We can pretend to be as normal as they want us to be. In fact, I suspect that some of the very people pretending to be citizens, marching door to door, are sleepers themselves. That is the best way to win. The question is: Are we willing to stay here and chance that? Should we find a place to hide and wait until we are called? Should we find a place to hide even *after* we're called?

We need more time.

I borrow Cecily's headphones and listen to the reports for hours. After I am done, Gray takes over. He drums his fingers on the table so Cecily will think he is listening to music. We are worried without letting it show on our faces. "We have a frequency in our wrists," Gray tells me. "I can't turn them off completely. It's impossible to take them out." He holds up his left hand. "They own us with this."

"How much time do you think we have?"

He shakes his head, and I lower mine.

The mob inches closer and closer to our side of the city every day. We have a few weeks left if we're lucky, but then this place will be overrun. Even the police officers with their riot gear cannot prevent it. We can hear them on the streets, the officers and the angry crowds, and it doesn't sound as if the officers are winning.

One morning I wake up to a dull pain in my wrist. I want to think nothing of it, but it is the same hand as my tracker. I hold it under the tap and run the cold water until the pain goes away. Just a few minutes later I catch Gray rubbing his own wrist. We lock eyes and quickly drop our hands.

The signal has finally been sent. Our handlers are calling us.

We are supposed to report to the flower shop. A lot of others probably already have and are hiding, getting ready to strike.

When I look in the mirror, I am surprised to find that I am older than the girl I was in the cottages. Surprised that I am not as eager to grab my gun and my knife as I once was. I am not nearly as focused. I am still me, and I want to live, but my head is spinning now. It is making it *difficult* to live.

Edith's dresses are loose on me; I make sure never to wear her prettiest ones. I wear only the ones that look the oldest and most ragged; seeming beautiful still doesn't matter to me. Each time I wear a dress I imagine the look of horror Gigi would give me, and I miss her, and that's what the dresses start to mean to me. They make me think of everyone—

Edith, Jack, Da, Gigi, the original Lirael—all at once.

Gray goes out and brings back books. For Cecily, the colorful kind. For me, anything that's on the lists of books to read before you die. I could paint, but supplies are expensive, and I am afraid of what would show up on my canvas. I'd rather send my mind away to a different world, and Gray understands this. There are so many books; I know I won't read them all before I die. But I sit in the bathtub and read as much as I can, and this is how time passes. Sometimes I find Gray sitting in a corner of the apartment, tinkering with watches like the one Edith gave me. "I didn't know you made them," I say.

"I started a few months after I became a Safe," he confesses. "I hated how easy it was for them to control us. The one you have is going to die soon."

I nod.

We are talking around it. The pain in our wrists.

I am about to go back to the bath when something catches my eye. I turn around again. Crouch in front of Gray. "Your hands are shaking," I say, grabbing his hand and holding on to it until he stops working.

He nods without looking up. "I don't have any pills left. I'm taking care of it. I'm going to pay a guy to make more, but first he has to figure out what exactly they've put in it. He'll make you some, too." He didn't tell me because he knew what I would do. I first glare at him, then count the number of pills I have left, plus the ones among Edith's things. I divide them evenly between us. Enough now to last nineteen days for both of us.

"It'll be terribly inconvenient if . . . you know . . . ," I say, "something happens to any of us right now."

"Right," he says, and I can feel his eyes on my back as I walk away. Back to the bathroom, where Cecily sits also in the bathtub. I round the corner, but then I poke my head out again.

"Right," I echo firmly, Madame style, but with an exaggerated accent.

His lips twitch.

These moments are rare. There is absolutely nothing to smile about, but we smile anyway.

I tell myself this is all a game.

At any moment it will end, just as quickly as it started. Like the afternoon I first realize that there is a girl in this world who must find Gray attractive. Several, in fact, and I cannot stop thinking about that. Who she is. What she looks like. Why she might like him. His good looks perhaps, his kindness, his one-sided smiles as much as his sadness, the fact that she can understand him. Understand where he is coming from and where he is going. He is young and old at exactly the same time, strong and vulnerable, too, a contradiction.

I am supposed to be playing hide-and-seek with Cecily, and the closet in Gray's room is our most obvious spot, but I'm so distracted that I don't care. I sit there, rubbing my aching wrist.

When Gray enters the room, I startle. He sits on the edge of the bed, takes off his boots.

"What's wrong?" he asks, frowning at me.

I realize I am sitting inside his closet in the dark. I am sitting there, thinking about him. I stand, shaking my head, and climb out. "Cecily and I," I say, pretending my face isn't hot, "are playing . . . hide-and-seek." As if he can't hear her counting down from fifty.

I go out to the living room. He stays in his room for a while before he comes out, and by then our hide-and-seek game is over.

I know all about this feeling. This new type of loneliness that creeps in the older we get. Suddenly the couch is smaller than it used to be, and I can feel Gray right next to me when Cecily stands. I jump up like the couch is on fire, and Gray actually looks stung. I don't know what to say. He and Cecily both watch me like I'm crazy. I pick up my coat. "I have things to do," I say, and pull on a hat. "I'll be back soon."

But I only sit at the top of the staircase of our building like an idiot. I sit there and close my eyes, and I try to remember *things*. All those *things*. The things that a girl tells herself so she doesn't start to notice eyes in a different way and wish that laughter were directed at her. I imagine Edith shaking her head at me. Her brother should not be part of my game. There should be another boy, and he should be easy to toy with, and it is *his* hands and *his* eyes and *his* silences I should notice. I sit there for an hour. Only afterward do I realize that Gray could see me. His stupid cameras watch everything. He could see me the whole time, sitting there. When I come back to the apartment, I read with Cecily and catch him watching me strangely. I look down, play with my watch.

We say nothing to each other.

I fall asleep, I think, but when I wake up, the light in Gray's room is on. I walk toward it before I realize what I am doing, and even after that. I don't knock. Gray is lying on his back on his bed. I tell myself that I notice the book he is reading first, before I notice that he isn't wearing a shirt. He sits up but doesn't say anything. Neither do I. I just turn off the light and stand there in the dark.

He finds me. He finds me in the dark and pushes my hair gently from my face. I pull him toward the closet. Maybe if something happens in the darkest corner of a room, where no one and nothing can see, it doesn't happen at all. I shut the wooden door, and we stand among the shirts and coats. Not moving, barely breathing. *Still*, the voice in my head chastens. *Still. You are doing something really, really bad, Lira. You are playing the worst game it is possible to play.*

I take his hand.

I cannot tell what he is thinking in the dark. And then he surprises me by hugging me. His chest is warm against mine, and I close my eyes. I hug him back. *This is enough*, I tell myself. *The game can end just like this.* But then he is pushing my hair from my face again and leaning down. His breath tickles my ear. "I want to kiss you out there in the light, Lira."

I flinch. I try to pull away, but I can't. "Why?" I ask.

"Because the world won't end. Because I want to see your eyes when I do. I know you, and tomorrow you're going to tell me to forget whatever is about to happen, and that's not going to work for me."

I say, "I was going to tell you that now."

Neither of us laughs.

He guides me out of the closet to the window without

ever letting me out of the hug. I can't breathe, but maybe that's the way it's supposed to be. I catch the reflection of the moon in his eyes as he lowers his face to mine. He kisses me with warm lips, the kind that is afraid of spooking a frightened deer, and holds his breath. When I don't run, when I lean closer, press my lips harder against his, he kisses me again as though he has been imagining this moment, this mistake, for much longer than I have.

CHAPTER 45

The sun rises somehow, and we have fallen asleep sitting upright underneath the window. My lips are swollen; my mind is numb. Gray kisses my hands and tells me that I am beautiful. His eyes are dark, intense, as if this means something wonderful to him when he says it. I kiss his eyelids and ears and run my fingers through his hair, over his chest, down his back. There are many scars with many stories and many stories with invisible scars, but Cecily will wake up soon. I smile my unnatural smile when he pulls me onto his lap, and I wrap my body around his. We have lost our clothes. We have lost our minds.

"When it's time to stop feeling this way," I whisper against his lips, trying desperately to rediscover the ground beneath me, "we have to stop. We'll know when and how to stop it."

"Okay," he says softly, not looking at me.

I don't meet his eyes either.

In the end I don't know which lies are the worst: the ones we tell ourselves in the dark or the ones we pretend to agree to.

The truth is that this morning my tracker wrist hurts worse than it did yesterday. In a different way than it ever has. The most searing pain I have ever felt, and my arm is heavy. Gray flinches when I touch his wrist. But we still don't acknowledge what it means: that we have to go. We have to go; it is not a choice.

I make breakfast with Cecily afterward. She brushes my hair. She sings me a song. I make her laugh at least twice, and then, when she isn't looking, Gray corners me in the kitchen with his lips. We kiss quietly, desperately, holding hands. "We'll wait as long as we can," he says against the back of my neck. I nod.

But it's time.

It's *time*.

CHAPTER 46

It is easier to imagine that they are not us. The boy and the girl at the end. For the girl's part, she'd always thought that in the end she would let her sister go. But instead all three of them fill a single trash bag with things from the apartment. The boy shrugs into a coat and leaves to find a truck that can't be linked to him. When he returns, the girl and Cecily are waiting by the door, packed, dressed. Not a single word is uttered. Not a single sound is made. The boy and girl do not look at each other, and even Cecily is smart enough not to ask questions. Today is different from every other day. Somehow she understands this as she crouches in the backseat of the car with her sister.

They have decided to run away from this war. To escape the city and find a safe place where all three of them can hide. They are not sure where exactly, but they know they have a better chance of surviving outside the city. And if they cannot save themselves, then they will find a way to save Cecily. That is the plan.

Barricades seal off every single corner of the city, but they drive to the weakest one, an electric fence protected by twenty guards with guns. They squat in an abandoned motel across the street for nearly a week, waiting and hoping for any kind of opportunity. But each day passes, and there is none. Not for the girl and boy. Not even for Cecily. This is the worst part. At the very least they have to get her to a safe place.

And now what?

"What's wrong, Lira?" Cecily whispers.

I open my eyes, and she's staring at me. I'm clutching my arm. Small beads of sweat dot my face. I am tired and dirty; my skin is burning up. I don't look at her. I focus on the small room we're hiding in, the broken glass and clothes strewn on the floors that do not belong to us. There are other people hiding all over this building, too.

"I'm fine," I tell Cecily in a shaky voice, but in that exact moment my head spins. We have been holed up in this room for five days now. Gray sits in his own corner with his back turned to us. It's bad enough for Cecily to see my face grimace with pain. Worse if she sees him, too, and harder to explain. She has to believe that at least one of us is strong. She has to believe that it is him.

The pain in my wrist radiates through my whole arm.

I get up and go to Gray. "Okay," I whisper. "Okay, the other plan. We hide her." And with those simple words it is over for the girl and the boy. We accept it. The impossible idea of freedom put out of our minds for good.

Does it mean anything that we tried?

It was stupid to try, wasn't it?

CHAPTER 47

I find Aunt Imogen hiding in the old apartment.

I am packing everything that matters—clothes mostly, our remaining cans of food—emptying the medicine cabinet, when I sense someone behind me. I am not usually so careless, and as I turn, my fist connects with a jaw. Aunt Imogen crumples to the floor. For a moment I do not recognize her. She is dirty; her hair is wild; her clothes are covered in dried blood. Her blunt butter knife clatters to the floor between us. I must look different to her, too. A hat hides my hair; a torn jacket covers my dress. The moment she recognizes me, my aunt bursts into tears. "I thought you were dead. Have you seen what is happening? I thought— Oh, God. Oh, God, Lira, where is Cecily?" Her voice becomes hysterical. "Where is Cecily?"

I step forward and place a grimy hand over her mouth, beg her to be quiet, but it doesn't help. Outside, someone screams, something smashes. Chaos spreads like wildfire. We waited too long. I should not have come back here. Gray told me so.

But I argued with him.

"I have all the supplies we need there," I said. "Food, bandages, medicine. If we can't go to the shops anymore, then we have to go back."

All these supplies are for Cecily. For wherever we hide her.

"I should never have left," Aunt Imogen is saying now, over and over. "You were all I had. I'm so—I shouldn't have . . ." Her words trail into incoherence. I catch the word *family*, but I don't know why blood means that she has to care about me when she has never even known me. I am not the one she has let down. Her niece is: the one who isn't here anymore because of me.

I let her hug me. I stand there stiffly until she is finished. Until she sees the lack of emotion on my face and finally lets go of me. Her crying stops abruptly; her hand flies to her mouth. I have misjudged her. She understands right then what I am. She scans the floor for her butter knife. I kick it out of the way and hold up my hands. "It's okay," I tell her calmly. "It's okay. Really."

"No, it's not." There is a hollowness in her voice. "No, it's not." Her whole body sags, but she forces her eyes to hold mine, and they are strong eyes. This is the first time I have truly noticed them. "Is she dead?" she asks finally. "Is my niece dead?"

It reminds me of the girl. It reminds me of Da. Of Gigi, as if they all are standing here right now, asking me, "Is she dead? Did you kill her? How could you? How could you? How could you?"

I breathe. I breathe again.

Seeing Aunt Imogen changes everything. The illusion of the three of us—me, Cecily, and Gray—that has been building up inside my head quietly deflates, and I feel relieved somehow. This is how it should be. How it should have always been.

I reach for the bag of things I have packed just as the door opens. My eyes focus on her shoulder. "We can save your lives," I say. I stuff the bags with more things. "Yours and Cecily's, but you need to listen. You need to do exactly what we tell you. Do you understand what I am saying?"

"We? Who is we?" she asks. And then she turns around. She looks relieved to see Cecily at first. Then she notices Cecily is holding Gray's hand, and her teeth clench. It is black and white for her. A monster and an innocent. Her eyes flicker to the floor, and I know she's gauging whether she can reach her butter knife first. She doesn't understand how easy she is for two sleepers to kill. If either of us had wanted her dead, she would be dead already.

"Is there anything you want from your room?" Gray asks Cecily. He doesn't wait for her answer. He just scoops her up and takes her there. Aunt Imogen starts to follow them, but then her eyes jerk back my way. I don't know who is more surprised: I with the gun in my hand or she. She looks at me in the worst way possible. There is power in that look, more than she knows, but I hold my gun steady. I keep my voice calm. "There is an old well at the orchard that Da turned into a storage room. It has—"

"I know what it has," she snaps. "I grew up there."

I nod. I search my pockets until I find the keys of the car we stole. "It's parked behind this building. Gray was going to take her there," I say. "That was—we couldn't think of a better plan." I give her the keys, the bag, the gun. "You have to go fast and you have to go now. Don't stop for anyone, no matter who they look like, no matter what they say, no matter how young or old they are. Just keep driving until you reach the trees."

I am not afraid of the look in her eyes when she weighs the gun in her hand. I say, "You need to keep it together for her, no matter what happens next. No matter what you see. You have to protect Cecily—can you do that?"

She pauses. After a moment she puts the gun inside her bag.

Gray and Cecily come out of the room. Cecily is holding an old teddy bear she's had since she was little, and she's crying. I don't know what she heard. I don't have time to ask. "You have to go with Aunt Imogen," I say, and force a smile as our aunt pushes past me toward her. Her aunt. Hers, not ours. When did I stop making distinctions like that inside my head?

Cecily cries harder. Her contorted face is focused on me. "You're leaving me, aren't you?" she asks, and then, before I can say anything, she is hugging me. Her tears stain right through my dress. I pat her hair, her shoulder, her arm. I do everything as robotically as I can manage. It is easier to forget a person who did not want you like you wanted her. Who did not love you like you loved her. Who did not cry a single tear to match what you shed for her, or so I tell myself. I push her away after she has hugged me only a moment.

Cecily stares at me. She can see right through my facade. A part of me even imagines that she might know what I am.

I can't bring myself to ask, especially when she starts to sob again. "I'm scared, Lira."

I press my lips to her ear. "Close your eyes and pretend you're somewhere else, okay?" I whisper. "Remember what it feels like to be a bird? Remember what it feels like to fly away?"

She wipes her eyes and nods, as if something between us is now settled. She hugs Gray and kisses his cheek. She is calm as she takes Aunt Imogen's hand. She looks back only once as they walk out the door. "You'll come back to the trees one day," she says. "There's Gigi's magic in the trees. And I've already asked it to bring you back." As surely as the sun sets and the world spins, Cecily believes this.

I watch her go with a smile on my face that disappears the moment she does.

I am a good liar.

Secretly I was done. I gave her up the moment Aunt Imogen turned up. I am not Edith. I have never once imagined having to look after anyone, have never wanted it. The same empty look clouds Gray's eyes. A bottomless sky that goes on forever. I do not even feel sad about losing that part of him. You have to let go of the stones if you don't want to drown. You must always know who you are; I tell myself I do.

And yet Gray and I don't report to our handlers for a week. We will be questioned and possibly punished for it. Yet we stay in his apartment without talking about why. He kisses me, and I kiss him back, and we hold each other and press our skins together. We confuse ourselves like this. We destroy ourselves like this.

Yet I don't ask him to let go. The boy who drowns me. I don't let him go.

I want Cecily to be right. That there *is* magic. For the first time in my life I want to believe in something better. I am giving myself permission to want that. Because the girl who turns off her watch one week later, who walks toward the flower shop where the rest of her team is already mobilized, that girl, and what she is capable of, and what she is incapable of, frightens me. She shrugs into her skintight fighting suit without asking any questions. She takes the safety off her gun without breathing.

Jack is my excuse. I feel sick inside as I tell them that I had to stay with him until he died. That I had to bury him. That it was a mission I had to see through to the end. This is not the best excuse, but since Jack died alone, there is no way of disproving it. I also tell them that I killed Cecily and Aunt Imogen. And even though I should have reported in immediately, staying with Jack implies that it is our people who matter to me. So after only an hour of interrogation they let me go with nothing more than a warning that they will be watching me.

But Gray doesn't have a good explanation for why he did not report in. His sister is dead, but the war is more important. It takes precedence over his mourning her.

They spend hours questioning him. Then they use their lie detector tests to ask him the same questions all over again. Finally they decide to punish him with a demotion. He has been such a good sleeper so far that he could easily be a leader, but when I see him again, he doesn't have the same badge I have on my chest. "It's better this way," he says with a shrug. "I'd rather not be the one giving the orders."

Before I can respond, I spot Julia walking in our direction. My body goes cold. Gray has his back to her. He is still telling me about the questions they asked him. Julia has her long hair twisted into a bun on top of her head like Madame's. "Gray," I croak, but that's all I can manage before she is standing next to us.

"Hi," she says.

I force my breathing to stay even. It would be stupid to confront her, not just today but ever.

I look at Gray, and his jaw is clenched, his eyes have gone dark. Julia does not seem to notice. She is wearing the same leader badge on her uniform as I am. She smiles. "I have been looking for you all over. We should ask to be assigned to the same places. They might say yes."

I'm not sure which one of us she is talking to. I have not seen her in two years, and Gray has not seen her since the farmhouse was burned down. She is acting as though Edith had not even existed. As though it were only ever the three of us.

Gray says nothing, so I have to speak. "I have already been assigned my commanding officer," I say. I try to force some kind of enthusiasm into my voice, but it doesn't work. I look away. "I'm supposed to be reporting in now."

"Yeah, me, too," Julia says. She looks at Gray's chest and frowns. "Hey, where's your badge? You're supposed to have a badge, too, right?"

I tense up. Gray actually takes a small, almost imperceptible step forward and then back again. His knuckles are clenched so hard behind his back that they are white. "I'm gonna go," he tells me.

"Oh," Julia says, taken aback. I am almost impressed by how unperceptive she is. When she says, "Gray, what's wrong?" I actually begin to fear for her life. Is it possible that she is this stupid? Or did she think that she had done such a good job that no one would ever guess?

I start to speak for Gray. "Gray is—"

But he is louder. "Edith is dead." His voice is cold, empty.

Julia flinches, and her smile wavers but only for a moment. She takes a deep breath. "Yes, I heard the farmhouse burned down. How terrible." The only sign that she is affected is the slight flush in her cheeks.

Gray turns away from her. "I'll see you later," he tells me.

"Okay," I say.

"Gray, wait. I'll come with you," Julia says.

I stare after them. Mostly after Julia. Is she doing this to be cruel? Or does she genuinely think that if she acts like the farmhouse did not happen, then it didn't?

I report to my commanding officer, a woman who gives me a bag filled with knives and guns and tells me to come back in the morning.

The flower shop is our headquarters, but it's the other abandoned buildings around it that are filled with sleepers, some of them already getting ready for bed. While everyone in my team eats and talks and goes to sleep, excited for the new day to come, I am not hungry, have nothing to say, and cannot sleep. So I am walking up and down the street around the flower shop, kicking at pebbles in the dark when Gray finds me. "Are you okay?" I ask him. What I want to know is what has happened to Julia. Whether she is still alive, whether we need to be worried.

"I don't know if I can work with her," he says, stuffing his hands inside his pockets. "I don't know if I can even stay in the same room as her."

I have just one plea. "Please don't do anything stupid, Gray," I say. And I cannot tell in the dark whether his nod means yes or no. We say good night, and I watch him walk away with his head down. I want to go after him. I want to wrap my arms around him like I did that first night in the apartment. But I can't.

When I get to the cots set up inside one of the empty buildings, I find that Julia has reserved one for me. She waves me over, and I lie down next to her, trying to keep my breathing even the entire time. I lie down next to Julia, close my eyes, and feign sleep, but when everything is dark and quiet, I sit back up. I suddenly don't know if I can do it anymore. I made Gray promise he wouldn't do anything foolish.

But I can kill her. I can give Gray and Edith and all the others at the farmhouse their revenge. No one would know it was me. I can be so quick about it that Julia would not even have time to open her eyes.

What would that make me?

For hours I sit there, staring at her, until I am so tired that I have to lie back down. But I barely get any sleep. I think of Cecily and Aunt Imogen and how people like them would never be alive right now if they'd been with someone more like Julia. Someone less like me.

When morning comes somehow, there is no blood on my hands. I pack my things and leave before Julia opens her eyes.

"Here is your list," my commanding officer tells me. They send me and several others back to the countryside. To my neighbors. Knock on the door. Smile and say hello, and then shoot.

They send me to Mathieu. He peers out at me from between the curtains and then rushes to open the door without thinking. Without wondering why I am wearing this uniform. "Where's Cecily?" he asks, looking past me. Expecting her and her mean looks, her bossy words, to flounce out of nowhere. Before I can even answer, before I can warn him about the other sleeper standing next to me with his gun, Mathieu is dead.

Then we enter his house and kill his parents, too. His

other siblings. People who do a double take when they see me and whisper, "Lirael?" Just before they die.

Later, in the bathroom, when I am covered in blood and I cry, I still see through my tears like I am supposed to. I still remember whom I am fighting for. They have trained me well. There is a softer part of me, of course, that remembers whom I am fighting against. That remembers that these people did nothing wrong. This world rightfully belongs to them, not us. But I do what I am supposed to. I sometimes have to whisper to myself in the mornings, as I get dressed, "Don't you dare fall apart now. Don't you dare." And sometimes, when we are receiving fresh orders at the flower shop, I stand close enough to Gray so our hands brush without anyone seeing, and that little bit of heat is almost enough.

Every moment of our lives is a domino piece. One slight action brings about a greater one. At first the world falls quietly. We move in the night like shadows, through houses and among people who once thought we were their friends. A waitress at a café. A teacher. A boyfriend. Sleepers do all the work. The people we bring from our Earth unpack their bags and move into the houses only after we've declared a town safe. We move on. As we travel, we sleep wherever we find room, in empty houses and on garage floors, and we raid whatever cupboards and fridges we come across. At the end of the day it is not the fact that we are at war that we remember but the smaller moments. The blood that won't wash from a stained shirt. The screams that keep us awake at night: You think they belong to the sleeper on the floor next to you, and then you think it is only a memory, only to find that it is you. You are screaming, but can anyone else hear?

For months and months and months.

If there are two versions of one person, which one deserves to live? Which one deserves to die?

Gray and I found two people who mattered. We saved them. Is that enough?

I don't see Cecily or Aunt Imogen anywhere as we replace their world with ours, person by person. I tell myself they made it to the well.

Somehow that has to be enough.

My mind rewinds to our last night in the apartment, when I whisper these words to Gray in the dark: "Did I make it easier for you?" He doesn't ask what I am talking about. He knows I am asking about what happened after he killed my alternate three years ago. After he completed my assignment for me. All the people he's had to kill since. Did killing a fourteen-year-old girl who meant nothing to him, who wasn't even his responsibility, make it easy to kill all the people he's had to after that?

He shakes his head.

He asks: "Did I make it harder for you?"

I shake my own head, but we both know that's a lie. I am suddenly so tired of all these lies. I want there to be only truths between us. I want to tear down anything else that is contrary, so I take a deep breath. "I lied," I say. "My grandfather was not a fighter." The horrible words echo in the moonlit bedroom, and my eyes blink at nothingness, at someplace beyond here where the memories float. "He did not kill his alternate. I did."

I look at Gray, frightened to have said the words out loud, but he only leans in and kisses me.

"When I got there and they were fighting," I say, "I knew the smart thing to do was stand to the side and wait. I could see that he had his hands around Da's neck. I even thought it would be better if Da was dead. But then I—I . . ." My voice trails off for a moment. "But it was too late. By the time I got back to Da, he'd lost too much blood. He was just—he was looking at me with these eyes, and then I realized that he wasn't looking at me at all, that he was dead."

"You regret it?"

I swallow.

I close my eyes.

In the end it is Lirael, the real Lirael, I consider brave. She was thirteen when she got her tattoo. It was the same week her father died of a heart attack, and she convinced some dirty-looking boy from the floor below their apartment to sneak her into his father's tattoo shop. To mark her skin before her grandparents came to collect her and her sister the next day. She lived in the city then. She'd seen the words graffitied on a wall somewhere, saying, "Let me be weak and know my flaws. Let me love and be afraid. Let me be foolish and sad, so that I can say that I was strong. I was beautiful. I was a fighter. I was fearless."

I watched her grit her teeth on the screen in the basement of the cottages. The boy called her an idiot, but he had a look of respect in his eye as he worked. She was thirteen, but she didn't give him a choice. "You have to save whatever you know right now," Lirael told him when he asked why, "in case you lose it. My father used to say that." Her eyes filled with tears. She terrified me. We were too young to be able to know and say things like that. How could I possibly become her?

"One day," she said sadly when he'd finished, "I am going to forget everything I've written here. And then maybe I'll look in the mirror and remember."

She didn't, though. She didn't ever forget. At the moment when it counted the most, I was the one who forgot. She fought me like hell. She was the strong one.

On this last night at the apartment I am supposed to be reading a book. Charles Dickens's *Oliver Twist*, but the words haven't stuck. Right from page one, they haven't stuck. I sit cross-legged on Gray's bed, trying to figure out what is wrong. And I am not thinking about my grandfather and how I shook him afterward and how I begged him to please, please, oh, God, please, open his eyes. As if begging can make a person undie. But we are only part of a cycle. I know that now.

Why do we ever think we can be infinite?

"If I can get us out of here, will you come with me?" Gray whispers. I open my eyes again. He's not looking at me, I'm not looking at him, but I hear the words anyway. The sudden desperation in them, as if he knows something I have not yet understood. "If I can find a place where no one will bother us ever again. Will you come with me?"

I don't answer. I look away.

But we both know.

We have broken our rule.

We have broken every rule.

CHAPTER 48

The first time I catch a sleeper girl crying in the bathroom of the diner we have just taken over, she hurries away ashamed, and I think nothing of it. Another time a sleeper boy misses a simple shot and almost gets us all killed. "What the hell?" I ask, but when he turns around, I see that his hands are shaking violently and his nose is bleeding.

Then it happens again, with another sleeper.

And again.

More and more of us falling apart. More and more and more.

By the time I understand what is happening, we have been rewriting the world for over four months. My commanding officer has put me in charge of a small town named Bayard, an hour away from Paris. She assigns fifteen younger sleepers to me, and together we form a team. For weeks we sweep through Bayard and surrounding areas with our guns, making sure no one is still hiding. We set up camp in an old diner on the outskirts of the town.

We are getting ready for bed one night when the phone rings. It's my commanding officer. After I give her our status report, she says, "All sleepers are expected to return to the city this Friday for a celebratory dinner. Lagrange Hotel, five p.m."

She hangs up the phone without waiting for my response.

I pass the message on to the others. "Great," one of them mutters underneath her breath. We all dread Friday, but it comes anyway. A bus arrives and takes my team ahead of me. I have been provided with my own car; one of the perks of being a leader. I leave, reluctantly, a few minutes after their bus disappears down the road.

We all have heard about these celebratory dinners. They are held in honor of the war's success. In honor of us.

The thought does not make me drive any faster.

I am fiddling with the radio when it happens. One minute

I feel perfectly fine, and then the next a steady flow of blood streams from my nose. The bus has disappeared, far ahead of me. I stop the car and climb out. I pinch my nose. When the bleeding doesn't end, I lie on the grass by the side of the road and wait, staring up at the blackbirds in the sky.

It starts to rain.

I have learned to love the rain. Sometimes I hold my head underwater in the bath and stare up at the ceiling, which appears vague and fluttery like a dream. I have a new theory about tears, whether in the bathtub or in the rain. They don't count because you cannot tell whether you are truly crying. We are 70 percent water, and water comes and water goes, and at the end there is no difference. Those are not tears you see. Those are not stories or feelings or anger, red-hot anger, leaking out of me.

Our war has been too successful too quickly. There are too many sleepers and not enough for us to do; that is why we have the time for frivolous dinners. We should be out there, fighting, but instead we are shipped off to places like Bayard. And I have not seen Gray in more than two weeks. I have no idea where he is stationed. I have heard that some of the very best sleepers have been shipped off to other parts of the world, to help in places that have had lower success rates. The rest of us are of very little use. I am afraid to return to the city and discover that Gray is one of the ones who have been shipped off. And I am afraid that Julia is not.

I only get up again because the raindrops hit me hard, make me splutter. In the car I take another dose of my pills. I have never taken them twice in one day before, but then again, my nose has never bled before. Since the pills have kept me healthy so far, maybe they can fix whatever is wrong.

I am soaked and covered in mud when I finally reach the city.

Madame meets me at the door of the hotel, and I am so shocked to see her that I trip up the last step. She looks exactly the same, not one gray hair more or less. "I've just arrived," she says, a small suitcase in her hand that I know I have to carry for her as a show of respect. "I understand you're stationed an hour away."

I nod, then think better of it. I pull my coat tighter around my body and croak, "Yes, ma'am."

We deposit her things at the front desk, and then, as I walk away, toward the floor I share with the other sleeper girls whenever I am in the city, I catch her amused stare directed at me. I see her eyes and know I have not disappointed her. This is how she likes to see me—tired and dirty, not looking my best.

I want immediately to change. Of course I want to change, but she ushers me back to her side. "Come," she says. "We're already late enough as it is." I have no choice but to obey her.

The closer we get to the hotel's banquet hall, the louder the noise and the more I shrink. But Madame's hand is firm on my arm. We are standing just outside the doors when she hesitates. I brace myself for more insults, but she is staring intently at my face, searching for something. Finally she leans back, satisfied. "You're sick," she announces, and I flinch. How can she know?

I yank my arm from hers. We stand there, sizing each other up, and I don't know what it means that I am suddenly no longer afraid of her. Since I left the cottages, I have known many people who were stronger, wiser, kinder, braver. *In the end,* I tell myself, *she is just a sad old woman. Why did I ever let her mean so much?*

I am proud of myself. Jack would have been proud of me, too. I square my shoulders, and I am about to walk past her when she speaks again, softly. She bends toward my ear, but I lean away from her. "We lied about what the pills do," she says, her words hanging between us, her eyes cold but not as empty as I remember. "The very last thing they have ever made any of you is healthy."

"What?"

I hear myself whisper the word, but she pretends she didn't say anything at all. Whatever she has just told me was not supposed to be said. She has broken protocol. But she quickly becomes the Madame I know, and she takes my arm again, pushes the door open. She makes me walk into the room with her. Makes me the laughingstock, because everyone else looks his or her best.

There are parties like these happening all over the world. Small gatherings of thank-yous for the sleepers, for the Madames, where we drink wine and toast one another. Already there has been a message from the president. There is money, and nice houses for those of us who still have families from our original homes. The world is whisper quiet, dark, just as we like it, and we pat one another on the back and say, "Well done."

We lied about what the pills do.

Those words are ringing in my ears.

Madame steps up onto the platform next to the others. She is the oldest one of them and perhaps the toughest looking. Though she smiles, she looks as though she does not recognize us, not really. We are simply her job well done. "Thank you, each and every one of you, for your service," she says. I am numb when I join the lines that form all the way to the door. When it is our turn, each of us steps forward. We kiss her cheek.

She offers the same words to each one of us. "You have done a spectacular job. This was impossible without you. This isn't their world. It's ours. And we have taken it."

I stumble away from her in a haze. My chest is heavy, and I don't remember how to breathe.

I stand at the back of the room, as far back as I possibly can. It's just as well that I look like a wet dog because everyone else leaves me alone. "You look—" Gray says, and I turn around, find him smiling as he looks me over. A sigh of relief escapes me. He is here. He is alive. "Give me a second," he says. "I'm thinking of it." He is even farther back in the shadows than I am. And his eyes have aged. There are only glimpses now of the boy from the cottages. I suspect I look the same.

I don't know how to function properly. I make my body face the party again. I stare straight ahead, clap my hands when I am supposed to, but when I can't hold it in any longer, I say: "Gray, the pills. The ones that are supposed to keep us well. The ones you had your person look into." *The ones I just took two more of, less than an hour ago.*

Gray freezes, hands in mid-clap, and then he slowly lets

them fall to his sides. "I wasn't trying to keep it from you. I just found out yesterday, and there was no way to reach you. I was waiting to see you face-to-face."

"Madame," I say, nudging my head toward her. I tell him what she said.

His jaw clenches almost immediately. "She said that to you?" he asks. "Why would she do that? Is she trying to flaunt it in our faces?" He looks like he wants to walk up to Madame and get himself killed, right here and now. But she wasn't smiling when she told me, the way she would have taunted us at the cottages. I don't know why she did it, but she wasn't smiling.

I don't tell him that. I take his arm. "Gray," I say, "what is in them?"

He is still looking over at Madame. "They didn't lie about the white pills," he says, through gritted teeth. "They've kept us healthy all these years. It's the blue ones that are the problem. They are just a bunch of poison capsules."

"Poison," I whisper, letting go of his arm.

He finally faces me, and his eyes are blazing. "They've been dormant in our bodies all these years. But now that the war is almost over and there are too many of us . . ." His voice trails off, but I can figure out the rest of that sentence on my own.

"How?" I ask, and my voice is pathetic with hope. I know the answer, but I ask anyway. "If the poison is dormant in our bodies, then it cannot kill us. Right?"

Gray stares at me for a long moment before he answers. He holds up his tracker hand. "When we were kids," he says quietly, "Alex and I used to talk about cutting off our arms so that if we ran away, they wouldn't be able to find us. Now it turns out that that's the only thing that would have saved us."

"Our trackers?"

"When they decide that a sleeper has served his purpose, they trigger his tracker remotely. It sends some kind of signal, and the blue pills are activated."

My head spins as I turn around again.

"The pills keep you healthy. Keep you alive." That's what they said.

I never once saw Madame take the pills, not in eight years. That's all I can think now.

Even if she had taken them in private, I should have found them when I discovered where she hid her stash of shortbread, or Edith should have when she went looking for Madame's best wine. To spend so much time rummaging through her things as cottage children and never once see her bottle of pills. She wasn't taking them. And when the nonsleepers arrive in this world, I have never seen them given the pills either. Yet they all are fine. It's possible that they are taking the pills and I haven't noticed, but I doubt it.

Those graphs Miss Odette printed every month. I thought they were studying my health. But they were only making sure the poison they put in our blood was contained.

"We've been killing ourselves," I say, my voice calm, my eyes still looking straight ahead.

Gray says nothing for a long time. Then, eventually: "Yes."

"So," I say, "this is really our farewell party. We just don't know it yet."

My mind goes numb. I do not know whether I am surprised that these few months of war are all they ever really wanted from us. There are thousands of us, and we were meant to be effective. Now they won't have to deal with the consequences of what we have become, what they have made us capable of. We won't be here much longer, and we are too weak to do anything about it. Some of us can barely stay standing. In the end there won't even be a story to tell. A woman will give birth to her baby, and she will whisper, "Look. Look at our world. Isn't it beautiful?"

And we will be their ghosts.

* * *

I cannot sleep after the celebration. I lie in my hotel bed, but the war is still not over behind my eyes. The dead die over and over again. In my mind, in my dreams. Everyone I have ever cared about. Alex, Edith, Da, Gigi, Jack. Every time I close my eyes, they are there.

I *don't want to watch anybody else die. I can't.*

There is only one death left. When it comes, I will not be strong enough to handle it.

In the morning Gray is waiting for me in front of my car. I don't know how long he has been out here or how he knew I would try to leave before everyone woke up. I unlock my car and stand with the door between us, the wind blowing my hair into my face.

"I think we should finish this," I tell him. "Before it gets . . . complicated." It already hurts. But I wear my mask. I don't want him to see how scared I am of whatever comes next. I don't want him to know that I always fail. At being there at the end. For everybody but myself.

I'll fail us both. I know it.

He just stands there, studying my face. He does not even look shocked. Perhaps he has also thought the same thing. "Is that what you want?" he asks finally, and there is only the slightest emotion in his voice.

I want to shake my head at the exact same moment I want to say yes.

"It was always going to end this way, remember?" I tell him. "We said we would know when it was time." I take a deep breath. "I've never thanked you for being my friend. For saving my life that night at the orchard. For helping me with Cecily."

He swallows. He looks down at his boots. "Lira," he says, but there's nothing else to add, and my name hangs in the air between us.

I steel my shoulders and stand taller. I climb into my car.

And when I leave the city, he lets me go. His team is assigned to a place hours away from Bayard, and I don't see him again for weeks. I tell myself it is better this way. To let us both down now.

I have already begun the process of becoming a ghost.

CHAPTER 49

After a few months I am back at the flower shop again. My assignment in Bayard is over. Is it intentional that Julia always winds up standing next to me on new assignment days, so that we are picked together? And then she smiles at me, as though she honestly means it.

Oh, I realize. She thinks I am like her. She thinks I walked away from Edith and Gray and everything that was wrong in the farmhouse. She doesn't know I killed Da's alternate. She doesn't know Cecily is alive.

"I can speak to someone for you," Julia says, leaning close

to me, and there is something horrible in her voice. A quiet respect for me, as if I am the inspiration for who she is. "When all of this is over, you'll be safe from—well—" She shrugs, and it confirms everything I already guessed. This new world we're creating isn't meant for sleepers. Handlers maybe, but not sleepers.

My hands are stiff at my sides. I make myself smile back. "Thank you," I lie.

I pitied Julia once, but now I find myself almost afraid. Of the cold twist of her lips, the scowl that she offers the rest of the world. She walks too fast, and I hurry to keep up.

I hope I look like her.

I hope I am nothing like her.

We are given water duty as our new job. We are allowed to choose two more teammates. Julia chooses Gray. She still doesn't notice the way he won't look at her when she talks, how he stands as far from her as possible, or the way his fists clench whenever he sees her.

I don't know anybody else, so I choose the other girl standing next to me. A girl with purple hair who tries to hide the fact that she cannot stop coughing. Her eyes are heavy, and she sways a little. I figure she will benefit most of all from water duty.

"I'm Leah," she says, holding out her hand.

Only then do we recognize each other. She used to make animal shapes with paper when we were in the cottages. We even slept in the same dorm.

She is not the same girl she once was, but I cannot figure out why. The purple hair? The sick greenish hue of her skin? Or is it the long scar down the side of her face? On their own, none of those things should make me forget her.

"Don't worry," she says with a sad smile. "Nobody ever recognizes me at first glance."

It has only been four years since the cottages. But looking at Leah makes it feel like a lifetime.

On our first day we row out into the middle of the water where the portal is. We sit in our boat and act like Madames. We pull out all those who come through the portal. There are fewer and fewer every day, which is just as well. We are becoming weaker. Our bones groan, our noses bleed, and we are only good enough for the water. Julia sits with Gray, says things to him, and he says things back. They have their backs turned to us, and every so often Julia leans closer to him. Hours pass before I understand that she is interested in him. That there is nothing wrong with being together now that the war is under control. A twinge of surprise and something else, something unidentifiable, passes briefly through me.

"They're having serious trouble balancing our medica-tion," Leah says, shivering violently underneath her blanket. I can hear the noise her teeth make each time they meet, and her eyes are yellowed, only half lucid. She has made only one paper bird today, a small pink swan that floats on the water for a full minute before it sinks. "But Madame says that they've almost got it."

"I'm sure she's right," I say.

The surface of the water remains calm. Nothing and no one come up from the portal. Gray asks how Leah is feeling and furrows his brows each time she leans over the boat to throw up. She wipes her mouth and apologizes afterward. "I think I had something bad to eat," she says, trying desperately hard to stay positive. I can see her veins through her skin.

I hear myself say, "It was probably the sandwiches Julia made."

"Hey," Julia says, but she's staring at Leah with something akin to horror. She meets my eyes, and I read her message there: *We'll make it. Me, you, and Gray. We won't be like her.*

Leah dies on our fifth day on the water. We've barely rowed out far enough.

We take the boat back to shore, and Madame has some-one carry her body away. I still remember the look of hope in

Leah's dull eyes. "Maybe the medicine is starting to work," she had said, staring up at the sky like it confused her. "I'm actually feeling kind of better."

"You look better," I'd lied.

At least at the very end it is a quiet affair, almost a secret. We fall asleep and don't remember how to wake up.

The next day Julia wraps her arms around herself, her eyes wide, and she is quiet. She sits with Gray. I sit on the other side of the boat, staring out at the water. Today we rescue a man and his entire family. They tell us, as we pull them out, that there is only 35 percent of our Earth left now. Less than half, and most of it in shambles. Only the mad ones and the sick ones are left. I stare into the water for so long that I don't feel Gray come up beside me, and we sit like that in silence. He watches the water, too, and then he puts his hand right next to mine on the edge of the boat so our little fingers are touching, but he doesn't say anything.

Behind us, the man is trying to have an animated conversation with Julia about what this new Earth is like. "Is it clean? Safe? Nothing disappearing?" he asks.

He gets a nod in response.

Julia is still shocked by Leah's death. At the inevitabilities that surely lie ahead for her. It has only just now become apparent to her just how disposable we all are. We have stopped taking our pills, but it doesn't matter now. They were never what we thought they were, and whatever button needed to be pushed to trigger their effects has been pushed. There is more than enough poison flowing in our veins to kill us.

She answers every question the man asks with "Yes." No matter what he asks.

"But how will we live?" the man asks. "What houses will we be assigned?"

"Yes," Julia says.

The following day she is the same way.

Despite what she did to Edith, it is getting easier to be around her. It is easy to see that she thought she was protecting herself all along. She did it wrong, aligned herself with the wrong people, but her goal was the same as that of all of us. To survive. To live.

I will never forgive her for her choice, but I cannot kill her either. The most I can do is keep my back turned and stare out at the water, thinking, I cannot die like this.

I cannot die like this.

Here, doing this. I cannot die like Leah, on a boat, pretending that I am going to get better. Buried by people who will not remember who I was the moment I am in the ground. I think this, standing next to Gray, our hands touching for the second day in a row. Today is going to be exactly the same as yesterday, minus the man we rescued. But then Gray turns to face me, waits until I meet his eyes before he continues. "You don't get to punish yourself, Lira. Every wrong thing you have done, I have done, too. We are exactly the same, you and I. Why do you think you're the one who deserves to be alone at the end?"

I shake my head. "Gray, I—"

"You're good in spite of what they wanted you to be," he says. "You're good, and that's why you're different, and that's why I love you. You think it's a flaw. That you have to hide it. But it's the very best thing about you. And there are many, many other things."

I open my mouth and shut it again. I do this three times before I give up. I look down at my arms. I am so cold these days I wonder whether the sun is playing tricks on us. Maybe it is really winter instead, and the stones on the ground are covered thickly with ice. Is anything in the world as real as we want it to be? "I don't know what to say," I admit finally.

Gray shakes his head. "I wasn't expecting you to say anything. But if you want to end this on the basis that things are going to get complicated, then you should probably know that they already are, for me." A small smile twitches on his lips. "And have been for a while.

"Give me a day," he says softly. He waits until I meet his eyes before he continues. "I know why you're watching the water like that. I've been thinking it, too."

He sits down suddenly. His body is dying, too. I sit next to him. Julia watches us quietly, her own eyes lost in a place I cannot imagine. I hate that she is here. I hate that neither I nor Gray has done something terrible to her yet. Worst of all, the way she doesn't mention the promises Madame has made her, of how we will be the only sleepers to live through this. She says nothing at all.

"Just one day," Gray says. He takes my hands, but I am the one who lowers my head to kiss his. Each one of his knuckles, which are bonier than ever now, and then his palms. He pushes the hair from my face like he used to, and when my eyes meet his, I am sad, but not really.

"Oh," Julia says suddenly, staring at us.

"Just one day," Gray says again.

I whisper, "Okay." He kisses me, and I allow myself to think the thing I have been thinking for nearly all of my years in this world.

I want my freedom.

I *want to go home.*

CHAPTER 50

We plan carefully. We have to ask for special permission from Madame, but that's easy. We tell her that we want to spend the morning on the beach instead of our rooms, so we can watch the sunrise. We are allowed to ask for things like that now. Sentimental things. Our favorite box of chocolates. A new pair of shoes. A new dress. Perhaps they feel guilty. Now that the war is mostly over and all that is left is a bunch of sick sleepers, the people of this world can tell themselves that they did only what they had to in order to survive. Perhaps they have decided that if they are kind to us, then they are not monsters. Especially now that we are almost dead.

In the state we're in, I suppose Madame assumes we cannot get up to much. She says yes without even glancing our way. I tell Julia about the plan when we are alone. I say, "You have to do this one thing for me. Because you said I was your friend."

She doesn't understand why I would want to leave. "But this is our home now," she tells me.

I shake my head, dismissing her words. "We need a boat," I say. "No one can know."

She is silent for a long time before she nods. "Okay," she says. "Leave it to me."

Gray drives us to the orchards with supplies for Aunt Imogen and Cecily. He has been doing this for months, even after I told him we were over. I suppose he and Cecily still enjoy each other's company. "She asks of you every time," he tells me, stopping the truck, but I just turn my head away and look out the window. I don't want her to see me like this.

But even as I watch him walk away, somehow I know what will happen. He will tell Cecily I am here. She will insist on coming up. Gray has walked only a few feet away from the car before I climb out. I pull the hood of my coat over my eyes. We don't say anything as we climb down the well. Cecily runs to him first before it registers that he is not alone, and then she squeals.

I wear the very best smile I have. It's not much, I know, but I wear it for her. I've never done that for anyone before. She tells me how terrible life is, living underground, all the things she misses doing. Meanwhile Gray is talking to Aunt Imogen. "When your supplies run out this time, come up," he tells her. "There's money inside that bag. It's enough for a place to live. When you come up, move far away from here, and wherever you go act like everyone else. Act like you belong there. The world is different now."

He doesn't tell her that there are pockets where the fighting is still strong, though. Where sleepers still work to control towns and cities that are run by members of the Resistance. They trained their own assassins—and possibly turned some of our own—to murder as many sleepers as they could. And they were even good at it. All those hangings. All those couples with red ribbons tied to their hands. Many sleepers, the healthy ones, have been shipped off to these locations. There will be no mercy for these resisters when they are captured. They will die in all the worst possible ways we can imagine.

That is what we have been told.

But a small part of me isn't so sure. A part of me wonders whether it is enough that there are people out there like Da was, like the real Lirael was, who are strong enough to try, to fight for their lives. And maybe eventually they will begin to win.

This is the version of the story that I secretly prefer, whether it is a fantasy or not.

Gray doesn't tell Aunt Imogen or Cecily about it. About the ones still fighting for the old world. With the way she looks now with her gun, it is the kind of thing Aunt Imogen might want to join. Might want to take Cecily along for. It is the kind of thing that will kill them.

In the end I don't remember saying good-bye to Cecily. Maybe I am still there in the orchards with her like she thought I would be. I think that, even as I spend the rest of the day with Gray on the beach. We don't do much. We kiss and we tell stories and we sit around a fire toasting marshmallows. The wind is our enemy, but we ignore it because Gray opens up his coat and motions for me to come closer, and when I'm cuddled up against him, he covers us both. I think I cry. I think I cry and cry and cry until I don't remember why I am crying. In those moments, if someone asked me what I wanted most from the world, I would say, "I want to learn how not to love, and how to unlove, and how to be content being alone."

Early the next morning Julia wakes us. "I have the boat," she whispers, and we all climb on board quietly. We row along the water. Even though we've made the trip at least a dozen times, our arms are tired today. There are moments when I cannot feel my legs. When the boat stops, I stand. I climb out of my coat and stand there in my simple clothes. Gray does the same. Julia won't look at either of us. I cannot believe that she is the last person I know at the end.

"You can come with us," I tell her, surprising myself, but she crosses her arms and shakes her head.

"Madame is on my side about this," she says. "There has to be a way to fix us."

I have never seen her look so young.

There probably is, I want to say. *They won't give it to us.*

I kiss Gray instead with all the strength I can muster. "I'm sorry I didn't love you earlier," I whisper. "It's almost over already."

"Is it?" He smiles.

We hold hands. We are young, but at the same time we are not. We are old souls. We are tired souls. At the last moment Gray hesitates, and I know him well enough to know why. His hand tightens around mine as he turns to look at Julia, and a big part of me breathes a sigh of relief. I've envisioned this moment for so long, but it did not belong to me, and I had no right to instigate it.

"I have to tell you something," he says quietly to Julia.

Julia's face changes, surprise to confusion, and then finally, finally it settles on something dull and broken that looks right through us. She understands, but Gray takes a deep breath and says the words anyway. "I know what you did to them at the farmhouse," he says. "To Edith."

For a long time Julia just stands there, not denying it but not confirming it either. Then finally, when she speaks, her voice is so small it almost doesn't exist. She is looking down at her hands, at her shoes, at anything but us. "We had a duty to our country." She sounds as if she is only reciting our sleeper anthem. "We had a duty to help our people, no matter what."

Gray shakes his head, his hand clenched around mine. And though his voice comes out soft, it is strong and unyielding. "No, Julia," he says. "That wasn't for our country. That was for you."

Instead of arguing with him, Julia turns to me. She is crying now, and I don't know whether it is because she feels guilty about Edith or because she doesn't like the things Gray is saying to her. She meets my eyes and pleads with me. "*You* understand, don't you, Lira?" she says. "You understand why I had to do it."

Gray is so mad he actually laughs.

"The irony," he says, "is that Edith's the only reason you're still alive right now. She would have asked us to let you go. That's the *only* reason."

Julia is staring at me, waiting for me to refute his words. To be on her side. She stands there with no apology written on her face. She feels bad, but if she had to do it over again, she would. I know she would. And I cannot forgive her for that.

"Good-bye, Julia." With those words, she finally knows how I feel.

I don't know what happens to Julia after that. Perhaps she sits crumpled in the boat for hours with tears running down her face, until she wipes them away and rows back to Madame, and Madame gives her the cure and she lives a full life. She becomes a teacher or a nurse or goes to the university while working as a waitress part-time. Perhaps she receives what she wants: her chance to live. In this war perhaps she is the only one who wins.

I don't know.

The water is cold. Difficult to swim through when your

bones are fragile, your muscles wasting away right before your eyes. At the end you start to ask yourself whether it is the right white light you are swimming toward. Whether it is light at all or just a trick the darkness plays on you.

CHAPTER 51

I was born in a house. I was born to a man and a woman who both were very poor. They worked in the circus, but that year half their staff and circus animals vanished into thin air just like that. They were not worried because the woman was about to give birth, and with my birth came all the money they would ever need. The day I was born, my father held me for about a minute. My mother did not hold me at all. "Give her to them," she said to her husband tiredly.

She was one of few women willing to have children

for the cause. For the sole purpose of populating a strange orphanage that had popped up in Paris.

My parents made many choices Lirael Harrison's parents never had to make.

And this one was one of them.

They called me Katy first at the orphanage. Before they knew what my name in this world would be. Before they started to shape me into a cottage girl. Before, when I thought I could be a dancer and a teacher and an astronaut all at once. When I thought I could touch the world. I was Katy until they broke her and swept away the pieces.

At the surface of the water, boats bob. Hundreds and thousands of boats people jumped from stretch out over the ocean. Boats that, when we hop from one to the other, eventually take us to land.

And there are other sleepers like us. A couple of handfuls who had the same idea. We pick out houses amidst the rubble and live there. Some want to live in mansions and penthouses, but Gray and I are satisfied by a small blue house with a mustard-colored roof. It has a tree behind it and two dogs that come begging for scraps every day.

Our Earth is quiet. Our Earth is peaceful. When we

arrive, a girl walks out onto the street and smiles at us. "The good news is this," she says, after introducing herself as Sibel. "Since we don't have alternates anymore, we won't disappear. We'll die the old-fashioned way. Although there is probably something you should see."

She leads us to one of the abandoned houses where all the furniture has been cleared out. "We found this," she says. The walls and the ground are covered in papers, notes, and calculations that I am not sure I understand. Mathematical equations, graphs, and charts. We stand there for so long, staring at the walls, that my legs begin to shake.

"Scientists were collecting all this information for years," Sibel says, "and nobody told us."

I run my fingers across one of the maps. Beside it is a picture of three Earths right next to one another. "What is it supposed to mean?" I ask.

Sibel points to the first one. It looks like a satellite photo, taken from space. "This is us. This other one is the planet that we just invaded," she says. "And this is the one that doesn't exist yet."

"Doesn't exist yet?" Gray says, frowning. We stare at the charts again, with new eyes.

A new planet is forming behind our dying one. Another

planet that will have people who look like us, that will have a portal in its ocean like ours. At some point there will be two planets again, fully formed. The notes scribbled on the charts say that this has happened twice before, and each time only one world was left. The first time there were no sleepers. The other Earth simply disappeared. The next time they carried out what they called their Replacement Initiative with sleepers. This is only the second time it has happened.

Gray's eyes are just as startled as I feel.

The world we just left behind will become like us.

It is a cycle. There is no escaping it.

There are always two worlds. One world destroys the other, and yet somehow there will be two again. An eternity of sleepers, portals, more orphanages and cottages.

Always.

Gray takes my hand.

"I love you," I tell him later, when we are alone.

He kisses my neck. "I'm happy whenever I'm with you," he says. "That's all I know. The world is terrible, and we both have done terrible things, but you, Katy, make me happy right here, right now."

I like being Katy again. I do not remember her, but I think one day I might.

Believing that there is more than blackness behind my eyes is the most important choice I will ever make for myself.

The future is coming, but this is what we are for now. A girl, a boy—and countless others, who just wanted to live. Perhaps we both die today. Perhaps only one of us, and we become nothing but ghosts, reminiscing about the past inside someone's dreams. Perhaps there is a cure, the end will slow down, and we will live until we are seventy.

Either way.

We will be here until there is nothing.

They say the world doesn't actually end with darkness.

Acknowledgments

I am indebted to my agent, Alison Fargis, for her passionate belief in this book, and to the team at Stonesong for their support. Also to my editor, Martha Mihalick, for her wisdom and insight and for getting my story; to Sylvie Le Floc'h, Lois Adams, Katie Heit, Catherine Knowles, Gina Rizzo, Katie Fee, and to everyone at Greenwillow and HarperCollins Canada. This book would not exist without my family and friends, who have been there from the very beginning. Thank you to my parents for never once telling me that I could not touch the stars if I wanted to. Thank you to my sisters, who save my life every single day just by being in it: I would save every version of you in every universe. Thank you to Natalya, Sarah, Rebecca—for not rolling your eyes when I told you I was writing a book. I thank every teacher, professor, author, poet, artist, and musician who has inspired me over the years. Thank you to my fellow 2015 debuts for writing fantastic books and making me wonder what I am doing among you. And lastly to *you*—yes, *you*—who are reading my acknowledgments page: thank you for letting me borrow your imagination for a little while.